"My apologies," Harris said. *"I wasn't making an advance. I was trying to hide you. I forgot myself for a moment."*

Why did it sting that his actions were based only on protecting her? "I'm not upset. I'm glad you're here. Being alone with a man is new to me, but it's nothing like I'd imagined it to be." It came with more powerful emotions. Desire. Happiness.

Harris looked at her. Watched her. Didn't say anything. His gaze drilled into her.

Finally he spoke. "Are you telling me you've never been alone with a man?"

Laila shifted under his scrutiny. "Aside from members of my family, I have not been alone with a man. Not in the way you mean." She had never before experienced the attraction or the connection she had with Harris. "It's well understood in Qamsar that an unmarried woman of a certain age isn't left alone with her suitors."

Dear Reader,

I'm excited to the share with you the third book of the Truman brothers miniseries. Harris's story takes place in a setting inspired by my husband's experiences living in the Middle East.

Harris is a distrusting FBI agent who needs Laila, a member of the Qamsarian royal family, to help locate and stop a terrorist. The search leads Harris to Laila's home country in the Arabian Peninsula. Away from the world he knows and the support of his family, Harris is tested by the rules and restrictions of Laila's conservative country.

Laila has her own ideas about life and love and is challenged by the changes in her world and by her attraction to Harris. To find happiness, they'll both need to set aside disappointments of the past and fears of the future and embrace a new life they never thought possible.

Happy reading,

C.J. Miller

PROTECTING
HIS PRINCESS

—

C.J. Miller

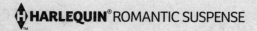

HARLEQUIN®ROMANTIC SUSPENSE

Recycling programs
for this product may
not exist in your area.

ISBN-13: 978-0-373-27847-3

PROTECTING HIS PRINCESS

Copyright © 2013 by C.J. Miller

Printed in U.S.A.

Books by C.J. Miller

Harlequin Romantic Suspense

Hiding His Witness #1722
Shielding the Suspect #1770
Protecting His Princess #1777

C.J. MILLER

is a third-generation Harlequin reader and the first in her family to write professionally. She lives in Maryland with her husband and young son. She enjoys spending time with family, meeting friends for coffee, reading and traveling to warm beaches around the world. C.J. believes in first loves, second chances and happily-ever-after.

C.J. loves to hear from readers and can be contacted through her website at www.cj-miller.com.

To our princess, Quinn. I wish you love, laughter and happily ever after.

Chapter 1

She would never enjoy a cup of coffee again. Laila removed her stained navy-blue apron and shoved it in the washing machine with the others. A few more tasks and she could close for the night, giving her feet—and her nose—a much-needed break.

Laila had been listening to the radio since she'd closed the store, hoping to learn new information about the situation in her home country of Qamsar. Her brother's regressive, conservative social policies weren't popular with certain factions in the country, and Laila hoped Mikhail would adopt a more moderate approach to ruling before tensions erupted into violence. Her mother feared civil war, and Laila feared for her family's safety. The broadcast had nothing new to report.

Laila double-checked the coffee, latte and espresso machines, and switched off the lights and radio in the back room. The only sound in the small café was the washing machine filling with water.

She jumped when she saw a man leaning against the café's glass front door. Deep blue eyes watched her. Laila crossed the room, her heart jittering nervously. He had visited the café dozens of times before, and each time, he had caught and held her attention. "Harris. What are you doing here?" she asked through the glass.

Had he not been one of her regular customers, she would have backed away, told him to leave and maybe even called the police. But Harris was a good man, charming, easy to talk with, and she'd developed a fondness for him. She looked forward to his visits, and though this one was oddly timed, a shudder of excitement piped through her.

"I tried knocking, but you didn't hear me," Harris said. "I need to talk to you."

Laila stared at him through the glass. "About what?" Growing up in Qamsar, even as a member of the royal family, she was wary of men. American men made her doubly nervous; though with Harris, her nervousness was centered on attraction not fear. Attracted to him and unsure how to strike up a friendship, her feelings for Harris confused her. In Qamsar, it wasn't appropriate to have a friendship with a man. Much about her life in America was new to her, including her job, which she'd taken to stay off her brother's radar and have money of her own. It was a freedom she enjoyed.

Harris pressed a badge against the glass. "You're in danger. I need you to come with me."

Laila leaned forward, examining the badge that contained Harris's picture and the words *FBI Special*

Agent. Surprise and alarm skittered across her skin. Harris had never mentioned what he did for a living, and she had never told him that she was the emir's sister. A stab of betrayal pierced her. She'd expected the American government to monitor her, but she hadn't expected Harris to be the one doing it.

Had danger traveled from Qamsar to find her in America? "Why do you think I'm in danger?" Her nerves tightened in her stomach and exhaustion fled to the corners of her mind.

"Please trust me. I don't mean you any harm," Harris said. He slid his badge into his pocket and held his hands out, palms facing her. "Let's talk for a few minutes without me shouting through the glass."

Laila unlocked the door and allowed Harris inside. "Is my family safe?" Her mother's safety was at the foremost of her thoughts.

"At the present the data I have on the situation indicates they are not hurt or directly in danger."

Which was not the same as saying they were safe. People in public positions during social upheaval were never completely safe. Since her father had died two years ago, her brother Mikhail had taken over as emir, and the shift of power had caused political and social rumblings that had only grown louder with time. "Then why do you think I'm in danger?" Laila asked. She liked Harris. Whenever he'd come to the counter to place his order, he had spoken to her and listened to her responses. His demeanor tonight was different than it had been in weeks past. His shoulders were tight; his carefree, flirtatious smile was missing and tension pulsed off him in waves.

"We've received intel that someone wants to hurt

you," Harris said. The tension she'd sensed was pent up in his words.

Laila forced her heart to remain calm. Growing up in Qamsar, political enemies of her father had often threatened her and her family. Threats weren't anything new. "The situation at home isn't good, and someone always gets the bright idea to intimidate my family and me in the heat of emotion. I don't take those threats seriously."

His brows drew together and his blue eyes sharpened. "You need to take this one seriously."

Laila wouldn't allow an American man—no matter how attracted she was to him—to scare her. Americans didn't understand the Qamsarian culture, and they didn't understand her family. "We can talk about this another time. I'm tired, and I have an early class tomorrow. My uncle will be expecting me, and he'll be worried if I arrive home too late."

Harris waited while she locked up and followed her to her car. "Please, Laila. I wouldn't be here if we didn't feel the threats against you were real and pervasive."

Laila pulled her car keys from her handbag and pressed the unlock button. The lights on her car flashed.

"No!"

Harris's shout echoed in her ears, followed by the sound of an explosion and the sensation of her body being slammed into gravel. She slid, the backs of her legs and her arms burning. Harris was on top of her, his body covering hers. Laila gasped for air, the heaviness of him stifling. She struggled to sit up. As he rolled to the side, pulling his phone from his pocket, she caught sight of her car. It was now consumed in flames.

Her mouth fell open. She hadn't expected this. Not while she was living in America. Car bombings didn't happen in suburban America. People were safe here, weren't they?

Who wanted to kill her bad enough to follow her to America?

Harris scanned the area, looking for anyone out of place. A bystander who might have seen something or even the bomber lingering to watch the fallout of his attack. No one except law enforcement and the first medical responders were on the scene.

Laila sat on the curb in the parking lot, a blanket wrapped around her. He'd had someone on his team call her aunt and uncle to let them know Laila was fine, painting the explosion as a car accident. The truth was more grim: a car bomb had been planted in Laila's car. If Harris hadn't recognized the high frequency whine of an explosive's timer engaging, she would be dead. The intel the FBI had gathered on the situation had predicted Laila and members of the royal family of Qamsar were in danger, though it was difficult to predict how or if an attack might occur.

The FBI's list of bombing suspects was short, mostly made up of members of the Holy Light Brotherhood, a terrorist organization that wanted Qamsar to remain isolated from "infidel influences." Those "infidel influences" included America as a whole, and with the emir negotiating a trade agreement, a female member of the royal family studying in America became an obvious target to anyone wanting to send a message.

Harris sat on the curb next to Laila. "How are you holding up?"

Laila watched him with tired, soulful brown eyes. "I'm in shock. I've read about bombings. I've seen it reported on the news, but nothing like this has ever happened to me."

The profile the FBI and CIA had created for Laila indicated she had lived a sheltered life. Living in America with her uncle and aunt, her mother's sister, was the first time Laila had been away from Qamsar and her life as a royal princess. After her father, the former emir, had died, Laila had come to America on a student visa and had enrolled in the University of Colorado in Denver. From what Harris had gathered, her brother was not happy about Laila living in America, but he hadn't outright forbidden it. "We'll make sure nothing like this happens again to you."

Harris had connected with Laila from the first day he'd met her. She went about her job quietly and efficiently, and she had intelligent, alert eyes. If she wasn't his assignment, he might have asked her on a date, and gotten a chance to know her better and uncover the passion he saw simmering below the surface. Then again it was better for him to keep his distance. His track record with women was embarrassing, and he wasn't ready to add another name to the list of failed relationships. When he was working a difficult case, those women were targets of his enemies, and none had proven able to handle the pressure or remain loyal when money changed hands.

Laila pulled the fleece blanket Harris had given her tighter around her body. Harris read the gesture as less from cold and more from discomfort. Was his presence making her uncomfortable because he was male? He and Laila weren't alone. The parking lot was filled with people: FBI agents and CIA investigators, along with local law enforcement. The FBI and CIA had teamed up to create a joint task force to shut down the Holy Light Brotherhood, starting with the head of the organization, Ahmad Al-Adel. When it became apparent Al-Adel had potential ties to the Qamsarian ruling family, the task force had become interested in Laila and how she could help find Al-Adel.

His CIA contacts had told him that, as a Qamsarian woman, Laila had had a conservative upbringing. Not conservative the way an American defined it. Conservative as in limited contact with men, chaperones when appropriate and never being alone or having physical contact with any male apart from family. Harris was doing his best to respect those boundaries, but the extrovert in him found it difficult not to touch her, not to let his gaze linger on her and not to overtly flirt with her. Laila was a beautiful woman. She spoke with a tentative formality, her accent light and pleasing to his ears. She was sensual and feminine, even if she tried to hide it behind loose and concealing clothing.

He moved a few more inches away to give her more personal space.

"No one can promise this won't happen again," Laila said.

Sadness drew a frown across her face and everything in him urged him to take action to erase her unhappiness. Seeing her upset affected him. He wanted to do something, say something, but he didn't have the words to make this better for her.

Tyler Morgan, Harris's CIA counterpart on the task force, arrived on the scene. He strode to Harris and glanced between him and Laila. "Is this the Princess of Qamsar?"

Laila flinched, and Harris gathered she didn't like being called a princess. He'd gotten the sense she was trying to blend with the Americans around her, and her Qamsarian title didn't help that effort. "Yes, this is Laila bin Jassim Al Sharani."

Harris introduced Laila to Tyler. Laila stood and nodded, though she didn't offer her hand in greeting.

"We need to talk with you," Tyler said and looked around. "In private."

Laila shoved her hand through her hair, forcing strands behind her ears. "It's late."

If she refused, Harris couldn't force her to speak to them, but he feared what would happen to her and her family without his team's assistance and her co-operation.

"It's important. We can speak to you at your home if you'd be more comfortable," Tyler added.

Her shoulders slumped in defeat. "I guess we can meet. I feel like I don't have a choice."

Harris wondered how much Laila knew about the political situation. Mikhail bin Jassim Al Sharani, Laila's brother and the Emir of Qamsar, was suspected of working with Al-Adel and the Holy Light Brotherhood. Harris doubted Laila was aware of how much danger the emir was bringing to his family and his country by engaging with a dangerous man like Al-Adel.

Laila rode with Harris and Tyler to her aunt and uncle's home. Her aunt Neha and uncle Aasim were waiting up for her. Laila reassured them that she was okay, and Harris explained he and Tyler needed to speak with her about the car incident.

Tyler appeared nervous and tense, watching the situation with an anxious energy that made Laila uneasy. She was grateful Harris was with her. He had a relaxed and easygoing presence that made everyone in the room feel comfortable. She got the impression that that was the image he was trying to convey to relax her. Underneath his quick smile, he was a force to be reckoned with.

"We need to find out from Laila everything she remembers about the incident while it's fresh in her memory. We think the man who caused damage to her car is a serial hit-and-run driver. We want to stop him before he hurts anyone else. Is it all right to speak with Laila alone?" Harris asked.

"That depends on Laila." Her uncle looked to her and waited for her response.

Part of the terms of Laila's student visa was that she comply with law enforcement. She'd known before coming to America that her brother was a person of interest to the American government.

At her quick nod of agreement, her uncle turned back to Harris. "We'll give you a few minutes of privacy. We'll be upstairs if you need anything. It is late. Please do not keep our niece awake too long. She's been through a trial tonight and needs her rest."

If it hadn't been two badge-carrying members of the United States, her uncle never would have agreed to leave her alone. American-born, her uncle was more progressive than her family in Qamsar, but he took his role as her guardian seriously.

Her aunt and uncle were one of the reasons Laila

believed Mikhail hadn't outright denied her coming to America for her education. Under their watchful eyes, she had thought she was safe. Were her aunt and uncle targets of the bomber, as well? Her aunt had distanced herself from the Qamsarian royal family when she had married Aasim, an Arabic-American small business owner living in Denver.

Laila took a seat on the tan suede couch and smoothed her dress over her knees. She'd worn this outfit to work a hundred times before. Now, with Harris, it felt too short and revealing. Add to it Harris making her feel hot and tingly, and the circumstances were compromising. She was grateful for the other man in the room even if he was quiet and on edge. "How can I help you?"

Laila studied Harris. Clean-cut. Shaven. Good dresser. Unless he had changed his appearance for this operation, she could see him being a man who followed the rules and kept out of trouble. He was taller than Tyler with broad shoulders, blond hair and lighter skin than most men from her country.

When she and Harris had spoken in the café, she'd thought him an intuitive person, or if she was honest with herself, she'd hoped it meant something more about their connection. Now she wondered if it was just a part of his agent training.

"We'd like to offer you protection," Harris said.

Suspicion swept over her. They'd demand something in return. If they wanted information about Mikhail, they'd be disappointed. She didn't have the inside track on her brother's plans for the country, and she held no sway over his decisions.

Harris smiled at her. The easiness of his voice disarmed her. "We believe the man who orchestrated the bombing is a dangerous person. We can keep you safe from him while we look for him," Harris said.

"What about my family? My aunt and uncle? My mother and brothers?" Laila asked. How in-depth was the information Harris and his team had gathered about the bombing? Was anyone at home in danger? Mikhail had his personal guards, but how well was he looking out for the rest of the family?

"We can provide protection for the members of your family in America," Harris said. "If anything happens to any members of the royal family on U.S. soil, negotiations between the United States and Qamsar get dicey. It's in our best interest to keep you safe."

Then their offer was politically motivated.

"Agent Tyler is with the CIA, and we're working on a joint task force. I have experience in the region from my time with the marines, and Tyler's been involved in the Middle East for most of his career," Harris said.

They didn't have to sell her on it. She welcomed help as long as the price wasn't too high. "What is it that you want from me?" Laila asked.

Harris met her gaze. Her body temperature escalated. "I want you to take me to your brother's wedding as your guest."

The emir's upcoming wedding was no secret, but his request was a surprise. Her brother's marriage was long overdue, and Laila had considered not attending the ceremony. She and Mikhail didn't see eye to eye on most issues, and Laila liked being out of the country and away from Mikhail's control. Though she hadn't forgotten her life in Qamsar, her lifestyle in America was fast becoming preferred. More comfortable dress.

Going where she wanted. Talking to whomever she pleased. She liked her independence.

"Why are you so interested in my brother's wedding?" Laila asked. It was the last place she wanted to be. Forget about bringing a spy into the compound, which would land her in a tremendous amount of trouble. Were they looking to get an edge on the negotiations for oil? Or was he offering to attend to provide protection?

"The men who we believe targeted you tonight might attend your brother's wedding. It gives us the opportunity to do some reconnaissance. If we locate them, we'll alert our law enforcement counterparts in Qamsar, and they'll apprehend them. We need someone to get us inside the wedding events so we can look for them."

"Who is it that you are looking for?" One of her brother's political enemies? Someone in America drawing her brother's attention here, making a point to Mikhail?

"We've heard chatter on our monitors about a conspiracy to harm you. Your presence and activities in America aren't appreciated by those who'd like to stop progress in Qamsar," Tyler said.

He wasn't directly answering her.

She looked to Harris to fill in the blanks. "We don't have confirmed intel yet, but we suspect the Holy Light Brotherhood, under the direction of Ahmad Al-Adel, wants a safe haven for his group, and he hopes to find that in Qamsar. Al-Adel wants to stop any trade agreements between America and Qamsar. We've taken a leap of faith telling you this," Harris said. Harris paused, as though not certain he should say more. "As

I've gotten to know you, I feel you're a good person who makes the right decisions."

On some level she trusted Harris, but Laila had grown up sheltered by her parents. She wasn't street smart, and it had been one of her dear mother's greatest fears when Laila had told her that she'd been accepted to the University of Colorado, an American university, that someone would take advantage of Laila's unworldly and naive nature. She and her mother were in touch daily, which Laila hoped lessened some of her mother's concerns.

"Why would this man be at my brother's wedding?" Laila asked. "Why don't you contact Mikhail and let him know who you're looking for?" Her brother wouldn't want to be involved with a terrorist. That could devastate the country.

Harris and Tyler exchanged looks. "We've reached out to you because we can't contact the emir directly. We cannot trust him," Tyler said.

Then Laila was hit with the second bomb of the night.

"We believe the Emir of Qamsar has voluntarily embroiled himself in a relationship with Ahmad Al-Adel, the leader of the Holy Light Brotherhood," Harris said.

Laila missed the next several moments of conversation. Her tired thoughts caught up to what Tyler was saying.

"The emir's wedding will bring Al-Adel out into the open. To miss his wedding would be a sign of disrespect between the two men. As a member of the royal family, you'll have access to places and events and people that outsiders won't. When Al-Adel arrives at your brother's compound for the wedding, Harris can alert the team, and Al-Adel will be captured," Tyler said.

Confusion spun through her. If Al-Adel was responsible for the car bombing at the café, as Tyler was implying, and Mikhail was working with him, had her brother tried to kill her?

Despite her efforts to stay unemotional and focused, the information was difficult to swallow, almost unbelievable. "My brother wouldn't do that. He wouldn't willingly work with a terrorist." Mikhail could be brutal and cold, but participating, even indirectly, in acts of terrorism against the United States, Europe and the Middle East was declaring a war he couldn't win. Qamsar was a small country with limited resources. Besides that, she was his sister. It was a huge leap from not getting along to trying to kill her.

"We have a financial trail tying the Holy Light Brotherhood to Mikhail. We have assets in the country who have substantiated rumors of the entanglement," Tyler said.

As much as she didn't want to believe it, doubts about her brother flooded her thoughts. If Mikhail had found a way to get more money, he might have agreed to work with Al-Adel. Mikhail was ruthless, driven and bent on gaining power. Even more power than he possessed as the Emir of Qamsar. Mikhail wanted a legitimate, prominent place on the international scene and would do whatever was necessary to get there.

Al-Adel's money would mean improvements for the country in places where Mikhail believed they were needed—in mosques and government buildings—without engaging in trade agreements with countries like America.

Blindly accepting their words as true could make a fool of her, putting her in a position to betray her country and her family for no reason. Then again, if they were right and Mikhail was working with Al-Adel, stopping him and evicting Al-Adel and the Holy Light Brotherhood from Qamsar would protect her country. Mikhail may be ousted from his position as emir, but cutting any ties with a terrorist group would be better for the prosperity of Qamsar. She was out of her depths and indecision rolled through her. "I can't believe this." She didn't want to believe it.

"We believe the emir wants to end trade agreement negotiations with the United States, but because the people of Qamsar want the agreement, Mikhail needs to force public opinion that America will cause greater harm than good. If something were to happen to one of the royal family, Mikhail would blame America and use the incident to incite anti-American anger," Harris said, his voice gentle.

Mikhail hadn't stopped her from moving to America. At the time she had believed he was too grief stricken over their father's death and too busy with his new responsibilities as emir to argue with her. She had been waiting for him to demand she return and had been surprised that he hadn't yet. Did he have another motive for allowing her to stay in America?

"You think my brother would arrange for someone to kill me just to sway public opinion?" Believing that Mikhail was working with Al-Adel was difficult. Accepting that he would kill her to forward his agenda was impossible. "He wouldn't do that, and even if you're right and my brother wants me dead, how does traveling to Qamsar guarantee my safety in any way?"

"No guarantees. But you are safer on Qamsarian soil. It makes it more difficult for Mikhail to pin an incident on America," Harris said.

"Difficult but not impossible," Laila said, reading between his words.

"If you agree to do this, regardless of how it plays out, I'll protect you and your family. I'll be there," Harris said.

"If I allow an American into my brother's compound, and he finds out, he'll kill me," Laila said. Any involvement with the American government, even manipulated, could be perceived as a betrayal of Qamsar by Mikhail. Though it would be harder for Mikhail to reach her in America, she would be at Mikhail's mercy when she returned home.

"If we think the emir suspects anything, we'll relocate you to the United States. We'll give you, your mother and your brother Saafir citizenship and a new identity."

Before coming to America, Laila's life had been decided for her. Having a taste of freedom, Laila didn't want to let it go and return to the life she'd had in Qamsar. She wanted to make decisions for herself and her life. Citizenship in America would give her that. Having Saafir and her mother with her would make that transition easier. Not having the deep love of America that she did, would they agree to relocate for their safety?

Mikhail's name was absent from the list. If he was working with a terrorist, he would face the consequences of that decision.

Chapter 2

Two weeks later, with the contract from the United States government locked in a security box at the bank, Laila and Harris were en route to Qamsar accompanied by Laila's uncle Aasim. They'd had to loop him into their ruse, and he had agreed to maintain his silence. He wanted no involvement in the politics of his wife's family. The Qamsar Embassy in America had also agreed to wait for the Americans to complete their investigation before releasing information that the Holy Light Brotherhood might have been responsible for the car bombing.

Their flight had lasted twenty-two hours, and Laila was grateful they'd flown first class. Though she and her mother had often traveled in style with her father, this was her first trip as the girlfriend of Harris Kuhn, fourth generation descendent of the former German royal ruling family and heir to a German shipping company fortune. Laila was presenting him to her family as the man who intended to marry her. Considering her family was likely planning to arrange her marriage with a man of their choosing, she was concerned about this aspect of their cover story. She only hoped Mikhail liked the idea of a wealthy European nobleman with ties to the German government and an international shipping company marrying into the family. Harris was assuming a certain attitude. An I-deserve-to-be-here, I-have-plenty-of-money attitude.

One that normally Laila found classless and rude. In this case Harris assured her that his behavior and arrogant attitude was important. Any show of weakness and the emir could exploit it.

Harris needed to strike a careful balance of strength and gentleness. If he came on too strong, Mikhail would dislike him and feel threatened. If he wasn't confident enough, Mikhail would dismiss him as useless and weak, and see no benefit in allowing his sister to have a relationship with him. Harris might even be asked to leave the wedding festivities. Mikhail was not known for his patience and calm demeanor.

For the trip Laila had chosen to wear an outfit more conservative than she'd worn in America. The fabric was light and cool, and she wasn't showing an inch of skin from neck to wrists to ankles. She wouldn't give her brother a reason to be annoyed with her. She wasn't Mikhail's favorite person. Far from it.

The drive to the emir's compound took forty minutes, and the last five were the most important. If Harris wasn't permitted inside for the wedding celebration, he couldn't look for Al-Adel. Laila had let her brother's event coordinator know about her plans to bring a guest. The liaison hadn't indicated it was a problem, and Laila hoped she would have heard—either directly or through her mother—if her guest wasn't welcome.

She was anxious, but Harris seemed at ease and was less apprehensive than her uncle, who wasn't happy about visiting Qamsar. Her aunt had stayed in Colorado, but Aasim had felt obligated to escort his niece since she was traveling with Harris and to attend the wedding as a show of respect to the emir. At her aunt's urging, he'd worn more traditional Qamsarian clothes. It was the first time Laila had seen him dressed in that manner.

Harris wore black trousers and a white dress shirt, the top button open at the neck and the sleeves rolled to his elbow. On his wrist was an expensive-looking watch. A simple, understated look and he owned it.

Their chauffer, provided by the emir, drove the black sedan to the entrance of the compound. The maroon iron gates were secured to a perimeter wall constructed of concrete, painted tan to reflect the rays of the sun. The smoothness of the concrete made it impossible to climb the fifteen-foot wall without ropes. Every ten feet along the top of the wall, a security camera was posted and actively monitored by the emir's private security staff.

Two security guards stepped out from the gatehouse, guns slung over their shoulders. Their khaki uniforms and patches on their shoulders identified them as the emir's private guards.

Laila glanced at Harris to gauge his reaction. He appeared unimpressed, though he turned to her and smiled. "Are you nervous about having me meet the rest of your family?"

For a minute she forgot the part she was playing. She focused. His question was a good first-meeting question. "My mother won't be pleased you're German." She gave herself a pat on the back for remembering his cover and playing along as if they were a couple. "But she'll be happy to learn you're converting to Islam." Harris had hoped that part of their cover story would convince her family to accept him. Converting was a coup for her family, at least, if it was reality.

Since agreeing to this mission, she'd been thinking that she could have a life that had previously been an impossible dream. The man who she married needed to be faithful and true, but his religious beliefs weren't as critical as being a good person, a partner to her. She wanted a man who would treat her as an equal, and with love, respect and fairness. If she married any man her brother had selected for her, she had no doubt those dreams would be out of reach.

The armed guards approached the sedan. This level of security was new. Did the additional measures mean her brother suspected a plot was afoot? Did Mikhail know his relationship with Al-Adel and the Holy Light Brotherhood put him and the people around him in a more dangerous position? Or did the influx of international guests attending the wedding, some who held visible and high-profile positions, call for enhanced security?

If they were turned away at the entrance to the compound, Laila would have fulfilled her part of their agreement and avoided the deception that would follow. It would have been a relief and a disappointment.

If Mikhail was working with Al-Adel, he had to be stopped for the good of Qamsar and for the royal family.

Harris's hand came over hers, his thumb rubbing hers slightly. The chauffeur lowered his driver's side window.

"Everyone step out of the car," the guard said.

Laila glanced at Harris, and he nodded. "It's okay, Laila. These measures are to keep everyone safe."

To keep everyone safe or to search for a traitor? Laila got out of the car on trembling legs. Her brother and his security team had eyes and ears everywhere. Did they know she had betrayed him? Harris circled to stand next to her, and her uncle took his position on her other side. If Harris's cover had been blown and her uncle was charged guilty by association, Laila would never forgive herself.

The guards patted down the driver, her uncle and then Harris. They reached for Laila, sliding their hands down her sides and letting them linger on her hips.

"Watch your hands," Harris said in Arabic, a hint of possessiveness in his voice.

The guards immediately removed their hold on Laila, appearing startled by Harris's words. Harris didn't flinch, and his piercing look communicated he was not backing down and might be willing to be more confrontational.

"We need your identification and to search the car and your luggage. Do you have any weapons you need to declare?" one of the guards asked.

"We don't," Harris said.

His answer surprised her. He didn't have a gun with him? She had wondered how he would sneak it into the compound, but walking around unarmed seemed dangerous. What if he was discovered as an American spy? Mikhail did not treat spies or traitors with leniency. He jailed them, or in some cases, they disappeared.

"If you could please stand over here." The guard gestured to his left.

Harris said he didn't have a weapon, but had he packed anything else that would get them in trouble? Laila's mouth went dry. Equipment Harris planned to install inside the compound? Some technical gizmo that would raise questions? The chauffeur popped the trunk, and the guards began their search.

Harris clasped his hands behind his back. He took sunglasses dangling in the front of his shirt and slipped them over his eyes. "It's hotter than I thought."

Was that a coded message? He was looking around with a bored expression on his face. How did he manage it? She felt as if she would sweat through her clothes and melt in a puddle of nerves.

Laila fiddled with the ends of her head scarf. Was Harris worried about what the guards would find? After several agonizing minutes, the guards put their luggage back in the trunk and opened their car doors. "Sorry for the delay. Enjoy your visit. *As-salaam alaykum.*" *Peace be upon you.*

"Wa alaykum as-salaam," Harris and her uncle said in reply. *And with you peace.*

Laila gave Harris extra credit for knowing the proper response. He had indicated to her he'd prepared for this operation. Perhaps he had prepared more than she'd thought.

They climbed into the car and drove through the gate into the emir's compound. Despite passing the security screening at the gate, Laila didn't feel relief that the first gauntlet had been passed. They were now in the lion's den.

The foyer of the emir's main house was four stories high, a large aviary filled with colorful birds hung from the ceiling. On ground level, blue marble fountains located on either side of the double mahogany doors of the formal entryway spurted water.

They were greeted by the emir's head butler who snapped his fingers for an attendant to appear and escort them to their room. Or more precisely, their rooms. Within the walls of the compound, Harris and Laila would not be permitted to spend time together in private without supervision. If they needed to speak alone, they would have to arrange a secret meeting.

With a bid goodbye, Laila's uncle followed an attendant to his room.

Once she was escorted to her room, another attendant waited at Laila's door, making it clear he wasn't leaving her and Harris without a chaperone. Never mind that she'd been living in another country where she might have been alone with a man at any time, in the emir's home, his rules applied. For that matter, in the emir's country, his rules applied. She'd grown up with the same rules and restrictions, but in the last couple of years, she'd grown accustomed to freedom. Being here already felt stifling.

She was Qamsarian royalty and with that came intrusions into every aspect of her life. She'd been raised to accept that her life was not her own. Only since the death of her father two years ago and her subsequent time in America had she questioned that eventuality.

"I'll unpack my things and take a shower. How about we meet in an hour?" Harris asked. "You can show me Qamsar. You've spoken so often about the souk, I'd love to see it. Maybe get a gift for your mother."

She and Harris would be staying in rooms on opposite ends of the guest corridor. Laila wished he could stay closer. At least within shouting distance. She'd never spoken to Harris about the marketplace, but Laila nodded along. If he needed to go to the souk, she'd provide what cover she could.

She closed the door to her suite. What would she do for the next hour? She should call her mother to tell her that she'd arrived. Her mother was staying in the family's country home about twenty minutes from the compound.

Nervous about speaking to her mother and giving something away, Laila stalled. She opened her luggage and hung her dresses and veils. The trip had pressed wrinkles into the fabric, but she could send them to be pressed later. She set her toiletries in the en suite on the counter.

She jumped at the sensation of hands on her waist. She whirled and found herself looking at Harris. His blue eyes were bright, and his full lips caught her attention.

"What are you doing?" she asked.

"I missed you," he said, his eyes twinkling in amusement.

Her heart rate jumped. He had? They'd been apart for less than twenty minutes. She pushed his hands away.

"I need to check your room," he said.

Disappointment plowed through her. He'd been teasing. Flirting with her. As part of their role or because he liked her? Before they'd left the States, Harris had made it clear, once he was in character, he stayed that way. It was easier to live the lie fully immersed, as opposed to switching roles. How much of his flirtation was the real Harris, and how much was him playing a role? It was their first day in this charade, and Laila was questioning their relationship. It was a disquieting emotional place to be.

"How do you know no one saw you come in here?" she asked.

"I was careful. I came in through the balcony." He pointed across the room to the sliding glass doors.

She hadn't heard him open the doors. Or land on the balcony for that matter. She needed to be more alert.

Harris walked around her room, fiddling with his cell phone. "I can't get a signal." He swung the phone in every direction. After several minutes, he stopped. "Your room is clean. Mine is not."

Laila lifted her brow. He'd been using his phone to check for surveillance equipment. "Your room is bugged?"

"Audio surveillance. Probably not video, but I can't be sure. I had to get creative with leaving my room. Good thing all of the balconies are close together."

"Did you remove the bug?" she asked.

"And tip off whoever planted it that I found it? No way. I'll wait for the right opportunity and have it malfunction. Closer to the wedding, when more guests are staying here, the staff will be stretched too thin to follow up on a broken transmitter. By then I'll have won them over with my charm." He grinned at her. His smile threw fuel on the crush she'd developed on him. Some men were too handsome for their own good.

"You won't win anyone over if someone finds you in my room." It would be a terrible breach of protocol and inappropriate at best.

His face reflected concern. "No one saw me. I needed to know you were okay."

Whenever he looked at her that way, his eyes bright and filled with emotion, heat spread across her chest. Did he mean what he said? Or was he being the German boyfriend? She couldn't bring herself to put it into words. It was too embarrassing and too needy to ask, "Do you like me or are you using me?"

It was better for both of them to assume the latter.

A knock at her door sounded and fear raced through her. Harris had to hide. If he was discovered in her room, she would be in serious trouble. Could he fit under the bed? Should he go out the balcony? Harris didn't wait for instruction. He was nearest to the closet, and he pulled open the bifold door, gestured to her and the suite's door, and then silently closed the door behind him.

Laila steadied her nerves and opened the door to her room. Mikhail was on the other side, hands clasped behind his back, a somber expression on his face. He stepped into her room and looked around. "Do you find your accommodations pleasing?" he asked.

Did he know something? Mikhail was her brother, but her nerves tightened, and her mouth went dry. He'd never been easy to get along with, and since becoming emir, he was more difficult, his temper on a hair trigger.

As a child, Mikhail had been hot-tempered. As a

young adult, he'd had an elitist, entitled attitude. Growing up, Mikhail had been close with her uncle, her father's youngest brother, Hakim. Hakim didn't believe in changing Qamsar's culture or in civil rights for minorities or the poor. He supported the old ways and believed that power was best placed with the royal family, and everyone else should do as commanded for the betterment of the country. Hakim was killed in a sandstorm when he was thirty, and his death had affected Mikhail deeply. Mikhail had admired him and his beliefs about preserving the culture of Qamsar. If Al-Adel was feeding into Mikhail's ideas, perhaps Mikhail had found the coconspirator he'd been missing since Hakim had died. It was the best explanation she could come up with for why her brother was so different from their father and her other brother, Saafir.

Instead of the guest suites, Laila would have rather stayed in her old room, but Mikhail had remodeled that part of the compound, and her and her brother Saafir's bedrooms had been repurposed. "Yes, thank you for your hospitality." Her decorum with her brother lacked warmth, but that had been the case for years. Despite her father's insistence they behave amicably with each other, they'd never developed a close relationship, and with the shadow of the car bombing looming, anxiety in her brother's company was high.

Mikhail lifted his chin, looking down at her. "I was surprised to learn you'd attend the wedding. You gave the impression you had too much work to do in America." The last word of his sentence sounded like he was spitting bile.

"I made arrangements. I wanted to be part of your special day. I know how important this is to you and

Qamsar." She hated lying. Was her face turning red? Heat flamed up her body, and her cheeks felt hot.

Mikhail nodded his approval of her decision. "I was worried you were turning into a liberal Yank."

Mikhail's dislike for America wasn't a secret. He wanted to move the Qamsarian economy forward and bring more wealth to the country. He saw America as both an impediment and a necessity to that end. Negotiating with the American government frustrated Mikhail. He was accustomed to having power, and as the smaller country with fewer resources, he had to compromise his goals to gain the support of the larger country. Turning away from working with America wasn't an option unless he could build a lucrative alliance with another country. The people of Qamsar wanted those connections, those protections and those ties to market their products internationally.

"Of course not. I am loyal to my country." She was betraying her brother by being here, by allowing Harris to spy on Mikhail's wedding and within the compound to find Al-Adel, but she was doing what was right for Qamsar.

"I heard about your car trouble in America," Mikhail said.

Her car trouble? Was he referring to the attempt on her life? Harris had discussed with her how to play it. "The authorities are looking into it. I am sure they will find the guilty person."

"Probably some hateful, anti-Middle Eastern American with too much time on his hands. Maybe you should take it as a sign to come home," Mikhail said.

Laila studied him carefully, looking for indications of guilt. Would he say more on the topic if she remained quiet? Mikhail wouldn't have set the bomb to force her to return to Qamsar. There were easier, less deadly ways to get her to leave America. Would he insist she move back? "I am enjoying my studies."

"Father always said you had an inquisitive mind and should be kept busy. That belief is the reason I haven't made you return."

At the mention of their father, grief brought tears to her eyes. Mikhail permitting her to study in America was out of deference for their father. She hadn't considered that.

Mikhail looked away. "We need to talk later about the man you brought to the compound."

He knew! Laila schooled her expression as panic raged inside her. Had she given herself or Harris away? Watching Mikhail's face, Laila didn't see signs of anger or danger. She calmed her racing thoughts. Her brother wanted to talk about the man who she'd brought home. If Mikhail believed Harris to be a spy or an American, they wouldn't have been allowed to enter the house.

A creak sounded in the closet, and Laila forced herself not to turn. Did Mikhail hear it? Her heart beat a nervous staccato. "We can talk about it now if you'd like." While Harris was close enough to protect her. Did Harris understand enough Arabic to follow their conversation?

"I have a meeting. I don't have time. I stopped in because Mother asked me to do so when you arrived."

An obligatory visit. "Thank you for saying hello." Did her voice sound higher than normal, or was it in her head?

Mikhail looked around the room again. Had he

heard Harris in the closet? Would he search the room before he left?

"As-salaam alaykum," Mikhail said.

Laila lowered her eyes to the floor. *"Wa alaykum as-salaam."*

Mikhail left the room, and Laila waited a full minute before she moved. Was he gone? Would he return? Harris stepped out of the closet.

"That was close," Harris said and his mouth twitched.

Was he enjoying this? "Too close. We need to be careful." Pangs of doubt played on her thoughts. When she had imagined herself speaking to her family, she was a good liar. They believed her. Could she maintain this lie while in front of them? She and her uncle had agreed not to discuss the operation inside the compound walls. She couldn't speak the truth to anyone and had to maintain her cover at all times. She felt overwhelmed and terrified. "Someone will find out. It's too suspicious."

Harris's eyebrows furrowed with worry. "Suspicious how?"

"I've never brought a man to meet the family."

"You've also never been on your own for two years," Harris said.

Time in America had changed her, but would her family view the change as too abrupt? "How can I play pretend around-the-clock?" She rubbed her temples where a massive stress headache was forming.

Harris pressed his lips together. "Let me offer a compromise." He took a deep breath, and she waited. "When we're alone in this room, you'll be you and I'll be Harris Truman. Anything you need to say to me or get off your chest, you do it here with me. The rest of the time, we stay undercover."

A small measure of relief passed over her. She wouldn't be alone in her room with Harris often, but he was offering her something. If their mission became too much, she had a brief sanctuary from the lies. "Thank you. Yes. Here it will be you and me. Out there," she said and pointed to the door, "it is Princess Laila and wealthy heir Harris Kuhn."

Princess Laila and Harris Kuhn were to be engaged. How would a woman in her position behave toward a man like Harris? Even if her thoughts had changed since living in America, the culture in Qamsar hadn't moved forward. She had no firsthand experience with men in that way, or in any way, but Laila was curious and hopeful about that part of her life.

Laila's gaze traveled to Harris's mouth. No touches or kisses. It was what a Qamsarian woman expected from a relationship until she was married, but Laila wasn't sure what she wanted from a relationship. If Laila had a German boyfriend, wouldn't their relationship be a mixture of the two cultures? She drew in the heavy air, feeling as if there wasn't enough oxygen in it. It was Harris. That connection, that electricity that never stopped flowing between them was making her think about relationships, desire and lust. Topics she'd put out of her mind, knowing they weren't available to her.

Until now.

Until the possibility of staying in the United States and building a life where she was more than a submissive wife and mother were on the table. The possibility of marrying for love. She could be herself in a relationship. An equal partner.

"Will your brother stop by to see you often?" Harris asked.

Though he spoke in Arabic, he had dropped his German accent. Hearing his American accent on the Arabic words for the first time since they'd arrived in Qamsar was startling. "Hard to say. We lived together before I moved in with my aunt and uncle. Mikhail and I have never gotten along," Laila said.

"We'll expect interruptions and be as careful as we can," Harris said.

"I was worried the guards would find something when they searched the car and our luggage," she said.

"Nothing to find."

Laila held her tongue over the barrage of questions. The less she knew, the better. She couldn't slip up and say anything in front of her family.

"I was planning to head to the souk and see the sights. Feel like helping me find my way?" Harris asked.

"We'll need to find someone to accompany us." Would that be a problem for him? What did he have planned? "Maybe after we do some shopping, we can have dinner with my mother at our family's country house?"

Harris nodded. "No problem. Let's find out how to get our hands on a car and an escort, and we'll go."

"I presume you'll leave the way you came in?" she asked.

He winked at her. "You got it. I'll meet you in the lobby in ten minutes." He waited at the balcony door for a few minutes before stepping outside.

The heat of the day rushed in, and Laila looked out the doors into the lush landscape. The emir's gardens were beautifully maintained, every walking path clear, the plants shaped and benches clean. Did Mikhail spend much time walking in the gardens as their father had? The emir's compound was the nicest place in Qamsar, containing the finest luxuries.

As a child, she had thought of the compound like a castle. Now it was large and foreboding, the last place she wanted to be.

Laila called her mother, disappointed when she didn't answer her phone. She left a message, telling her mother she'd arrived safely and would see her soon.

She checked her appearance again in the mirror. If she was having dinner with her mother, it would be best for her to wear something less wrinkled. She selected a white dress that had the least crumpled fabric and wrapped a navy head scarf around her hair. Her dress was loose and comfortable, and would be cool in the heat of the afternoon.

After pulling on a pair of flat, plain shoes, she left her room and locked the door behind her. Not that she had any expectation of privacy. Mikhail would make it his business to be aware of everything that went on inside his compound. If he wanted to go into her room, he would.

Harris was waiting in the lobby for her, leaning against the wall, hands casually in his pockets. He had covered his head with a *ghutra*. Though it wasn't expected for him to wear it, it would help him blend. With sunglasses over his eyes, he'd be less identifiable, his blond hair and light skin an obvious difference from most native Qamsarians with their darker skin and hair.

"Ready?" he asked. The German accent had returned.

Laila nodded and clasped her hands in front of her. Harris didn't touch her. Didn't try to. He followed her to the lobby where Mikhail's butler explained the car situation. A driver would escort them to the souk and serve as their chaperone and security detail.

Harris didn't seem upset by the arrangements. If he was planning to smuggle something into the compound to help them search for Al-Adel or to keep them safe, how would he do so with the driver watching them? The security guards at the front gate would search them and the car again. What was Harris planning? Their mission was to find Al-Adel and alert Harris's team if they saw him or heard rumors about his arrival. Would Harris need a weapon to protect them if someone uncovered their real objectives for being at the wedding?

On the drive to the souk, Laila spoke to Harris about her life in Qamsar. Harris asked questions to spur the conversation. To anyone listening, it was a casual getting-to-know-you-better conversation.

When they arrived at the souk, the driver got out of the car and followed them. His behavior indicated his presence wasn't a negotiation. Laila and Harris wouldn't be alone for any portion of the trip.

In the busyness of the marketplace, Harris and Laila walked beside each other, not touching, the driver close behind them.

The marketplace was flooded with hundreds, if not thousands, of people. The CIA had told Laila to assume she was always being watched. It left her with an eerie feeling. She hadn't considered that Mikhail would place surveillance devices in the guest rooms. If she did anything wrong, anything out of place, it could be reported to her oldest brother and put her status with Mikhail in jeopardy. Laila didn't believe her brother held much regard for her, but at the best, he was indifferent. Earning his displeasure risked the operation.

Harris slipped on his dark sunglasses. For someone who looked foreign, he blended remarkably well.

"How are you enjoying yourself so far?" Laila asked him. Though he wasn't visiting for pleasure, and though the circumstances weren't ideal, she wanted Harris to have something good to say about her country. Wanted him to see the beauty around them. Most of what he knew about the country might be negative, but the emir's possible relationship with a terrorist didn't describe the country as a whole.

"Things are going well so far. How are you feeling?" he asked. He glanced at her and then returned to looking around the crowd, strolling slowly through the cobblestone streets. They skirted around a fenced-in area containing herd animals.

The driver stayed close behind them. Laila wished he would give them space or at least pretend as if he wasn't hanging on to every word they spoke to each other.

Her nerves were wound, but overall, she was fine. "It's nice to be home. I've missed my mom and my family. I love my life in America, but when I'm there, I'm aware I'm a foreigner."

Harris nodded in understanding. "I know what you mean. Whenever I travel abroad, it's not only how I look that makes me stand out from the locals. It's not knowing the customs and culture. I feel like I make insulting mistakes." With the exception of a brief time in her room, he hadn't dropped his German accent for a moment since they'd arrived. How did he stay perfectly in character? She felt as if she needed to check every word that left her mouth to be sure she wasn't blowing their cover.

"Do you have anything you're looking for specifically? I can take you to the best shops with the nicest wares. I know an antique dealer who sells some unique pieces." Was he eyeing something in particular for his mission?

"I read that the marketplace is the perfect location to shop for perfumes and carpets. My family might like a few local specialties as gifts. And of course, I'll need something for your mother."

It would make a good impression that Harris had gotten her mother a gift. "My mother is a practical woman. She won't expect anything elaborate." Anything too elaborate and Mikhail would take possession of it. She and Harris had discussed purchasing a gift for her mother before leaving the United States. If she and Harris were to become engaged, a gift of equal measure to Laila's social status would be expected from him to her family. Since their relationship was a sham, Laila didn't think putting the CIA through an additional expense made sense. By the time it became important for Harris to give Laila's family a lavish gift, the ruse would be up. For now, a thoughtful trinket was best.

"I'll let you give me guidance on what to get your mom. In my country, flowers and wine are appropriate. I'm guessing there's another protocol here." A man walking in the opposite direction bumped her, and her shoulder brushed Harris's.

Harris reached to steady her, his hands on her for only a moment, but it was heated enough to sear her to the core. "Are you all right?" he asked, shooting an annoyed look in the direction of the man who'd jolted her.

Laila wished she had brought a hand fan. It was too hot. The souk was crowded, and without the wind blowing, it was stuffy and confining. She wouldn't focus on how it felt to touch Harris. "I'm fine. I'm thinking my mom might like a small piece of artwork, like a statue or a landscape painting. One of her hobbies is painting scenery. Or maybe a set of worry beads." Her father had several worry beads he'd gotten at important dates in his life, among them when he'd become emir, when he'd married Laila's mother and when each of his three children was born. To continue the tradition and have Harris present her mother with a set to mark the occasion of their meeting would have significance to her mother.

In the event her mother grew to like Harris, she would be disappointed when she learned Harris and Laila's relationship was fake. Perhaps the worry beads and her mother forming any connection to Harris were a mistake. Before she could make another suggestion, Harris answered.

"That sounds great. We can also look for something for my mother and two sisters-in-law. I've heard the perfumes here are the best. I think they would get a thrill out of a special perfume."

Laila had known the stakes before she'd agreed to this. Being in Qamsar was harder than she'd imagined. She reassured herself that her deception was only required for a short time, and she was doing the right thing for her country and her family.

Harris was talking like a tourist. She had assumed he had a secondary motivation for coming to the souk. Maybe she'd been wrong. She'd been anticipating a cloak-and-dagger routine. "I know a shop that sells amazing scents. I'll let you know when we get there."

They were beckoned to a jewelry stall. "You wish to buy something for your beautiful lady?" the vendor asked, holding out a few necklaces for Harris to see.

Harris turned to her. "See anything you like?"

He wanted to buy her something? It wasn't necessary. Or was this part of the role he was playing: rich German heir? Would the girlfriend of such a man decline the gift, or would she be so accustomed to being spoiled that accepting would be natural?

Laila was overthinking. She wasn't pretending to be anyone. She was herself. "You don't need to buy me anything, Harris. But thank you."

"I have beautiful gold bracelets. They would look lovely on your lady," the vendor pressed.

"She's already lovely," Harris said.

The compliment tickled her insides. The vendor held a gold bangle bracelet with silver threading in the shape of ivy wrapping around the gold.

Laila gasped. It was a beautiful piece. "This reminds me of a ring that belonged to my great-great-grandmother. This has the same ivy pattern set against the gold."

"If we can work out a price, I'll take it," Harris said.

Laila whirled to him in surprise. "You don't need to buy that."

Harris negotiated with the vendor and smiled when they struck a deal. He turned and presented it to Laila.

"I saw how you looked at it. You can wear it to your brother's wedding. It's my special gift to you."

She slipped the bracelet over her hand onto her wrist and secured the safety clasp. "Thank you. This is nice of you and unexpected." It was the first piece of jewelry, or any gift she had received from a man she wasn't related to. "You didn't have to buy this."

Harris lifted a brow at her. "I know I didn't *have* to. I wanted to. Is there a place where you'd like to stop for a few moments to get something to eat? I'd like to look around on my own. You can stay with the driver."

Laila glanced at the driver standing a step away, watching Laila with annoyance in his eyes. Was he irritated he had been sent to babysit her, or did he have some personal problem with her?

"Maybe we should stay together," Laila said. Was Harris safe alone?

"Perhaps I should take you to see your mother first, and then return?" he asked.

Stash her somewhere first? Was what he needed to do that dangerous? What if something happened to him? How would anyone know? He could disappear in the country and never be heard from again.

"I'd like to stay together," she said. She should go along with whatever he said. It had been the plan when leaving the United States, but now she was worried about him.

Harris looked at her, studying her face, perhaps trying to understand her reasons without asking the question. "All right. If you insist."

She processed the words. Had her refusal caused a problem with his plans? He wouldn't argue in front of the driver and raise suspicions.

Harris continued walking and stopped at a stall where the vendor was selling shoes. He picked up a pair and turned them over. "Are these leather?"

The vendor nodded. "The finest leather. Soft. Will contour to your feet the more you wear them."

Harris held up his hand. "I'll take two pairs. And a pair for the lady."

Laila didn't think the shoes were attractive. They looked like shoes to wear on a construction site, heavy and durable. She opened her mouth to protest and then thought better of it. The CIA had asked her to go along with Harris when possible, and since they were in front of the vendor and the driver, no point in arguing with him. If he wanted to buy ugly shoes, then fine.

The guard escorting them leaned in close to look at the shoes. Was something wrong with them? Why did he seem interested in Harris's purchase? He hadn't cared when Harris had bought her the bracelet.

With the laces knotted and the shoes thrown over his shoulder, Harris continued along the marketplace. He bought a few bottles of perfume for the women in his family and an ornamental carpet, the items she'd expect a vacationer to buy. He was playing his role well.

At an artist's shop, he purchased a strand of rose-colored glass worry beads for her mother. It was delicate with the colored spheres catching the sun.

"Did you get what you needed?" she asked.

"Almost everything," Harris said. He looked ahead and continued walking.

Laila kept waiting for something to happen. For a man to lean out from an alley and draw them inside and give them a package. For someone to slip Harris a bag. For Harris to pick up a lone package off the sidewalk, left by another asset.

A man walking by stopped and pointed to Harris's shoes. "I can take those off your hands if you'd like."

Harris shook his head. "The stall ahead on the left sells them. You'll have your pick of color and size."

"I'd prefer shoes that were broken in," he said.

"Can't help you there," Harris said.

The man looked between her and Harris a few times. She stepped closer to Harris, unsure if the man was considering mugging them or stealing the shoes. It struck her as odd, since the shoes weren't remarkable or expensive. Whatever the nameless man was thinking, he decided to leave them alone and hurried in the direction of the shoe stall.

"That was strange," Laila said.

Harris made a noncommittal sound.

Was that conversation some coded exchange of information? "You bought those ugly shoes—" The guard was hanging on to every word, and Laila stopped her train of thought.

Harris's eyes widened slightly. "Hey, they are not ugly."

For a moment, she worried she'd offended him. Then she saw the amused gleam in his eyes. What good were ugly shoes? Was he trying to smuggle something inside them? Laila hadn't seen him pick up anything and put it inside the shoes. Did he have a gun stashed somewhere? Would he risk it, knowing they'd be searched, and if caught, they'd be in danger? American spy movies had her imagination running untamed.

"Whatever you say," Laila said. "Don't think you're wearing them to the wedding."

"But I bought a pair for you so we'd match."

She scrunched up her face. "Gee, thanks. I'll return the favor sometime. Maybe you'd like to wear matching head scarves."

Harris let out a bark of laughter. "Perhaps. I wonder what your family would think of that."

They'd think he was crazy. His blue eyes shone in the sun. He was a beautiful, captivating man. One who could make her think he had feelings for her, who could make her believe their romance was real. No matter how Harris looked at her or how he treated her, she had to keep their objective at the front of her mind. He was in Qamsar to find and stop a terrorist. He wasn't interested in falling in love, least of all with her. "If you dressed like a woman, my family would have questions," she said.

Harris grinned at her and molten heat rolled through her.

"I'm ready to leave whenever you are. The heat is getting to me," Harris said, plucking at his shirt.

Based on his nonchalant response, she was alone in feeling the chemistry between them. She refocused on the mission. If Harris had been in the souk for information, except for his strange and brief interaction with a man offering to buy the shoes, Laila hadn't seen anything unusual. She couldn't have explained the purpose or reason for the interaction if questioned.

If anyone asked her what she and Harris did in the souk, she could tell the truth. He'd bought presents for his family, a bracelet for her, a gift for her mother and ugly shoes. The driver would corroborate her story.

"I'll call my mother and see if she's ready for our visit," Laila said.

Laila took out her cell phone and dialed her mother.

Her mother answered on the second ring. "I was hoping you would call again. I missed your first call by ten minutes."

Laila's chest filled with happiness at the thought of seeing her mother. "Harris and I are finished at the souk. Are we too early for dinner? I wouldn't mind extra time to visit with you." She and her mother had kept in touch over the phone and with almost daily emails, but talking in person was better.

"I can't wait to see you. I've been calling you, but the calls went straight to voice mail," Iba said.

"The signal is sometimes weak here," Laila said.

"I'd love to have you over, but didn't Mikhail tell you?" Iba asked.

Laila's stomach knotted. "Tell me what?"

"He's invited guests in town for the wedding to the compound tonight. He has a special announcement. I don't know what it is. I was getting ready to leave now." Her mother sounded reserved and tense.

A special announcement sounded ominous. Maybe it was something to do with the wedding, or maybe it was another opportunity for Mikhail to make a declaration about how he planned to keep his family under his thumb. More monitoring. More check-ins. More rules. "Okay, then we'll see you there."

Dread and worry heavy in her stomach, Laila said goodbye to her mother and disconnected the call. "Change of plans. Mikhail is having a dinner and making a special announcement tonight."

The corners of Harris's mouth turned down. He addressed the driver. "Sounds like we need to return to the compound."

The driver glanced at his watch and nodded. "It would be offensive to be late."

Why hadn't Mikhail mentioned anything when he'd stopped by her room earlier in the day? If the news was bad, maybe he didn't want to give her a chance to run. What if Mikhail's special announcement was her engagement to one of his lackeys?

Chapter 3

Harris preferred sticking to plans. It was easier to put contingencies and backups into place when he understood the factors at play. A special announcement by the emir didn't have a pleasing ring to it. Harris wished he could make contact with the Bureau before the dinner and figure out who or what had changed in the political environment, but making contact when it wasn't an emergency was a mistake. Harris had a German number to call for check-ins, the cover being that the number belonged to his brother. But Harris couldn't get information or ask questions without risking someone overhearing his conversation. The CIA wasn't sure how technologically advanced the emir's security team was. Until Harris had a better sense of their abilities, he'd assume them to be masterfully skilled and be extra careful about calling his fake company from his cellular phone.

Harris and Laila returned to the compound. After another search of the car and themselves, they were allowed inside. First hurdle passed. They hadn't given his shoes, carpet or perfume a second glance. Lucky for him.

His assessment of the emir's security team's abilities moved a notch down from masterful.

Alone in his room, Harris turned on the radio and tuned to a station playing soft, relaxing music. He killed the lights. He'd checked for bugs again, but without more sophisticated equipment, he couldn't be certain if more had been hidden while he was out of the room. In the dark, he removed the thin plastic blade and small bottle of glue secured to the lining of his suitcase. He got into bed, pretending to need a nap. Jet lag. Long flight. Sleep was plausible.

Underneath the covers, he slit the heels of the shoes and removed the surveillance equipment. Five bugs in all, equipped with video and sound. If he needed more, he'd make contact with his asset and get a message to his team. He glued the soles back on the shoes.

Then he waited. For fifteen minutes he pretended to rest. Shortly thereafter he slipped two of the bugs into his pocket and got out of bed, leaving the rest tucked inside the pillowcase.

While getting ready and moving around the room, he made his bed and hid the rest of the bugs. If his room was searched while he was away, he risked trouble, but how often could his things be checked? The emir had nearly a thousand guests invited to his wedding, many of them staying at the compound.

Every room couldn't be searched daily. At some point, his would be again, but he'd place the devices soon in a predetermined list of locations. Based on what the CIA knew about Mikhail's compound and from the information Laila had supplied about the layout, the target locations were Mikhail's private quarters and offices on the east wing's second floor, the main dining area being used for entertaining guests and the library where Mikhail often retired in the evenings with colleagues. Getting to the emir's private quarters and the library would be difficult, but Harris would find a way.

The CIA had attempted to recruit a domestic employee on the inside to assist with this job. As yet they'd met with failure. Most of Mikhail's staff were too afraid to speak to someone about the emir, worried it was a trap testing their loyalty, and were unwilling to put their lives and families at risk.

If the CIA had placed someone on the inside, when he checked in with Tyler, the CIA agent playing his brother, he'd get the coded message. From what Harris could tell, the mission was going well. He'd picked up the bugs from the souk and gotten them into the compound without detection.

Laila was doing an amazing job as his girlfriend. She was appropriately affectionate with him, which in this world consisted of long looks and smiles from under her lashes. Old-fashioned flirting. He enjoyed it more than he should.

Playing the part of Harris Kuhn, German tycoon and heir who wanted to marry Laila, made it hard to separate the fantasy from the reality. The reality—that she was an asset, and he was involved in a dangerous mission with multiple lives at stake—was harsh. The fantasy—that Laila was his girlfriend, that he would steal kisses from her when he could, that he would sweep her off her feet and take her away from this world—was a lie.

His attraction to her and their chemistry was part of the reason this mission worked and created a believable situation. It was also the reason the operation was more difficult.

He had to stay in character and still maintain his distance from her. If he became emotionally involved, his judgment would be skewed. He'd been in that position before and wouldn't allow it again.

Harris changed into another outfit he'd been told by his contacts in the CIA was appropriate for a German to wear to a formal occasion in Qamsar. Harris didn't realize the agency had experts on such details, but he'd learned a lot about the CIA in the past few months. They had resources he didn't have with the FBI, including international experts on language, culture, protocol and politics. A knowledgeable staff was available 24/7/365 during a mission in case the situation went off the skids, and he needed advice or help. The CIA had a budget that supported the extensive resources Harris couldn't have hoped to have at the FBI.

Even so, this operation was Harris's first experience with the CIA, and he wasn't sure he liked working with them. They were more secretive and seemed to have hidden agendas. Part of him worried they weren't being forthcoming with him about this mission. Did they need access to the emir to stop a terrorist and preserve negotiations for oil, or did their interest lie elsewhere?

Harris was meeting Laila in the lobby at seven

o'clock. He arrived a few minutes early and watched the people around him. Others were milling around, greeting each other and talking. Harris had chosen this location on purpose, planning to keep his and Laila's meetings public to clarify to anyone watching he understood the boundaries. He needed Mikhail to accept him, and feel Harris was respectful of their culture and traditions, not to kick him out and blacklist him because he'd crossed a line.

Sticking to the rules, appealing to Mikhail's sense of social climbing, playing on his interests and making it clear Harris's family's shipping company was useful would keep Harris in the compound long enough to complete his mission. He'd set the bugs, watch when and where he could, and hope they'd find Ahmad Al-Adel.

Laila stepped into the foyer and glanced around, searching for him. He stole the moment to take in her beauty and grace. He'd been prepared to keep his eyes pinned to her face, but his gaze wandered down her body. Her navy dress covered her from wrists to ankles. The light blue embroidery along the sleeves, neck and length of the dress suggested shape around her curves. She'd applied more dramatic makeup than he'd seen her wear in the past, emphasizing the darkness of her eyes, the deep pools of brown a man could lose himself in if he wasn't careful. Her hair was covered, and when she reached to adjust her head wrap, he saw gold bangles on her wrists, including the one he had bought for her in the souk.

He'd purchased it to stay in character. In pursuing a woman's affections, a man as wealthy as Harris Kuhn would buy his girlfriend whatever she wanted.

But seeing Laila wear the bracelet brought him a certain amount of pride and pleasure that had nothing to do with playing a part. She was a beautiful woman, and she deserved beautiful things.

Seeing him, a smile lit her face, and she strode toward him. "I hope you haven't been waiting long."

"I didn't want to be late and get off on the wrong foot with the emir and your family." Not only did Harris not want to miss anything—or anyone—he was playing the role of nervous suitor meeting Laila's family for the first time. "Nervous suitor" would be early and fidgety.

She glanced at his feet. "You aren't wearing the shoes." She seemed a bit relieved.

He grinned. "I have to break them in first. But once I get them ready, they won't leave my feet."

She laughed. "Oh, good. I can't wait." The smile on her face reached to her eyes. He was mesmerized by her. Entranced.

Which made it easier to play this part. No danger of anything coming of it, not in the long run. Not only did his relationship history prove he couldn't make things work, his job also required he give her space when they returned to the United States. He wouldn't make the same mistake twice and get involved with someone while he was working.

After the mission, he'd never see her again. Sadly it was the way most of his personal relationships ended. He'd been trained to analyze people and scrutinize their relationships, he could create profiles of men who were good and bad at relationships, but he couldn't manage to keep one of his own. Worse still, some of the women he'd been attracted to in the past had been disastrously flawed. The last had betrayed his undercover identity to the target of an investigation, putting him and his team in grave danger. If her betrayal hadn't been discovered, he'd have been killed.

Saying he was bad at relationships was an understatement.

"I'm anxious about tonight, too. I can't wait to see my mother and my family, but I'm worried about what Mikhail wishes to tell us," Laila said.

"I'm sure everything is okay," Harris said. He had the same worry, but if anyone was eavesdropping, he wanted to come across as confident in Mikhail and reassuring to Laila.

Without touching, Harris escorted her to the dining room.

The maître d' for the evening seated them close to the head table where the emir and his bride would sit. It was a terrible view of the dining room entrance. Harris wished they would have been placed in the back. It was a large event, and Harris wanted to get a look at the attendees.

Two dozen tables seating ten each were covered in perfectly pressed white linen cloths and immaculately displayed dinnerware. Maroon carpets blended with the cherrywood of the chairs. Staff stood around the edges of the room, waiting to spring to action when summoned.

"Is something wrong?" Laila asked Harris, leaning closer to him and keeping her voice low.

Had he been scowling? He adjusted his expression to neutral. "I'm keeping an eye on things. Waiting for your mother." Looking for faces he might recognize, like any of the known members of the Holy Light Brotherhood.

Laila nodded and lifted her water glass, taking a sip. "Nothing to worry about. She'll like you."

Harris wasn't sure about that, but his primary goal was to watch the crowd. Though he could have spent the evening watching Laila, her elegant movements, the delicate way she lifted her glass and set it down, that wasn't part of the mission, either.

Harris forced his eyes away from Laila and looked around the room, constraining his expression to remain blank as his gaze landed on royal family members in high-ranking political positions. Such people wouldn't impress a wealthy German business heir.

"Mother." Laila rose to her feet. She looked as if she wanted to run to her mother in greeting, but protocol and decorum stopped her.

Harris stood and waited. No denying it was Laila's mother. They could have been sisters; they looked so much alike.

Laila's mother was escorted by an older man. Laila hugged her mother and the two clasped hands, looking at each other as if they had much to say. The pair had great respect, love and admiration for each other. Harris got an inside look at why Laila had agreed to take a risk in exchange for a safe life in the United States for her mother. Her mother's happiness and safety meant a great deal to her.

The man approached Laila and Harris, extending his hand in greeting to Harris. "I am Khalid bin Jassim Al Sharani. This is my late brother's wife, Iba."

Laila and her mother broke apart, and Iba turned to Harris. Her eyes were as sharp and intelligent as her daughter's. Harris got the impression neither woman missed anything.

Harris introduced himself and waited for Khalid to continue.

Khalid gestured for everyone to sit. "We were surprised to learn Laila was bringing a friend to the wedding. In the past Laila has preferred to be on her own. She's always been an independent woman. Aasim has only good things to say about you, Harris, but he admitted he didn't know you well."

A test, Harris was sure. "Laila and I have been friends for some time. I was pleased to be invited. My family has vacationed in this area, and they've always spoken highly of Qamsar. This is my first time in the country."

Khalid took an ornate ceramic cup from the center of the table. Almost as soon as he turned it over, a waiter appeared with a carafe in his hand and poured coffee into the cup. "Where did your family vacation?" Khalid asked, not acknowledging the waiter except with a wave of his hand.

Harris was prepared with a lie. "They stayed in Cyprus, near the beach at the Palm Hotel."

Khalid liked Harris's response, whether the reference to the elite area of Cyprus or the luxuriousness of the Palm Hotel impressed him. Harris was glad he hadn't made an enemy of Khalid. Yet.

"What do you think of our country?" Khalid asked. He took a sip of his coffee.

Harris glanced at Laila and her mother. Laila was staring intently at him, worry written on her face. To anyone watching, she was nervous about the scrutiny her suitor was receiving from her uncle. Harris knew the truth. She was worried he'd make a mistake and say something to incriminate them.

Harris was too practiced and too deep into the part. He wouldn't let on who he was or why he was in Qamsar. "I've only seen the compound and the souk. Everything has been great. Of course, part of that is having an excellent tour guide to tell me about the area and the history." He inclined his head toward Laila.

Harris glanced at Laila and was struck once again by how beautiful she was. It was difficult for him to keep his eyes off her. Even showing almost no skin, her clothing loose and her hair covered, she was breathtaking. He'd always thought women in lingerie or wearing provocative clothing drew a man's attention. In this case, Laila drew his attention without giving anything away. She redefined sexy.

Harris was saved from more questions. A hush fell over the room as the emir entered with his future bride, Aisha. Mikhail wore a dark suit, western-style, and his bride looked happy in an orange dress, a head scarf covering her hair and neck. Mikhail stopped to speak with several men waiting near his table. Harris watched and smiled, mimicking the other guests around him.

Aisha's father was a prominent businessman in Qamsar, and their marriage had been arranged when the two were infants.

The emir's brother, Saafir, sat at a table near the head table, a teacup between his hands. He appeared somber. He wasn't mingling with other guests, and he didn't appear thrilled to be at the dinner. Was there bad blood between the brothers? Resentment that Mikhail, as the older brother, had inherited his position and his fortune? Very little had been available to the CIA and FBI about Saafir's personal life.

Harris memorized the faces of the men Mikhail seemed closest to and made a mental note to speak to them sometime in the next few days if he could. After several minutes Mikhail stood behind his table and gestured to his bride who sat at his side, gazing up at him. She had nailed the role of adoring wife. How much of her behavior was genuine, and how much was an act? Appearances were important to the royal family, but was Aisha pleased about her arranged marriage?

"Thank you to everyone for attending tonight's festivities, the first of many we have planned over the next several days. Some of you have traveled a great distance to wish me and my bride a happy life together."

The emir looked around the room. "Because you are my family and my closest friends, I have some upsetting news to share. I considered keeping the news secret to not put a blight on the festivities, but I want everyone to be alert and aware and not confused by gossip."

Laila tensed. Next to Mikhail, Aisha shifted in her chair, a frown on her face.

"My security team has learned that a member of the American government has attempted to infiltrate my home and to intrude on my wedding."

Laila's shoulders hiked, and Harris worked overtime to school his expression. He hadn't been discovered. He'd been careful. Sweat dripped down his back. He wasn't armed at the moment. If he had to get out of this room with Laila and her mother, it would be difficult to get past the security and staff.

"He's been apprehended and will be dealt with swiftly and sternly," Mikhail said.

Not him, then. Relief washed over Harris and on its heels, more questions. Who had Mikhail jailed? Harris wasn't aware of another American posted in the compound for the wedding. His communication with the CIA was limited, and he needed to be careful how and when he checked in. He'd have to do what digging he could to uncover if Mikhail's announcement was being used as a warning or if it was the truth.

If it was the truth, Harris needed to do what he could to free his fellow American or gather information so that he could be freed. Was the CIA aware an American had been on the premises and had been captured?

While the emir's wedding may mean a moratorium on government-sanctioned deaths for a few days, Qamsar wasn't known for its leniency or for fair and unbiased trials. They weren't known for having trials at all for suspected spies.

"I have invited many important guests into my home, and they are to be treated with respect," Mikhail said. "I have friends all over the world, from countries who are not always allies with each other. But here, inside my home, those resentments are not welcome. This is a place of sanctuary."

Important guests. Were any of those guests Ahmad Al-Adel? Harris hid his amusement over Mikhail's announcement implying he wasn't looking to make enemies and wanted peace within his borders. If he was working with Al-Adel, he was joining himself to a man who had many enemies and left a path of destruction in his wake. Mikhail was not interested in having friends all over the world. His dislike for America was strong in his policies and his resistance of America's attempts to finalize trade negotiations with Qamsar.

"I will not allow violence or deception to mar my wedding," Mikhail said.

Aisha forced a smile. It must be the one she pasted on when in public. Having this news delivered close to her wedding couldn't have thrilled her.

Did she know anything about the captured American? Harris's team hadn't determined if the arranged marriage between the emir and his new bride carried any real trust or intimacy or if the arrangement was purely a political and social agreement. If Aisha knew something, could he ask Laila to find out more information?

Harris immediately retracted the thought. He wasn't putting Laila further at risk to pry information from her brother's future wife.

Mikhail glanced at Aisha. "No more of this talk. I want everyone to enjoy themselves. Please make my home your home."

Had Mikhail stopped speaking of the American because he saw Aisha was upset? Doing so would imply actual feelings between the two, and it might mean Aisha knew something about the American spy. Harris would have a hard time speaking to Aisha. Aside from being a male, he wasn't a relative and had no reason to approach her.

Dozens more waitstaff filled the room, distributing the first dinner course: beef kabobs with peppers and mushrooms; a vegetable salad with tomato, cucumber and chickpeas sprinkled with feta cheese; and couscous with dried fruit.

The conversation at the table returned to Laila and Harris.

"Laila tells me you are converting to Islam," Khalid said. "I was encouraged to hear this."

"Yes, that's my plan. I know to start a life with her, I need us to have a strong foundation, and that means a belief system that guides us both," Harris said.

Iba and Khalid nodded their heads in approval. "What do you do for a living?" Khalid asked.

Of course, that would be important. His job would need to be the right status for someone like Laila. "I'm taking a leave of absence from the family business to focus on my studies. After I complete my education in America, I'll return to Germany and take over running the financial side of my family's company. My father felt it was important for me to have a strong education to best help the business."

"And what business is that?" Khalid asked.

Did he not know? Harris would have assumed when his name appeared on the guest list, the emir's staff would have checked him out. Or perhaps Mikhail had and had not shared information he'd found with the rest of the family.

"Uncle, please," Laila said. "You have days to get to know Harris. You don't need to ask him so many questions."

"I don't mind talking business," Harris said. "My family runs an international shipping company. Kuhn Freight will transport anything, anywhere, anytime, by land, sea or air."

"Anything?" Khalid said with a smile. "Sounds like a big company."

"It started as a small company," Harris said. "Just

my great-grandfather and his brother. It's grown in leaps and bounds. We primarily help with international moves and work with businesses that transfer their employees to another country for work. But no job is too large or too small." Let that get back to Mikhail. He'd have to see the value in ties to a shipping company with great resources and connections.

"Why don't you tell us about your studies?" Iba asked her daughter.

"I'm working on my thesis with my advisor. It's taking longer than I had planned, since I had some additional classes to complete before I started the program, but I'll present it next semester," Laila said.

It was the first Harris had heard her speak of her education.

"A man may not like for his wife to be more educated than he is," Iba said quietly. "Perhaps you should enjoy the learning, but not pursue the degree."

Hurt shadowed Laila's eyes. She'd wanted her mother's support.

Though he felt strange saying anything, he interjected, "It's wonderful for Laila to have a master's degree in communication. So much she can do with that. My parents are pleased to know she'll be helpful in the family business," Harris said.

Laila beamed at him.

What were her plans with her degree? Before he'd offered a new life in America, had Laila planned to forget her education after she entered into an arranged marriage?

Laila took control of the conversation, telling her mother and uncle about her classes, and her options for the future. She walked just shy of stating she would not return to Qamsar, though her relationship with Harris implied it.

Making a note to ask her more about it when they were alone, Harris half listened, half scanned the room around him, trying to place names and faces. He'd been given a list of invited guests that were of interest to the CIA. That list ran over four hundred people long. The total invitee list was well over a thousand.

Harris had an encrypted, protected program on his phone that would allow him to check faces later, but for the present, it was safest to observe.

He felt eyes on him and noticed someone in his peripheral vision looking in his direction. Harris forced his gaze to his dinner and then back to the person watching him. Harris didn't recognize the man, his dark hair and beard giving him a generic, unremarkable look. He wasn't tall or short, broad or slim, no outstanding features. The type of person the CIA loved to have on their team.

The last Harris had heard, he was the only CIA or FBI resource assigned inside the compound. Then again, he hadn't known another American spy was being placed inside the compound. Were more agents here to deliver a message to Harris or to support his mission? Or did other operatives have their own agendas?

The CIA operated differently than the FBI. The FBI shared information, and when he was working a case, Harris had access to everyone and everything about that case. The CIA liked to keep information compartmentalized. Perhaps they thought it would limit exposure. If one agent was captured and knew nothing about another, not even torture could drag the information from them, and a multipart mission could find some success.

Harris returned his attention to the conversation. Laila was speaking about her classes the next semester and the research project she was working on with one of her professors. When she was given a new identity, her life would change dramatically. Leaving her school and abandoning the ties she'd made would be difficult for her.

Harris took another look around the dining room and disappointment surged through him. No sign of Ahmad Al-Adel, and therefore nothing to report. He hadn't expected it to be that easy. But he had hoped.

Their first wedding event in the compound had gone well. At least Laila believed so. She could tell her mother wasn't thrilled with the idea of Harris being German and interested in her daughter, but she wasn't opposed to it enough to forbid it from happening. Harris mentioning his plans to convert to Islam had taken the edge off her disapproval. Laila had spoken to Saafir briefly, and he had expressed his happiness that she had met someone in America and appeared content with her life.

Harris had asked Laila to meet him somewhere private after dinner. With the number of people moving around the compound, and the eating and socializing going on well past midnight, she and Harris had agreed the courtyard gardens would suffice for a meeting. It was cold enough at night that not many people would venture outside, and the fountains, gazebos and palm trees gave them enough hiding places that she and Harris could speak without being seen.

Laila stepped into the gardens, the cold of the night sending a shiver up her spine, and she pulled her wool wrap tighter around her shoulders. Her excuse for being outside was to get fresh air. It sounded ridiculous even to her, but if she wanted to talk to Harris alone, this was the best option.

She had a thousand questions about the events of the night. Harris wasn't obligated to tell her anything about what he'd learned, but Laila needed some salve for her nerves. She was worried about the American spy who Mikhail had captured and concerned what it would mean for her and Harris. Had other CIA spies gotten access to the compound? Was Harris aware of them and keeping her in the dark? If so, what did that mean for her role in bringing Harris to the compound? She hoped she hadn't made a big mistake.

Harris appeared so suddenly, Laila bit back a scream. "You scared me," she said.

"Sorry about that," Harris said. "Are you cold?" He didn't wait for her answer and took off his jacket and put it over her shoulders. It smelled of him, the light scent of sandalwood and spices.

She couldn't wait to ask her questions. "What did Mikhail mean by an American getting into the compound?"

As her eyes adjusted to the dim lights of the gardens, she read worry on his face.

"I don't know. I found that odd, as well. Any Americans on the list were invited guests, at least to my knowledge. I'll need to find out what happened. It could be a bluff to scare anyone thinking of snooping around. Or maybe it's part of his plan to turn public opinion against Americans, painting them as spies trying to sabotage his wedding."

Mind games were Mikhail's specialty. She didn't point out that Harris was a spy who would ruin the emir's wedding if Al-Adel was found in the country. "My mom didn't like that you weren't from our country."

Harris tucked his hands into his pants pockets.

She was struck by his boyish charm. As a former American military man and FBI agent, he had deadly talents, ones she wouldn't test, but he had an honest and open way about him. He was easy to trust. But wasn't that the point? Getting people to trust him was part of the job.

"I know she wasn't thrilled with me. I expected that. I'll have to win her over. I think telling her I was converting helped."

Did he care about her mother liking him? They weren't a real couple. It shouldn't matter what her mother thought. As long as she didn't hate him, openly oppose the relationship or have Khalid protest their involvement, she and Harris could struggle through this assignment without her objections becoming another obstacle.

"How are you doing? Has it been difficult for you to be here?" Harris asked.

The question caught her off guard. Since arriving in Qamsar, she'd had an eerie sense of impending doom. So far the dropped bombs hadn't been what she'd expected. Mikhail hadn't announced her engagement to one of his lackeys. Mikhail hadn't refused to allow her to return to America, though he had suggested it would be better for her to stay in Qamsar following the car bombing outside the café.

An American in custody was unsettling, as was Mikhail's warning to his guests. Foreign governments had taken an interest in the Emir of Qamsar, and his announcement made it clear his wedding wouldn't distract him from his vigilance.

"I'm fine. Worried about whoever Mikhail has in custody," Laila said. Though they weren't in her room, Harris was behaving differently toward her than he had in the company of her family. He was standing closer, and his focus was more intensely on her. Her conservative childhood beliefs battled with her new perspective on relationships. Leaning in and touching him was natural. Only knowing their relationship was make-believe stopped her.

"I am, too. I'll see what I can find out about it."

The sound of footsteps approached, and Harris pulled Laila behind a gazebo and against him. She could feel his breath on the top of her head and his heartbeat pounding in his chest. Wrapped in the band of his arms, she was warmer, safer. He wouldn't let anything happen to her. Laila wanted and accepted the comfort of his arms around her.

She had never touched a man this way. She'd never been hugged by anyone except her family, and even then shows of affection were infrequent. Her body stirred, and she rested her head against his chest and fisted his shirt in her hands, holding him to her. How would it feel to kiss him? To feel the press of his mouth hot against her, the way she had imagined a kiss would be? Curiosity and desire created a heady mix, which confused her and made her light-headed.

Harris wasn't her boyfriend or a man she was promised to marry, and yet being in his arms felt right. She felt alight with excitement.

"I think they're gone," Harris said. He stepped away and straightened. "My apologies. I wasn't making an advance. I was trying to hide you. I forgot myself for a moment."

Why did it sting that his actions were based only on protecting her? Being alone with a man was unfamiliar to her. What could she say to let him know she wasn't offended without sounding forward? "I'm not upset. I'm glad you're here. Being alone with a man is new to me, but it's nothing like I'd imagined it to be." It came with more powerful emotions. Desire. Happiness.

Harris looked at her. Watched her and didn't say anything. His gaze drilled into her.

Finally he spoke. "Are you telling me you've never been alone with a man?"

Laila shifted under his scrutiny. She wasn't ashamed of how she had chosen to live. It was, after all, a deliberate choice. Her aunt and uncle were trusting, and she could have secretly dated men in America. She'd been asked out a few times by customers in the coffeehouse and had declined their invitations. "Aside from members of my family, I have not been alone with a man. Not in the way you mean." She had never before experienced the attraction or the connection she had with Harris.

Harris stepped closer. "How is that possible? Have you seen yourself? You're gorgeous. How do you keep men away from you?"

Laila blushed. The compliment heated her insides. "It's well understood in Qamsar that an unmarried

woman of a certain age isn't left alone with her suitors. My father or mother chaperoned dinners, and my
father was planning to select someone for my marriage.
He died before he'd made the final arrangements." With
the power and influence her father had held, he should
have arranged a match when she was young, as he
had done for her brothers. But his relationship with
Laila had been different. Her father had admitted he
was having trouble letting go of his daughter, and had
wanted to find a good man with honesty and integrity
who would treat her well.

"The first man you want to be with is your husband." He spoke it as a statement, not a question. His
voice lacked incredulity. He sounded as if he was trying to understand.

"My parents' plan was that I only ever be alone with
my husband. In America, I wondered about that choice
and if it was right for me." The darkness hid the red-
ness that burned on her face. She'd been too direct.

"Now that your future is more open, how do you
feel about that?"

She hadn't entirely processed what would change
for her when she started a new life in America. She
was concentrating on the part of the arrangement that
would keep her family safe and her from being married to someone Mikhail had chosen, likely someone
she would find awful. She put the conversation back
on comfortable ground. "I want to be happy. In America, I will learn to date how other modern women do."
Though she had worried about an arranged marriage
with someone Mikhail would choose for her, she hadn't
had the same fears when her father was alive. He would
have seen to it she married someone good and kind.

"You no longer want an arranged marriage?" he asked.

Once she was living in America, she wouldn't have the means to arrange a marriage. She'd need to break ties with her past life and find someone on her own. "It might not be an option without a male in my life to arrange it or the connections to find someone. I suppose my mother or Saafir could help, but we'll all have to find new lives and build relationships. I could find my own suitors." Couldn't she? Could Harris be one of them?

"I'm responsible for your health and well-being. I put you on this track, and if it goes off the skids, I'll know I had a hand in that. If you end up married to a jerk you meet in America, I'll hold myself accountable."

She wasn't planning to let her life veer off course, and she wouldn't marry a jerk. She might be inexperienced, but she had good instincts. "You seem to believe I'll make bad choices. I'm capable of finding a good man." She wasn't sure what qualities she would look for. Those things had been in the hands of her family.

He called her out of her worry. "How will you know the good guys from the bad? You don't have experience seeing through someone's lies," Harris said. "The world is full of liars."

He was included on that list. Their entire relationship was a deception. "Perhaps your line of work has made you jaded. Not everyone prides themselves on being a liar or needs to lie every day to get their job done."

He winced. "Low blow. But truthful. Believe it or not, outside my work, I am an honest man."

She challenged him right back. "Is that what your ex-girlfriends would tell me?"

His shoulders lifted. "They might. They would probably tell you I'm too busy and too involved in my work to be a decent boyfriend."

Disappointment fluttered through her, and she got the sense he hadn't finished his thought. Everyone had flaws, but his sounded like he'd rather spend time working than with his woman. "Would they be right?"

"Maybe. I always thought, for the right woman, I'd work less and find a balance."

"I had hoped for the same. That is, to find a man who would allow me to work."

"What do you plan to do with your degree?" Harris asked.

"I'd like to work for a small company. Help with PR and marketing. Flex my creativity but still get home by dinnertime to be with my family."

"Those dreams are possibilities now. Find the right man and the right job, and nothing will stop you."

Laila shivered. Possibilities. Her life had been defined by the opposite. By boundaries and distance and following directions given by others. Her first venture into making her own decisions was attending the University of Colorado. She had loved the freedom and being away from the watchful eye of her family in Qamsar.

Another sound of footsteps and Harris grabbed her again. She didn't move or speak, afraid they would be discovered. She inhaled slowly, and the masculine scent of him tickled her senses. She wanted to kiss him. Everything in her clamored for it. She would be miles behind her peers in dating skills and at a disadvantage.

Everything she knew about dating came from friends' stories, books and movies.

Wasn't Harris the perfect man for a test run? Good-looking, probably a great kisser and temporarily in her life. If she made a mistake with him or made a fool of herself, in a few weeks, it wouldn't matter.

When the footsteps faded, she didn't draw herself away. She lifted her head to see what he would do.

"Sorry, again. Instinct took over," he said. His arms remained locked around her.

"This isn't so bad," she said. How did she encourage him to kiss her? In movies, it seemed as if an invisible force drew two people together, as if both knew when it was the right moment. Her skin tingled, and her stomach tightened.

Indecision wavered on his face. "You don't want this."

"Sure I do." Her cheeks heated at the bold words and their implication.

Harris searched her eyes. "These are a lot of changes for you in a short time. I don't want to put pressure on you or make you do something you're uncomfortable with."

In this moment, she didn't feel pressure. She felt desire and longing. She couldn't put into words exactly why she was encouraging him to kiss her. "I'm not uncomfortable." Maybe anxious. Curious. Questioning her life and her decisions. Open to new experiences.

Didn't he want to kiss her? She was out of her element. Unsure. And she yearned. That was the only word she could accurately apply to the situation. He was touching her, and she wanted more. What harm could one kiss do? She wouldn't sleep with Harris or let it go further than a kiss.

Decisions about men and relationships had always been made for her by other men. This time she was making the decision. She wanted this to happen. She was ready.

Harris lowered his mouth and brushed his lips to hers. Heat shimmered from the contact across her entire body. The tip of his tongue outlined her mouth. He was playing with her, exciting her, and she loved every moment.

Laila put her hand on the back of his head and brought his mouth full against hers. She melted into the kiss. Surrendered. Her lips burned with white-hot awareness. It felt natural, and her body felt primed and ready. His kiss affected her in ways she hadn't considered. Her prior plans to wait for her husband before touching a man had meant a lifetime of physical loneliness.

Until she had kissed Harris, she hadn't cared about chemistry. Feeling the blaze of passion, she suddenly understood it wasn't something she could pretend to feel with a stranger or manufacture in a marriage.

With perfect clarity, she knew her life had veered off the well-worn path beaten by her mother, her grandmother, her great-grandmother. Her doubts cemented into fact. A companionable, arranged marriage wasn't enough. She wanted more. Deserved more.

His mouth drifted to her cheek. "We have amazing chemistry."

"You've said that all along." And now she got it. Truly understood the difference between liking a man and feeling a soul-deep pull toward him.

He moved his hands to her elbows. "Tell me what's going on in your head."

She couldn't define a precise emotion. She felt light-headed and excited, hungry for more and anxious for another kiss. She couldn't take it back or return to a place where she'd accept a loveless arrangement because tradition demanded it.

"Are you disappointed?" he asked.

Of the chaotic swirling emotions she felt, disappointment wasn't one of them. "Of course not."

"We should be more careful," he said.

About letting it happen again? Or about letting it go too far? She couldn't bring herself to ask.

"I should get you back to the party," Harris said.

Now disappointment streamed through her. Their interlude was over as quickly as it had begun. It had irrevocably changed her. What was he feeling? She hadn't thought about what she wanted her first kiss to be. It had always taken place in the context of her wedding night, with her husband.

Not in the courtyard under the cover of night with an undercover FBI agent who, for all she knew, was playacting even now. "We can't be seen together entering the compound," she said.

"I'll follow in the dark. No one will see me. I want to be sure you're safe."

She didn't have anything else to say on the matter, her feelings a kaleidoscope of emotions. For the first time, her future wasn't defined by what another man decided for her.

Laila was deep in thought and jumped when she crossed into the path of two of the emir's security guards. She didn't dare look behind her to be sure Harris was well hidden.

"What are you doing here alone?" one of the men asked.

"Getting some fresh air," she said. Harris's jacket was slung over her shoulders. Would they realize she was wearing a man's jacket? Had they recognized her as the emir's sister? Her heart beat faster.

"Women are not permitted to be out here alone," the guard said.

"Something bad could happen." The leer the second guard gave her sent a shiver of fear down her spine.

Harris was close, watching over her, and he wouldn't allow them to hurt her. But if he had to defend her, if he was forced to reveal himself, he would risk both his cover and his stay in the compound. Mikhail would take the word of his guards over his sister and her German suitor.

At least his leer told her that she hadn't been recognized. The emir's sister would garner more respect.

"I'm returning to the party now," she said, lifting her chin and squaring her shoulders.

They exchanged glances, perhaps considering questioning her further. They made the right decision and stepped to each side of the path allowing her to pass. Laila hurried into the house, hoping they hadn't seen Harris or stopped to speak with him. Finding them both in the courtyard would raise questions she couldn't answer.

Chapter 4

Harris should be tired. On the heels of a long flight and a day of surveillance, he should be ready to crash.

And yet he couldn't settle down and sleep.

That kiss. The potent, amazing kiss he'd shared with Laila. He hadn't expected it, and he shouldn't have let it happen. Laila was a virgin. An untouched virgin. Harris hadn't encountered a woman like her—and not just the pure-as-the-fallen-snow thing—in years. She was innocent and naive when it came to men, and he'd gone and kissed her.

He blamed this mission and his terrible judgment when it came to women. He'd sunk too deep into character, worried he'd give himself away to the emir, and now he didn't know where Harris, FBI Agent, began and Harris, German heir, ended.

He couldn't allow a kiss to happen again. Laila deserved passion and love from someone who could give her the life she wanted. Even before she had told him of her plans, his profiler training had her pegged as a woman who'd want it all: a successful career, a devoted husband and three adorable children. She'd volunteer at her children's school and make friends with the other moms, give her husband attention and affection, and stay on the ball at work.

If Harris got involved with her, he'd be risking the mission and breaking protocol, plus he had a messy history of getting involved with women who asked more of him than he could give, who expected him to be someone he wasn't and who either betrayed him or let him down.

He loved his job and sometimes that meant traveling at a moment's notice. He'd had to cancel plans, miss vacations, be a no-show as a plus one at a wedding. The women he'd dated didn't have patience for his excuses. They didn't understand the work he did, and in many situations he couldn't tell them much about it. They'd get frustrated and then disinterested. A few had become angry and vengeful. Harris always sensed when the breakup was coming. Once over email, twice over the phone, four times in person, he'd gotten the speech that started with, "I need a man who can be there for me. Be there when I need him."

Harris had shouldered a large portion of the blame for his failed relationships. He'd worked hard to make the breaks as clean as possible. He'd wished them well and moved on with his life. At least, almost all of them. His last girlfriend, Cassie, had been the exception. Her betrayal had left him for dead, and that he couldn't forgive or forget.

Part of him felt like a failure for being unable to maintain a relationship for more than a few months. His brothers—as wild as they were and as intense as their careers could be—had found and married strong, capable, beautiful women. Every time Harris visited with his brothers and their wives, he was reminded of what he'd given up by making the career choices he had and not finding the balance his brothers had.

His mother had warned him that he might one day look back at his life and regret how he'd spent his twenties and thirties. On some level Harris agreed with her, and on another he thought the right woman would understand and not ask more of him than he could give. The right woman would stand by him when life was difficult.

Tired of lying in bed unable to sleep, Harris got up and used the bathroom in his en suite. He cleaned his hands and then splashed some water on his face. The bed was comfortable, and the sheets were soft. Sleep should be easy.

He returned to bed, and the indicator on his phone blinked red twice. A message. Pulling the phone into bed, he typed in his password, pressed his thumb over the fingerprint reader, navigated to the application masquerading as an e-calendar, where he typed another password and waited.

Three full minutes passed, and he was prompted for a third password. And then he was in.

He almost laughed at the CIA's complex message retrieval system. Every message sent from his phone was encrypted and could only be decrypted at CIA headquarters with the proper software. Anyone who picked up his phone would have a terrible time getting his private messages, and even then they were seemingly innocuous. If his phone went missing, the CIA could access the phone remotely and wipe its contents. High-tech stuff, which he enjoyed, but Harris preferred working for the FBI. Harris didn't like the overt paranoid thinking that the CIA operated under. His FBI team was straight shooting and open with him about issues related to the case at hand. Harris felt as if the CIA held back, giving him the bare minimum he needed to do his job. This joint mission with the CIA would bolster his FBI résumé with interagency experience and give him access to more opportunities in the Bureau.

The CIA liked their covert rendezvous. Like the man in the souk who had asked about buying his shoes. An asset confirming Harris hadn't been discovered nor did he believe Mikhail was suspicious of his presence at the compound.

The text message waiting for him was in German from his "brother" Brady, also known as Tyler. "Mom wants to have steaks on the grill and try out some new recipes as soon as possible. Reilly has a new puppy. Mom doesn't think he can handle it."

Harris translated the message easily. The CIA needed to set up a meeting with him to talk about another agent or asset they had inside the compound. The person wasn't trusted by the team, and Harris suspected he or she might have been brought on due to circumstances, likely someone with access to the compound or a guest of the wedding.

Harris wondered if the message referred to the American spy who had been captured by the emir or perhaps the man he'd sensed watching him earlier that night. He'd talk to Laila tomorrow, get the rundown of scheduled wedding events and look for downtime to arrange a meeting. Harris didn't want to miss an event where Al-Adel could appear. Once he had a good time to meet, he'd call back and leave a message.

He stretched out in the bed and tried to get some rest.

When he awoke, a mild headache pulsed at his temples. He looked at the clock. Nine o'clock. Laila may have slept late, as well, trying to catch up on the rest they'd foregone while traveling. He reached for his phone and dialed her. In addition to his room being bugged, it was possible for the calls to be intercepted within the compound walls, and she knew not to speak of anything mission related.

She answered on the third ring. "Hey, you. How'd you sleep?"

"I didn't wake you, did I?" he asked, sitting up in bed.

"No, I was up. I just got out of the shower. I'm getting dressed for breakfast with my mom. You're welcome to join us."

His masculine brain caught and held the first part of what she'd said. *Shower.* Was she wearing a towel and nothing else? His body reacted to the image, and he was glad he was alone so no one saw his lower half saluting the idea. "Give me twenty minutes and I'll join you."

"No problem. I don't want to make my mom wait, so why don't you join us on the upper veranda?"

Over breakfast he could ask about the day's wedding events, a neutral, safe topic. "Sounds great."

Fifteen minutes later he strolled onto the upper veranda, scanning around him for Ahmad Al-Adel. He spotted Laila and her mother on the far side, their table shaded by potted palm trees. He hated to impose on their meal. Their heads were bent together in conversation, and both were smiling. When he drew closer, they looked at him, Laila with a smile on her face and Iba with a nod of acknowledgment.

"Good morning," he said, standing at the table and waiting to be invited to join them.

"Harris, please, sit down," Iba said, gesturing to the free chairs around their stone-topped table.

Iba didn't seem surprised to see him. Laila must have mentioned he'd be joining them.

Harris wanted to tell Laila how beautiful she looked this morning, her face lit by the indirect rays of the sun and the smile on her face captivating. However, commenting on her appearance wasn't the right thing to do. Especially not in front of her mother.

Laila's hand touched her lips, and Harris wondered if she was remembering the kiss they'd shared. It had been an amazing kiss. Explosive. Unforgettable, no matter how hard he worked to smudge it out of his memory.

A waiter took his order, and without a menu Harris assumed anything was an option. Eggs, sausage, toast, orange juice, coffee and a muffin. Maybe food would chase away the dull jet-lag-induced headache that throbbed at his temples.

The atmosphere on the veranda was much less formal than the dinner event the previous day. Guests arrived and left on their own schedules.

"I'm sorry I slept so late," Harris said. "I hope I didn't miss anything important." After seeing them together, he wished he would have delayed longer to give Laila and her mother time to talk.

Laila shook her head. "Nothing wedding related is planned until later today. My mother and I are meeting Aisha and some other family for bridal henna."

Perhaps then would be a good time for his meeting with his CIA contact. "I can't wait to see how it turns out." He caught the words and rechecked. Was that the wrong thing to say? Was the henna for a husband's eyes only?

Iba laughed. "Relax. I understand you are not from Qamsar, and I don't know how many of our customs my daughter has talked to you about. Given her love of all things American, I imagine not many. You don't have to worry over every word."

Laila beamed at her mother. "Mom, did I tell you that Harris's mother and father work together in the family business?"

"No, you didn't," she said. "How do your parents keep business separate from family? My late husband's job took his every waking minute, and I'd have to remind him that Laila, Mikhail, Saafir and I were here." She spoke with fondness, and Harris got the impression her relationship with her husband had been balanced, less of a male-dominated marriage and more of a partnership. Was that relationship to credit for the changes in the Qamsarian culture in more recent years? Women had been given more rights, and while their status was not equal to men, it had improved from when they were treated like pets. If Mikhail had his way, he'd turn back the clock on the cultural progress in Qamsar. How did Iba feel about her ruling son's stance?

It wasn't the time to question Iba. She had asked

about his family. "My mother is a strong woman," he said. His mother had been a CIA operative for most of her career, and had worked in the field on difficult and dangerous missions. "She keeps my father in check." The truth. His father had been a navy SEAL, strong and resourceful, but when it came to his wife, he had a soft spot. Their marriage had sometimes been difficult with travel schedules and three sons, but they had worked at it and were enjoying their retirement.

The waiter brought Harris his food. It smelled and looked delicious.

"When Harris returns to work for the family business, he'll help Qamsar," Laila said. It was an angle the CIA had wanted her to play up when possible. "Harris's company can help improve our imports and exports, maybe put some of our local specialties and crafts on the international market."

She was amazing. He didn't detect a hint of the lie, and he was great at reading people. Maybe, like him, she was sinking deep into the part she was playing.

Mikhail would see a side to the shipping connection others might not. If he was working with Ahmad Al-Adel, he could use shipping connections to move goods for the terrorist organization and call upon family loyalty to demand discretion.

"It's been difficult at times," Iba said. "My late husband wanted to improve the country's construction programs. We're restricted by the international marketplace. When we can't get the best or least expensive materials, we're forced to shoulder higher costs."

Iba wasn't a wife who had let her husband work while she stood by idle. Harris got the impression that, publicly acknowledged or not, Iba had taken an active role in her husband's career. It had to be difficult for her to lose control of that power in addition to losing her husband.

"Perhaps after the wedding, we can talk about some options," Harris said, feeling a twinge of guilt in knowing that, by then, they would be in America and his lies exposed.

Though Laila knew the truth about him and what he was doing in Qamsar, Harris couldn't stop thinking about how, post-mission, their relationship would be over, as well. She'd have a new life in America, and he'd be onto the next assignment.

Though it had always been the case, the more time he spent with Laila, the less he liked the idea of never seeing her again.

Harris remembered he'd brought the worry beads to give to Iba. "Laila and I picked something up for you at the souk." He took the decorated cloth bag out of his suit jacket pocket and handed it to Iba.

Iba looked from it to him with an expression of genuine pleasure on her face. "Thank you, Harris. You didn't have to buy me anything."

Sure he did. The pleased expression on her face alone made the small effort worth it.

She opened the bag, and after a moment of staring at it, she lifted her face, her eyes misted with tears. "My late husband collected worry beads. I guess Laila told you that. He marked every special occasion with them. When we were married, though it wasn't a traditional gift, he gave me a beautiful set. This is wonderful. Thank you so much."

Laila squeezed her mother's hand, and the look on her face when she smiled at Harris made him feel like a hero.

After breakfast Harris sent a reply message to his CIA contact indicating he could meet that afternoon around 2:00 p.m. in the souk. The confirmation came almost instantaneously.

In the meantime Harris had to get the monitoring devices placed throughout the compound. Laila knew her way around, and she'd agreed to help him. Some locations would be more accessible than others. Placement in the main dining area would be easier than getting close to Mikhail's private quarters.

If Ahmad Al-Adel was attending the wedding, Harris guessed he wouldn't arrive too early, or if he did, he would lay low. Being an internationally wanted man, Al-Adel would be cautious. Making an appearance at the emir's wedding would be a calculated risk, but one he might take to show Mikhail that he trusted their relationship.

Harris had read everything he could find on Ahmad Al-Adel, and he didn't believe the man was capable of giving respect to another human being. If Al-Adel showed up, it was because he needed Mikhail. With so many countries unwilling to negotiate or assist Al-Adel, Mikhail was one of his last remaining allies. In return Mikhail got unlawful muscle to enforce his will, even if what he wanted was outside Qamsar law. The money Al-Adel funneled into Qamsar was another bonus.

Harris met Laila at the entrance to the main dining room as they had planned. Though he had hesitated about involving her, the CIA hadn't been able to acquire the floor plan of Mikhail's private quarters, and Laila gave him a cover if anyone spotted him. Though it was a stretch, Laila had slightly more reason to be in the emir's private quarters than Harris did. Pretending to be lost would never work.

"Let's position the simplest ones first," Harris said. "Then we'll try the difficult ones." Even if they couldn't get access to Mikhail's private quarters, the CIA would have electronic eyes inside the compound.

Laila nodded. "It's too bad you're not a woman. Women are overlooked. You and I could walk around freely."

He wouldn't ask Laila to place the devices without accompanying her. He couldn't put her at additional risk. Was she implying he should go undercover dressed like a woman? The idea didn't thrill him, but he would do what he needed to do. "Wouldn't my build give me away?"

Laila shrugged. "Might make someone think you're a rather large woman, but generally, you'd be okay."

"If we need to use that technique to get to the private locations, we will." He'd call that option: last.

"You could dress like one of the servants. You know how people can be about housekeepers and staff. They don't see them. We can blend into the background."

Not a bad idea. He could dress as a butler or guard, though hiding his skin and hair color would be more difficult without something over his head and face. "Let's see how many of these we can place without needing to dress in drag."

The bugs were manufactured by a private contractor. If found, no one could tie them to America or the

CIA. If the emir's security team discovered a device, it might cause another search of the guest rooms or increased security. Harris was counting on the security staff being distracted by the influx of guests and missing the tiny bugs, the size of a number-two pencil eraser.

The easiest place to plant a device was the main dining room. It was near lunch, the room was busy and Laila explained the artwork along the wall as they circled the room. Harris removed the sticky tape on the back of the tiny device in his pocket and held it between his two fingers. He rested his hand on the railing between the doorway and the open seating area. He wrapped his fingers around the wooden bar and pressed the bug into place.

With a final push on the device to ensure it stuck, he took out his phone. A few finger presses later, he had the confirmation text message that the CIA was able to connect to the device.

The CIA now had surveillance inside the compound. They could watch the dining area twenty-four hours a day, and if Al-Adel stepped foot in that room, the screeners at the CIA would know. Even if he was wearing a disguise, their facial recognition software would peg him.

"Laila, how lovely to see you."

Harris slipped his phone into his pocket and turned toward the sound of Laila's name. An older woman accompanied by a serene-looking man approached, her arms outstretched.

Laila introduced Harris to her second cousin on her father's side, Betha, and her husband, Abdul. Betha was obviously pregnant, though Harris didn't mention it as he wasn't sure of the protocol. As they spoke, Harris felt someone watching him. He turned. The man he'd seen the day before, the plain, unremarkable, possible CIA agent was looking in his direction. The man averted his gaze when Harris met his stare.

Perhaps the camera he'd installed had caught the man's image, and Harris could have his resources search for the stranger's identity.

Harris wanted to ask Laila if she knew the man, but asking her now would draw attention, and if the man was CIA, he'd want to stay unnoticed. The CIA liked their agendas to stay secret and their agents to work alone, and Harris was playing by their rules during this mission.

Laila and her cousin were finishing their conversation with an exchange of pleasantries. Harris nodded at them and let Laila lead them away.

"Do you see that man…" Harris let his voice drift off. The man who'd been watching them was gone.

"See who?" she asked. Her eyes were the most expressive he'd encountered. He could read her emotions in them: concern, curiosity and excitement.

Harris slipped another bug into place to give the CIA a 360-degree view of the room. "Twice now I've noticed a man watching us. I was curious if you knew him."

"Next time he's around, signal me," Laila said. "Why don't I show you the library? It's where Mikhail sometimes entertains his male guests following a dinner."

A great place to hide a bug. If Mikhail met with Al-Adel, he might use the library, or would Mikhail invite him into his private quarters? Harris hoped Mikhail would have at least some sense to keep boundaries between him and one of the most dangerous men in the world.

Laila had never been invited into the library. Her father had spent evenings there with Mikhail and Saafir, smoking the hookah, and talking politics and business.

Checking first that the hallway was empty, Laila opened the door to the library and she and Harris slipped inside. Laila closed the door quietly behind them. This early in the day, the room was vacant. The heavy maroon curtains were pulled away from the windows, allowing in the sunshine. The windows were high on the wall and opened, fans spinning to air out the tobacco smoke.

The room smelled of mint tobacco, a favorite flavor of her father's. Years of smoking in this room made it impossible to get the smell out of the walls and carpets. Memories of him sprang to mind, and Laila's heart clutched in her chest. It had been years, but some days the grief was as raw as the day he'd died.

On the far wall, a portrait of her father hung. His kind smile, his laughing eyes and his regal and distinguished look brought fresh sorrow to her heart. He had been a good man, and she could never have imagined how her life would change after he was gone. Her father had been a strong, unwavering presence in her life and without him, she, her mother and her brothers were missing the anchor that had grounded them.

Her father had never gotten through to Mikhail, but he had kept Mikhail's ideas from tipping too extreme. Without her father as a counterbalance, Mikhail let his philosophies rule him.

Laila was aware she was alone with Harris. She took a deep breath and hid her sadness. She was helping Harris, and it wasn't the time to get upset about her father.

Though she doubted the room was on the compound's surveillance system, she kept her distance from Harris. Someone could walk in on them, and she wouldn't put herself in a questionable position. She had put them at enough risk being together in the library. She struggled to recall what she knew about the books in their protective glass enclosures, some of them old historical texts and first editions of local writers. Telling Harris about the books was perfectly acceptable.

Harris circled the room, looking at the books and likely searching for the best place to secure another surveillance device.

He was facing away from her, and Laila let her gaze wander over him. His clothing was well tailored and fit his body, accenting his wide shoulders and lean hips, his pants sitting over his muscled backside and long legs. He walked with confidence, his stride strong and sure.

She wanted him to kiss her again. Last night had been exhilarating. Now that she'd kissed him, she needed another taste. Once hadn't been enough. Was he thinking about it at all? Would she ever meet another man who made her feel the way he did?

In all her life, Harris was the first man who made her feel the crackling of lust and the heat of desire. Maybe it was the first time she'd allowed herself to feel something. Maybe he was the right man at the right time. Their relationship was fated to be brief. She could keep it light and fun, maybe share more kisses and manage to hold on to her heart.

"How do I open these cases?" Harris asked, pointing to one of the cabinets.

"Mikhail keeps the keys under his desk." She strode across the room and felt under the middle desk drawer, pulling a key off a hook. "See something that interests you?" she asked.

She handed Harris the key, and he put it in the lock and twisted it. Lifting the glass door, he took a book with a navy cover and a rock on the front, a bright light shining behind it.

"What is that?" Laila asked. She'd never seen the book before.

"The rock and the light are signs the Holy Light Brotherhood uses," Harris said.

"They are popular images in Qamsarian literature. If it is from the Holy Light Brotherhood, why would Mikhail keep it in here? This isn't a secure location."

Harris opened the front of the book. "I can't read Arabic as quickly. Tell me what it says."

Inside the pages were handwritten in ink, the book only half filled. She scanned the pages and didn't recognize any of the handwriting. It wasn't Mikhail's. It looked like at least three separate people had written inside the book. "It's a list of events and their dates, some of them natural disasters, some political milestones and some are names I don't recognize."

"Does it say anything about the Holy Light Brotherhood?" Harris asked.

Laila continued to skim. If someone caught her and Harris in this room snooping through Mikhail's books, she had a lot of explaining to do. "I don't see any reference to that."

On the last page, a name caught her attention. "It has my brother's name." Surprise and sadness created a heavy mix of emotions.

"Mikhail's?"

"No. Saafir. It says Saafir is to be welcomed into the light before Mikhail's wedding." Laila's stomach dropped to her shoes. Not Saafir. He couldn't be involved. Both of her brothers wouldn't allow the Holy Light Brotherhood to draw them into their clutches. Mikhail had always been hungry for power, angry at the world and focused on getting his way. But Saafir was easygoing and cared about others. He was less concerned about pressing his agenda, which almost never had anything to do with personal gain, and was more focused on helping the people around him. For all the compassion Mikhail lacked, Saafir made up for it in spades.

"What does that mean?" Harris asked. "What makes him part of the Holy Light Brotherhood?"

Thinking aloud or did he need an answer? "I don't know anything about the inner workings of that organization. Does he have to prove himself somehow? A show of loyalty?" A chill of disgust traced down her spine. She couldn't picture Saafir and Mikhail working together, much less Saafir working with the Holy Light Brotherhood. Laila shook loose her thoughts. "Saafir wouldn't hurt anyone." Even as children, Mikhail had had a darker side to his personality. But not Saafir. He had a heart of gold. He wouldn't get involved with terrorists. Not willingly and knowingly.

Harris took out his phone and snapped a few pictures of the pages of the book. He then set it back on the shelf. "I'll see what I can do about getting more information on this. If they are planning something, we need to get in front of it and stop them," Harris said. He moved toward Mikhail's desk, slipped his hand under it, likely placing a bug.

Laila locked the cabinet and replaced the key under Mikhail's desk. She followed Harris to the door and bumped into him when he stopped abruptly. She braced her hand on the door, and he grabbed her arm to steady her.

Heat shot from his touch up her arm and to her core. Their gazes met and held. Heat and excitement rushed into the space worry had occupied a moment before.

"Excuse me," he said. He didn't release her.

She didn't want him to. Was she bold enough to pull him deeper inside the room, press him against the wall and kiss him? She'd seen it done in movies. Was she sexy enough to pull it off?

Harris's survey drifted from her eyes to her lips, where it lingered a moment before plunging lower.

Her long dress suddenly felt too revealing. Barely any skin was showing, but his look devoured her as if she were stark naked in front of him.

"Laila," he said. Her name on his lips sent a shiver down her spine.

"Yes?" she asked. Her adrenaline was pumping, fueled by the danger of being discovered, fear for her brothers and the excitement of being alone with Harris.

Footsteps and voices sounded outside the library doors. Harris dropped his hand from her arm. He waited a moment, and then pulled open the door and moved out of the library. He gestured for her to follow.

Laila didn't recognize anyone in the group retreating down the hallway.

A blush darkened her cheeks, and Laila slowed her thoughts to calm her racing heart. They had remained on platonic ground except for an innocent touch. Not so innocent thoughts, but Harris didn't know about those.

"Lead the way," he said.

Laila reassured herself no one had seen her in the library with Harris, and no one was paying attention to them now. If anyone asked what she was doing with Harris, she'd been showing him around the compound to see the artwork and telling him about some of the historical artifacts that decorated the area.

Their next location was Mikhail's living quarters. Mikhail had remodeled the compound after her father had died, closing off part of their family home for his private use. Located on the east side of the house, access from the main part of the compound was barred by a set of double doors. Entrance required authorized access via a fingerprint scanner and password.

Though Mikhail had changed the rooms, she knew another way inside. "We should take a walk outside. I can show you the gardens."

"Sounds like fun," Harris said. He was letting her take the lead. She knew what she was doing. Growing up as the emir's daughter had its advantages.

They walked in silence to the northeast gardens. They weren't alone. Guests and family members were enjoying the landscaped grounds. Tables were set in the shade, with carafes of coffee and pitchers of water on the tables.

"Security has to be getting more challenging with so many people," Harris said under his breath to Laila.

"After the front gate checkpoint and dropping bugs in some guests' rooms, I think Mikhail is hoping for the best." Not that Laila believed her brother had gotten sloppy or that his people weren't well trained, but with the influx of people, the security team would be forced to adopt a different set of rules and procedures.

"Let's hope that our things stay in place." Their *things* being the devices. If security swept the area, they'd find and remove them. Then the hunt for whoever had placed them would begin.

Harris had assured her the design wasn't traceable to any company or to them.

"Mikhail is spending the day with our mother and his bride's family. He shouldn't be in his private quarters."

"Excellent," Harris said.

Mikhail's private living area overlooked the gardens and the garages that housed his car collection. Tucked in the corner, beneath the emir's private balcony, was the service entrance. Laila and Harris wandered through the gardens.

Laila stopped and pointed to a plant, hoping anyone watching would think she was telling Harris about the local vegetation. "The housekeeping staff arrives at 7:00 a.m. and 7:00 p.m., so it's unlikely we'll run into anyone. The door may be unlocked. If not, can you get it open?"

Harris's eyes twinkled with amusement. "I take great pride in telling you that I can."

His boyish charm made another appearance. That quality was alluring, and she wouldn't have expected it from someone in his line of work.

"How do you learn something like that? Did you take a class?" she asked.

"I've had some training. Some of it from my family. You'd be surprised how much you can learn from brothers who are mischievous."

Another mention of his family. He had told her that he was involved with his job to the point that his personal relationships suffered, but it sounded as if he kept his family ties tight. "You never have time for girlfriends, but you make time for family. Isn't it a matter of priority, then?" The words flew from her mouth before she could censor them.

Surprise showed on his face for an instant. "I'm not sure whether to be insulted or not. But you're right. It is about priorities."

Laila adjusted her head scarf over her hair, needing something to do with her hands. "But nothing comes before your job."

"Are you asking me or telling me? I love the work I do."

He'd mentioned that before. Laila looked around to be sure they were alone. "Even when it involves dangerous situations and difficult people?"

"The danger keeps things interesting and the people are the best part. Especially when I work with people who are doing their best to make a difference. To make things better or to right a wrong." His gaze pierced her.

He was talking about her. She didn't want him building her up as a hero. Her personal motivations weren't entirely selfless. "I didn't do this for some greater good. I did it to protect my family and my country, and give myself the chance to have the life I've longed for."

Harris took a few steps away. She followed. "I don't

believe that. You wanted to look out for your family, but after I told you the circumstances, you would have helped us anyway. You've never mentioned your desire to seek revenge against the people who tried to kill you with a car bomb. Your motives aren't centered on your personal agenda or need for vengeance. Your new life and whatever you choose to do with it are a bonus."

Would she have done this without the promise of a safe harbor for her and her family from the inevitable fallout of Mikhail's involvement with a terrorist? Did the car bomb have anything to do with her decision? Ahmad Al-Adel was a cruel and evil man. She wanted him stopped. If she had done nothing, and Al-Adel or his network of terrorists had hurt someone else, she would have had a difficult time with that. Guilt would have swamped her, and she'd feel responsible for the consequences of her inaction. "Maybe I've spent too much time in America, but doing nothing can be as bad as doing evil."

"All that is necessary for evil to triumph is for good men to do nothing," Harris said. "I remember hearing my dad speak that quote to my brothers and me."

Movement out of the corner of her eye caught her attention. One of the housekeepers was leaving by the service door. "Someone's leaving! Let's try the door now." Harris might have been able to pick the lock, but this was easier.

They moved toward the service door, catching it before it slammed shut. Laila and Harris slipped inside. Her eyes adjusted to the change in light, the darkness of the interior space confining. She could hear washing machines and dryers running. With the extra guests staying in the compound, Laila would bet the machines were seeing much more use. Had Mikhail changed his staff's hours or increased the number of housekeepers working during his wedding? Would anyone be in his private quarters or were most assigned to the guest suites?

Mikhail had changed many things about the compound. Was she overestimating her ability to guide Harris?

Laila reassured herself. Mikhail didn't allow video or audio surveillance in his private quarters. They'd just need to watch out for Mikhail's staff.

Laila crept to the closet on the right and opened it. She held up her index finger for Harris to wait. Going inside the closet, she removed her dark head scarf and tied it around her waist. She took one of the housekeeper dresses from a hanger and slipped it over her own. She wrapped the tan-colored head scarf that matched the housekeeper's dress over her head.

In the closet were a few other outfits. The largest was a gardener outfit complete with hat to protect the head and neck from the sun. She grabbed it.

When she stepped out of the closet, she didn't see Harris. Where had he gone?

He appeared around a corner. "I thought it was better if I didn't wait in plain sight," he whispered.

"Good idea."

"That's a good look for you," he said.

She rolled her eyes. The housekeeper uniform was meant to differentiate the staff from guests and the clothes were stain proof, the fabric easy to wash, coarse and unappealing. The high neck and length of the uniform covered her dress.

She handed Harris the gardener's outfit. "Not feminine and it should fit." Harris quickly tugged it on over his clothes.

"It will be difficult to explain why a gardener is inside," Harris said.

"Maybe you can say you came inside for extra tools or towels." She shrugged. "It was the largest masculine outfit in the closet."

"Let's aim to not be seen," Harris said, pulling the hat low over his eyes.

On the left were stairs leading to the emir's private quarters. She pointed to them, and she and Harris scaled them as quietly as possible. The creaking of the steps had her flinching. Laila paused for a minute to see if anyone would appear to investigate the noise. No movement. They continued to the second floor.

When she was younger, she, her cousins and her brothers would play hide-and-seek in this part of the house until the housekeepers chased them away. Exploring the compound had been a childhood game, and her father's security team and household staff had been endlessly patient when Laila would attempt to go somewhere she wasn't allowed. Her game exploring had taught her the compound inside and out.

The hallway was empty and with any luck, most of the staff were cleaning rooms other than the emir's quarters or working outside. The door at the end of the corridor opened into Mikhail's living quarters. Laila held the entryway doorknob in her hand. She turned it slowly, opened the door and peered into the hallway.

She could feel Harris behind her. He wasn't touching her, but he was close, the heat of his body radiating into hers. She should have removed her dress first before putting on the housekeeping uniform. This was nerve-racking work, and she was too warm.

Seeing no one in the hall, she stepped out and kept her head down. Mikhail's office was ahead on the left. She gestured to Harris to wait and tried the door herself.

It was locked.

She walked back to the service entry where Harris was standing. "It's locked."

"I'll get us in," Harris said.

He hurried to the door, and Laila stayed close to him, looking left and right for anyone to approach. He removed a small tool set from his pocket and withdrew two thin pieces of metal. He inserted them into the door, and turned them left and right.

Sweat broke out on her back. If they were discovered, they were in serious trouble. Her disguise might fool someone from a distance, but Mikhail would recognize her and jail them both. He was obsessive about his privacy. "Hurry," she whispered, knowing he was doing his best.

"I've almost got it."

Male voices floated down the hallway.

Laila grabbed Harris's arm in alarm, terror rocketing through her. The service entry was too far away. They'd be seen. Would they be overlooked? What if it was someone who had worked for Mikhail long enough to know that they didn't belong?

A closet two doors away was their best option. Praying it was empty enough for two people to jam inside, she opened the door and shoved Harris in first. She climbed into the closet with him.

Her ankle twisted on something, and she fell against

him, sending objects clattering. Harris's hands gripped her shoulders to steady her, and they went stock-still. She couldn't see, and if she moved, she risked knocking over more items and creating a racket.

The male voices continued to get louder. Had they heard the commotion she and Harris had made?

Laila closed her eyes and tried to place the voices. One might have been Mikhail's. It sounded muffled through the door, and she couldn't be sure. The other, she couldn't place. He didn't have a Qamsarian accent.

"The last delivery went without issue," the unidentified man was saying. "I was pleased your team managed the work with competence."

Mikhail snorted. "You expected something less? My people are trained and capable. Let me get you the documents, and then I must return to my commitment. I didn't expect you so soon, and if I'm gone too long on state business, my bride will have questions."

Laila could feel the rise and fall of Harris's chest, his hard body pressed to hers. As much as she needed distance to breathe and cool off, she dared not move for fear something else would shift and tumble to the ground, bringing Mikhail to investigate.

Her brother sounded annoyed. As the emir, his days were filled with making decisions, giving and receiving advice, and fielding questions. An interruption to his wedding should be expected, at least in part. Who was Mikhail talking to and what important state matter had drawn him away?

Laila heard a door open, likely the door to Mikhail's office. The voices became too soft to hear what they were discussing.

"Is he talking to Al-Adel?" Harris asked in a whisper.

Fear flickered in her stomach. "I don't know what he sounds like."

"The accent isn't Qamsarian. It could be Al-Adel or one of his Holy Light Brotherhood cronies," Harris said.

Her calf was pressing into something, and Laila tried to lift her foot and find a clear space on the floor.

"Hey, hey, watch your knee," Harris said, turning his hips.

She blushed in the dark. She'd forgotten how close her body was to Harris's. How delicate their position. "I'm sorry. I was trying to find a better way to stand than this."

She moved and hit something on the floor. It made a noise that probably sounded a hundred times louder to her than it did to Mikhail, if he'd heard it at all.

"If we had been a minute sooner, our bug would be in place, and we could have heard what they are talking about," Harris said, moving his arms, keeping them around her, but giving her a place to shift.

"They might meet again," she said.

"Maybe. It sounded like they were concluding a transaction."

Was he unaffected being this close to her? How long would they be trapped in here? The closet was stuffy, and her double layers were making her too hot. She suddenly felt light-headed. "I need to take off my dress," she said.

"What?" he asked, incredulity injected into the drawn out word.

"I'm wearing two dresses. I'm sweltering. Between that, the zero air flow and you pressed against me, it's like an oven in here." It had taken her thirty seconds to get the dress on, and now she felt like a bungling fool trying to remove it. The rough cloth stuck to the fabric of her dress, pulling both when she tried to draw it over her head.

"I got a quick view of what's in here before it went dark. We don't have much room to maneuver. Let me help. If you pass out, we'll have more problems."

Harris knelt and his head was by her breasts and then between her legs. She couldn't see anything, which heightened her awareness of him. Moving could create more noise. She stayed still and tried to think about other things, boring things.

He was shifting items slowly, carefully, and his hand brushed her legs. Torrents of heat rippled up her body. This was a slow, sensuous torture. Her body was overreacting to him. Her inexperience with men was causing this disaster.

Most women would be indifferent to a man touching their leg in an innocent way. Most women wouldn't care about a man kneeling in front of her. But for Laila, every aspect of the experience was new and exhilarating.

Like that kiss, the kiss that still burned on her lips. Harris couldn't have known what he was doing was making her hot and achy. He'd think it was the stuffiness, the clothes and the closeness. But it was him. Her body responding to him. She couldn't stop it.

His hands touched her side, perhaps feeling his way in the dark. Then his hands were on her arms, and he was pulling the dress free of her. Though he couldn't see her, Laila scrambled to ensure her gown was in place, everything covered. The housekeeper's head scarf had come off, and she searched for the fabric until she found it, her hand brushing Harris's.

The sparks of heat jolted her.

"You're cute when you're flustered," he whispered.

"How do you know I'm flustered?"

"Your breathing," he said. "Short, shallow breaths. Do you feel better without the two dresses?" he asked.

"Yes. I don't know how the staff works in those things. They are heavy and hot."

"They probably don't double up on their clothes while they work," Harris said.

Of course they didn't. "They also don't work in a two-by-two enclosed space pressed up against another person." The verbal reminder she was thigh to thigh with him vibrated in the air with hot dark tension.

"This is a compromising situation. The second time I've found myself with you in my arms, alone and in the dark," he said.

The kiss. It *was* on his mind. "It will sound like we're making excuses, but it's the circumstances. We're not planning to be together like this." She wasn't. No scheming on her part to be alone with him.

"I'd like to say I'm smooth enough to manipulate the situation to get you alone like this, but I can't lie. Ending up this way is pure accident." His hand touched the side of her face, and she leaned against it, letting his fingers caress her cheek. The sensual slide of his hand delivered an important message.

He wanted to kiss her.

A moment later, his hand cupped her chin, and his mouth found hers in the dark, tasting, touching and moving slow. As if they weren't trapped in a closet in the emir's personal quarters in danger of being discovered.

Her pulse hummed with excitement, and she shifted, bringing her hips closer to his. The telltale reaction of his lower half gave away that he liked this kiss. He was in to her. If he was playing a part, the kiss would have been all technique, no physical reaction. Or is this what a kiss did to a woman? Tricked her into believing it had emotional impact when it didn't?

His hands slipped around her, resting on her lower back.

He broke the kiss, and his body tensed. The sound of a door opening had her heartbeat escalating for a different reason. Neither of them moved.

The male voices they'd heard earlier were speaking in hushed tones and moving away from them.

Another few minutes passed. Her neck hurt from the strange angle she was holding it, and her left leg had started to go to sleep. She dared not move.

"I think they're gone," Harris said.

After several awkward shifts, he reached the door and cracked it open, peering out into the hallway. Laila worked to put the housekeeping dress over her clothes. She straightened the cloth. Harris had left the tiny closet.

When she pulled herself together, she found him slipping inside the emir's office. He had jimmied the lock that quickly.

She followed him inside, closing the door behind her. Harris positioned the bug on a bookshelf behind the emir's desk. It would give a view of the emir's computer and any guests he had in his office.

"You're sure your brother wouldn't permit video or

audio in his office?" Harris said, looking up and around the room for surveillance devices.

"He treats his private quarters as just that. Private. He doesn't allow his security to monitor the area the way they do with most of the rest of the compound." At least her mother had mentioned that to her when she was explaining Mikhail's remodeling. Harris set up the second device to monitor the doorway.

With a swift nod Harris gestured for her to follow him, and they vacated the emir's office, locking the door behind them. Laila and Harris fled for the relative safety of the housekeeping stairwell.

Chapter 5

Though he was cutting it close, Harris would be on time for his meeting in the souk with his asset, the same man who had stopped him previously to ask about the leather shoes he was carrying. Missing a potentially important conversation between Mikhail and someone in his office upped Harris's determination to catch Ahmad Al-Adel and the emir in the commission of a crime. He would do what was necessary to find Al-Adel and then alert his FBI team to apprehend him, striking a devastating blow to the Holy Light Brotherhood.

Harris planned to review the pictures of Al-Adel's known associates. He'd been fixating on Al-Adel, but the terrorist could have sent someone as his representative, a trusted associate or a family member involved in the Holy Light Brotherhood. If he was planning to attend the wedding, Al-Adel wouldn't travel alone, and spotting someone with known ties to Al-Adel might help Harris figure out if and when the terrorist leader would appear in Qamsar.

Outward appearances could be changed, but Harris had a knack for remembering faces. Some faces played on his mind long and heavy, like a certain beautiful, off-limits woman he'd kissed—twice—in the past twenty-four hours. He'd almost wanted her to stop him, to tell him that she wasn't interested in kissing anyone but her future husband. But once she was in his arms, rationalizations and realism evaporated.

He'd been tempted, if only for a moment, to take it further. To invite her to his room. To see where their physical relationship would go if left unchecked.

He'd squashed that line of thought in a hurry. Kissing her was one thing. Taking her to his room crossed another, more serious line. It would compromise their cover and her reputation with her family. Even with her as a willing partner, his conscience would have gotten the better of him.

She'd made it clear what she wanted for her future. Laila was waiting for the right man, a man she would marry. She was conflicted about her views of relationships, the differences between Qamsarian and American culture drastic and having an effect on her beliefs. Harris hadn't intended the kiss to place her in a regrettable situation.

The idea of Laila finding a husband nagged at him. Maybe he was worried about her making good decisions when it came to men. She didn't have dating experience, and that could mean her suitors would take advantage of her. Harris felt responsible for her, even though when this mission was over, he needed to let her go. She was only in his life for a short time.

To get to the souk, he'd had to use the emir's car service again. He'd rather have driven himself, and save the time it would take to ditch the driver and ensure he wasn't being followed.

The market was busier than it had been during his previous visit. Harris strolled along the shops and bought another bottle of perfume. He purchased water from a teenager selling bottles from a cooler filled with ice. He wasn't followed. He doubled back several times to be certain and followed FBI protocol to ensure he wasn't being tracked.

The meeting place was an outdoor grill. He was to order the grilled chicken platter and take his dish around the side of the building as if looking for a quiet place to eat. He located the grill, and after paying for his meal, he circled the building. The chicken held little appeal, slipping in the grease on the plate, but he enjoyed his thirst-quenching bottle of water.

He sat against the tan stucco wall and sipped his drink. A black van with tinted windows and rust around the wheel wells pulled up in front of him. Harris rose to his feet. Two men got out of the van and stood in front of him. Neither were the man he'd met in the souk earlier. "Get in the van."

He wasn't expecting this type of meeting. He'd thought they would stay in the souk and talk. But he went along with it. He climbed inside the van, and before he sat on the bench seats, the van lurched forward. A cloth was tied around his eyes and rope around his hands.

"Is this necessary?" he asked. He didn't like not

knowing where he was going, and he hated his arms being secured.

No one spoke.

If anyone had witnessed this exchange and reported it to the police or the emir, it would raise questions. Unless this *wasn't* his asset, and someone had uncovered the plan and taken advantage.

Harris didn't have a weapon. He hadn't acquired one or figured out how to get it inside the emir's compound yet. His cell phone was tucked in his pants with the GPS activated and sending a signal to the CIA. If he went missing, they'd know where to look. Unless he was killed and his body ditched before the CIA could send help.

But if these guys wanted to hurt him, they would have at least taken his phone.

The van stopped, and the side door was jerked open. The blindfold was removed from his face, and his hands were untied. His eyes adjusted to the bright light of the sun, and he squinted and tried to orient himself.

He was led to a run-down motel across the street from where the van had parked and to the second floor. His escorts stopped in front of a room with a rusted red door and missing numbers, and pushed it open.

Inside the man he'd noticed watching him at the emir's compound was waiting. Not the man he was expecting. Why hadn't the CIA told him he was meeting someone new? Or meeting someone who was also working the operation on the inside? It was another way the CIA was different, and it wasn't a difference he liked. He preferred to work on a team where the members were forthcoming about their plans and agendas. He didn't know how his mother had dealt with that ambiguity throughout her career.

The men who had escorted Harris to the motel left. The room had two single beds, worn and dirty carpet, and scarred furniture.

"I can see from your reaction, you recognize me," the man said, standing from the plastic chair where he'd been sitting.

Not trusting this situation entirely, Harris tested him. "How long did it take you to get here?"

"About half as long as it took you," the man answered.

It was the test question for this mission, and the man had answered correctly. Tension unwound from Harris's shoulders. "Why the theatrics? If I was seen getting taken from the souk, it would be hard to explain this."

The man waved his hand. "No one saw us, but I am sorry about their approach. We have private military contractors working with us, and they err on the side of aggression. They treat everyone like an enemy and trust no one."

Harris had to trust this man understood the politics in Qamsar better than he did. "I didn't realize we had anyone else on the inside."

The man reached into a minifridge and pulled out a can of soda. He tossed it to Harris. "I was late to the game. I managed to get invited to the wedding due to my connections with Aisha, the emir's bride. Her brother and I were old friends from grade school, and haven't been in touch in a decade and a half."

Which raised more questions than it answered. "Then why did we need to use Laila to get inside?"

The man gestured for Harris to sit on the edge of one of the beds. Given the smell and look of the room, Harris preferred to stand.

"She's part of the royal family. She's an insider. Besides, this mission is too critical to put it on the shoulders of one person. You aren't as experienced with the agency as I am, and we never planned this mission to be worked from only one angle," he said. "By the way, you can call me Devon."

The CIA hadn't trusted Harris enough to tell him about the players on this mission. They'd led him to believe he and Laila were the only ones in the emir's compound looking for Al-Adel. "I have questions." A lot of questions, but he guessed he wouldn't get many answers. Everything he wanted to know would be classified as "need-to-know," and Harris was someone who didn't.

"We can exchange information, but I don't want to disappoint you. I've got intel, but it might not be what you're seeking." With that, he sat once more in the plastic chair.

"Tell me what you know about the captured American," Harris said.

Devon took a sip of his soda. "We're working on that one. Tricky business."

"Then it wasn't a bluff by the emir?" Harris asked. Part of him had been hoping the captured American was a ruse, a warning to the guests who might have been approached by other international police and criminal investigation agencies for information.

"We know he was working inside the compound gathering intelligence. He'd been employed by one of the vendors handling the emir's wedding and was undercover as a caterer or waiter. He was discovered by his employer and turned over to the emir."

"How many of us are there?"

"That's the part that makes this confusing. We believe he's American, as does the emir, but he isn't one of us, and we don't know what agency sent him," Devon said. "We're working to find out if he is still alive and, if so, his condition."

"Back up a minute. Not one of us?" Harris asked, thinking it over. If he wasn't CIA or FBI, who was he, and what was he doing working this operation? Perhaps he was a spy from another country.

"We're thinking he's black ops and either works for a part of the government that doesn't exist," Devon said, finger quoting the words *doesn't exist,* "or he's some other operative altogether. Either way, we can't leave him inside. We need you to press Laila for information about where he is. He isn't being held in the prison in Qamsar. We need to know where else the emir might hold prisoners."

"When I spoke to her about this, she didn't know anything," Harris said. Laila had been as worried as him. "And if he works for another agency, how do you know they aren't staging a rescue mission?"

"We don't. We have many questions and few answers. We need Laila. She might hear rumors. The women in the compound are much chattier than the men. Or Laila might be able to talk to her brother or Aisha and find out more information," Devon said.

Harris wouldn't throw Laila in harm's way. She was helping him get inside the emir's circle to look for Al-Adel, not rescue the captured American. If asking too many questions put her in danger, he'd get the information some other way. "You're willing to put a civilian in the middle of this?" Harris asked.

Devon shrugged. "We'll do what's needed."

Cold. Devon wasn't the first CIA agent he'd encountered with that attitude. It surprised him the CIA was willing to go out on a limb to help someone who wasn't their own. He had a feeling Devon was withholding information. "Why do you care so much about this American?" Harris had to know the stakes.

"He knows something, and we need to find out what it is," Devon said. "Otherwise he would have been expelled from the country, not jailed. He's being kept for a reason."

Then it wasn't a humanitarian mission. It wasn't in the name of the American spirit that the CIA wanted to free the jailed American.

Harris could ask around and keep his ears open for rumors. "I'll see what I can find out."

"I know you placed the devices. Nice job," Devon said.

"I was late." Harris told Devon about what he'd heard while outside Mikhail's private quarters and his suspicions that the man had been either Al-Adel or from Al-Adel's terrorist group. He left off the part about kissing Laila and holding her in his arms. The CIA didn't need to know about that.

"But you didn't see the man the emir met with?" Devon asked.

"No," Harris said.

"Was that because you were distracted by Laila?"

A direct question. He had been distracted. But even if he had been alone in that closet, he wouldn't have revealed his presence to get a look at the emir's counterpart. "I didn't see the man because the emir's return was unexpected, and we had to hide." He worked to keep defensiveness from his tone.

"You're looking out for Laila. That's good. Just don't look out for her so well that you miss what's happening around you."

"I haven't missed anything," Harris said. He hated that Devon's words had introduced doubts. How much did Devon know about his last operation with the FBI? Did Devon know that Cassie had almost gotten him and his team killed? If he did, he had to also know that Harris had learned his lesson. He was focused on this mission. Nothing would sway him from their objectives.

"Has Laila told you anything about her family that would help us? Anything that ties the royal family to the Holy Light Brotherhood?" Devon asked.

Harris didn't realize the CIA thought Laila knew anything. His defensive response rose and he tempered it. Laila was rapidly becoming special to him, but he understood the boundaries. If she knew something critical, they needed to hear it. "I haven't asked her anything directly, and she hasn't mentioned anything I found relevant to this operation. Do you need me to ask her something specific?"

Harris would ask Laila whatever they wanted. She wasn't involved in anything untoward. She was as innocent as the word.

"We don't believe she or her mother are involved in Mikhail's relationship with Al-Adel. They aren't part of the emir's innermost circle and likely not privy to his dealings with the Holy Light Brotherhood."

Did Devon know anything about Saafir's connection to the Holy Light Brotherhood? "What about his brother? What is Mikhail's relationship with Saafir?" Harris asked.

Devon tilted his hand back and forth. "Not great. They get along in public, but they keep their distance in private. They are different in their goals for the country and their methods of handling people. Saafir has a soft side. Mikhail seems to have callused his."

Had that changed? Perhaps Saafir and Mikhail had grown closer and were working together toward a common goal. Without more evidence, Harris wouldn't make an accusation against Saafir, but the nagging suspicion remained. "Laila and I saw a book in Mikhail's library with the Holy Light Brotherhood insignia on the front. The book mentions Saafir. I took a few pictures and passed them on."

Devon's eyebrows shot up. "No one mentioned them to me. Is he in this with his brother?"

Harris wasn't the only operative given incomplete information. "I don't know. I don't think Laila believes so."

Devon nodded. "What do you believe?"

"She's a good judge of character, but she's not objective. I'm not ruling anything out. What about our primary objective? Anything more on that?" Harris asked. As far as he knew, Al-Adel hadn't been seen on the premises. Perhaps intel had picked up his movements elsewhere in the country.

"With the devices in place, we're checking the video consistently. We haven't given up on the idea that he'll show."

"Intel doesn't have anything more recent on his movements?" Harris asked.

"Nothing in two weeks. He's been quiet. Nothing

on the wires and nothing from our assets," Devon said. He shifted in his chair. "Let me level with you. This is your first CIA mission. It's easy to get overwhelmed. Some think you might not pull this off. That you're too softhearted to use whatever means necessary to get the information."

Harris squashed the urge to disagree immediately. He had a reputation within the Bureau for working well with victims and witnesses, for being good at sympathizing. He could do his job and be human about it. "I know what the situation calls for, and I know what is and isn't appropriate."

Devon ran his palm over his jawline and appeared skeptical. "When you're deep undercover, it's easy to forget. I've seen Laila. She's a beautiful woman. I don't want you to make a mistake with her that will damage your reputation. I've seen it a hundred times before. Guy meets a pretty asset, starts to have feelings for her and then when it's time to get the intel or uncover a rat, they hesitate in order to protect the pretty asset."

Laila's face sprang to mind. Laila was a charming woman. He didn't bother denying it. He was attracted to her. What man wouldn't be? Her innocence was refreshing, and her intelligence intriguing. "She and I are working well together. Our cover hasn't been blown, and part of that is because we make a believable couple. I have no reason to suspect Laila is involved with Al-Adel or the Holy Light Brotherhood. But if anything turns up that she's involved, I won't protect her. I know what my job is." He spoke the words with confidence. Laila hadn't done anything wrong. She wasn't involved with Al-Adel.

"Just don't make your affair with her too believable and get sucked in," Devon said.

"I won't. I've got this under control," Harris said. He'd learned his lesson. Relationships and covert operations didn't mix. Yet his reaction to her name told him that his control was precarious and could easily slip from his grasp.

Laila hadn't spent time with her dear cousins in too long. The henna ceremony was a wonderful place for the women in her family to get together, gossip and catch up on their lives. Men were excluded from the treatment area since hands and feet were bared.

More than one woman her age was pregnant, some with their third or fourth child. They were making their arranged marriages work. Had she been too hasty in writing off the idea of an arranged marriage? In many ways it was simpler. Fewer emotions were involved, less confusion, not so many decisions. And less room for errors, like errors involving kissing a man she had no future with.

Before coming to America, Laila had wanted to be married to someone her family approved of. Now she wanted both that and to marry someone who made her feel the way Harris did. Exhilarated. Hot. Achy. Alive.

Aisha's hands and feet were being decorated, and several other henna artists were working on the bride's and groom's families.

Laila waited for her turn, sitting between her mother and her cousin Betha. Betha, six months pregnant, was glowing with happiness and excitement. She was also the biggest gossip in the family, and Laila knew she was about to get an earful.

"Laila, tell me about this German man who's courting you," Betha said, leaning close but not lowering her voice.

Laila could have sworn every ear within ten feet perked at Betha's words.

With her mother's eyes and a dozen ears pinned on her, Laila struggled to remember her lies. She took a deep breath and felt her cheeks heating. She hadn't expected the blunt question. Lying when put on the spot was harder than Laila had imagined.

"Oh, she's blushing! She's in love," Betha said, clapping Laila on the back and giving her a hug.

Laila glanced at her mother. Iba's face didn't give away much of a reaction. What was her mother thinking? Was she disappointed? She'd been polite to Harris when they'd had breakfast that morning and had seemed pleased by his gift. Was she worried her daughter was making a mistake? Laila wished she could tell her mother the truth. She reassured herself it was only a matter of time. When she and Harris came clean, her mother would understand why she had lied, and why she had brought Harris to Qamsar. If Mikhail was working with Al-Adel, he needed to be stopped. Finding a terrorist and protecting her country was worth causing her mother some worry about Harris.

"We met at the coffeehouse near my school," Laila said. How could she change the subject? Didn't they have wedding things to discuss?

"Did he ask you on a date? What did you tell him?" Betha asked.

Part of her interest was probably in the cultural differences, and how she and Harris were handling them. Mentioning in front of everyone that her relationship beliefs were evolving and changing didn't seem smart at the moment. "I told him the truth. I had a different idea about dating than he did, and if he wanted to see me, he needed to be serious about courting me, and he had to speak to my uncle and meet my family."

"He didn't turn away and run?" Betha said. "I knew I would marry Abdul from the time I was five years old, and until the day before our wedding, he still broke out in a sweat whenever he saw me."

The women laughed. Good. Maybe they would talk about something else. Share their stories of commitment-phobic men.

"If he was willing to come to the emir's wedding and meet your family, he must be serious about you," Betha said.

Darn. Not as easy as she'd hoped. "He wants the same things I do. A family and a stable home." Laila glanced at her mother. Still showing no reaction, she was watching and listening. "His family owns a shipping company in Germany, and that could be a match Mikhail approves of. It could help the country to have access to quality import and export services."

Iba stroked Laila's head. "That's my daughter, thinking like a businessman."

"But she's right, Aunt Iba," Betha said. "The emir likes to have business ties within the family. That could win him over. You know, since Harris isn't Muslim." Count on Betha to speak the honest answer.

"Yet," Laila said. "He's converting." She felt as if she'd spoken the lie a hundred times since arriving in Qamsar. Why couldn't she just tell the truth? She didn't care what Harris believed in, as long as he believed in her.

The women around them nodded their approval.

"What does Noor think of this?" Betha asked. "He thought he would claim his bride when you returned home. Imagine when you showed up with another man!"

Laila repressed the shudder than went through her. She'd worried Mikhail would think to pair her with Noor, and hearing it confirmed, she felt as if she'd dodged a bullet. Not only was Noor one of Mikhail's best friends, he was a mean little troll to the women in his life. He was even nasty to his own mother. "I haven't seen Noor or spoken to him since I arrived. Harris hasn't spoken to Mikhail yet, so we'll see. I'm waiting for him to speak with my family before I start making plans for the future." It hurt to speak the words, hurt knowing she wouldn't have a future with Harris or anyone else, until she was settled in America and could figure out what to do.

Laila wanted to move the conversation along to other topics. She lowered her voice, keeping the conversation as close to her and Betha as possible. "I think it's more scandalous that an American is being held for spying. How ridiculous! Spying on what? Someone's wedding?" Laila laughed, pretending to be unaware of Mikhail's association with a suspected terrorist. Was the rumor mill churning with information?

"I heard the Americans sent a spy to look into the guests at the wedding. They are looking for a wanted criminal," Betha said in a near whisper.

She had it partly true. "With the security Mikhail has on this place? He's not letting any criminals sneak inside and ruin his wedding," Laila said, trying to prod her cousin for more information.

"What if the person the Americans are looking for is an invited guest?" Betha asked, leaning close, her eyes glimmering with excitement.

She had more to tell. Laila needed to get it out of her without raising flags she was digging too deeply for information about topics she shouldn't care about. "Powerful people associate with other powerful people," Laila said. "If some of the men in attendance are of interest to America, I don't find that surprising."

"I heard that the spy wasn't executed because Aisha didn't want it to mar her wedding week. But as soon as the ceremony and celebration end, Mikhail won't wait," Betha said.

Aisha glanced in their direction at the sound of her name, casting them a curious look. If she had been closer and already not engaged in a conversation with other friends, she might have given her opinion on the matter. Had she heard what they were discussing or just her name?

Laila's heartbeat escalated. If Mikhail was planning to kill the American spy, they only had a few days to find and release him. "Mikhail might try to get information first. Find out if he knows anything useful," Laila said.

"No, Mikhail probably wants him dead before he can slip away and deliver information back to America," Betha said.

Implying the jailed American had discovered something that Mikhail didn't want to get out. Laila and Harris had overheard Mikhail talking to someone in his office, perhaps someone in Al-Adel's inner circle. What else had Mikhail done? Maybe he'd gotten in over his head, and the American spy had discovered a secret the emir wanted silenced.

"I wouldn't want to spend the last of my days in the Cinder Block," Betha said.

The Cinder Block, the nickname for one of the most dangerous locked-down prisons in Qamsar, was located outside the compound walls and guarded twenty-four hours a day by the emir's private guards. The facility held political prisoners and traitors. Few survived inside and most disappeared without a trial or explanation.

"What does Mikhail think the American spy knows?" Laila asked.

Aisha turned to face them again, a frown across her face. It was enough to make it clear she had heard at least part of their conversation, and she didn't like what they were discussing.

Iba gave Laila and Betha a stern look. "This is not polite conversation for ladies to have. Please, this is a wedding celebration. Let's speak of happy things."

Laila let her mother turn the conversation to a new boutique that had opened near the souk that carried fine linen, light as air and beautiful.

If Mikhail was planning to execute the American after his wedding, they only had a few days to get to him. How would anyone get inside the Cinder Block and free the American spy?

Laila admired the henna on her hands and feet. The artists had done a beautiful job, the lines and designs intricate. She opened her closet to select an outfit for dinner. A knock sounded on her door, and before she could answer it, it opened, and one of the emir's housekeepers stepped inside the room. Laila grabbed a dress off the rack and held it over her bare feet.

The housekeeper averted her eyes to the ceiling. "The emir wishes to see you."

Fear and panic flailed in her stomach. Had she asked Betha too many questions about the imprisoned American? Or had Mikhail realized she and Harris had been in his private quarters? Her heart beat faster, and her mouth felt dry.

"May I ask why?" she asked, stalling for time. Could she get a message to Harris? She didn't want to join the American spy in the Cinder Block. If no one knew where she was, she might never be found.

"The emir does not explain himself to me."

"Very well," Laila said, adjusting her head scarf. "Please give me a moment to finish dressing." She didn't wait for the woman to agree. She slipped into the bathroom and put on a pair of shoes. Maybe this wasn't a personal audience with him. Maybe Mikhail was calling together the family to discuss the details of his wedding. Laila pulled her phone from her pocket and sent Harris a text: Called to meeting with Mikhail. Without more information she didn't have anything to add.

At least if she didn't return, Harris would know the last person she had seen. Though she felt guilty for thinking of her brother as a villain, she had always thought Mikhail had a dark side, and what she was learning about him made her nervous.

After checking her attire in the mirror, she exited the bathroom. "I'm ready."

With her knees trembling, she followed the housekeeper to the library. Panic had sweat breaking out on her lower back. She'd never been invited into the library before. Had Mikhail found the device they'd hidden inside? Would he ask her about it? She was a terrible liar and would break under pressure.

"Sister, please sit," Mikhail said, gesturing to the leather couch across from the chair where he was seated. Mikhail waved a hand to dismiss the housekeeper. They were alone.

Laila waited for him to continue. It wasn't her place to speak. She tried to interpret his posture and expression. Was he angry? Enraged?

"I had a conversation with Abdul a few minutes ago," Mikhail said.

Abdul, Betha's husband. Laila worked hard not to squirm and to keep her hands from shaking. If she showed fear, Mikhail would pounce and exploit that fear. What had Betha told her husband? Laila replayed the conversation looking for places where she might have made a misstep or pressed too hard.

"He mentioned your friend from Germany works in the import-export business."

Laila nodded. "Yes, his family runs a shipping company." She could have said more, but she wanted to know where the conversation was leading.

Mikhail gestured to his computer. "I looked him up online. The company is internationally known and has a superb reputation. They ship to almost every country in the world."

Laila wasn't sure what he wanted her to say. Was he testing her knowledge of Harris's job? She wouldn't necessarily know much about it. "That's my understanding."

"They don't currently import or export anything to

or from Qamsar," Mikhail said. "I would like to change that. Has Mr. Kuhn expressed the intention of courting you?" Mikhail asked.

Laila's heart rate slowed a fraction. Mikhail's interest in the shipping company was the outcome Harris and the CIA wanted. They had gone through a great deal of effort to set up a fake company and to establish Harris Kuhn's background in Germany. "Yes. He spoke to uncle Aasim in America, and I made it clear to Harris that he had to meet you and earn your approval of the match. He is converting to Islam, as well." She looked at her lap and tried to appear meek.

"I will have a talk with him soon," Mikhail said. "That is all. Good day."

She was dismissed. Tension floated away. Mikhail would never confide his private or business concerns to a woman, even if that woman was his sister. He hadn't found the devices, or if he had, he hadn't tied them to her and Harris.

She needed to warn Harris about the purpose of the meeting Mikhail would arrange and prepare him for what was coming so Mikhail wouldn't have the upper hand. And she needed to tell Harris about the Cinder Block, and her suspicions it was where Mikhail was keeping the captured American spy.

Laila was pacing in her suite when Harris entered her room through the balcony after receiving her text messages. He was relieved she was safe, but frustrated that the first afternoon he had left her alone, the emir had pounced on her.

The sight of her spread a warm awareness over his body. Harris closed the balcony door quickly behind him. "Are you okay?" he asked in English, remembering his promise to be himself in the privacy of her room.

She nodded. "I'm fine. Worried. Where were you?"

He wouldn't lie, but it was better if no one knew the details. "I met an asset in the souk."

Laila knew there was more to the story. He could see it in her eyes. She didn't question him further. She understood the boundaries. "I have something important to tell you."

What had happened at her meeting with her brother?

A combination of concern and fear played on her face. "I heard a rumor that the American spy is being held in the Cinder Block."

"The emir didn't tell you that, did he?" Harris asked, confused about her text message and this information.

"No, I heard it from my cousin Betha," she said.

Harris swore inwardly. The Cinder Block was on the list of possible places where the CIA suspected the unidentified American spy could be imprisoned. It was well guarded, and known for horrendous conditions and for vanishing prisoners. "Did she know anything else?" He needed to find a way to rescue the American. Prisoners didn't last long inside. They either died from the atrocious living conditions, or they were executed at the emir's command.

"Betha said they plan to kill the American spy after the wedding. I didn't want to press too hard and blow our cover. Mikhail approached me this afternoon about your intentions with me and your job. He wants you to tell him you're planning to marry me."

The second part of her information struck him almost as hard as the first. It had been the plan, and he'd known that he might be approached about his relationship with Laila. Harris was prepared to speak to the emir about his intentions, and to lie and tell him he planned to propose marriage as soon as he had her family's blessing. Lying about his relationship with Laila bothered him. Would anyone pick up on the guilt he felt over those kisses? Or would that simmering attraction help make his lie more convincing? "Is the emir expecting me to approach him, or will he approach me?"

Laila stopped pacing and stood in front of him. She looked up at him with her deep brown eyes. "He will likely speak to you. But, Harris, when he asked to see me, I almost had a heart attack. I thought he might have uncovered what we were doing."

Was she referring to the espionage or the kisses or both? "He can't know." They'd been careful.

"Mikhail has security everywhere. What if one of the cameras caught us sneaking around?" she asked.

"Then it looks like we were sneaking around, trying to find a place to be alone."

Laila's eyes widened. "How is that better? You know dishonoring my family is almost as bad as being a traitor."

Harris rolled the information around. He had been careful about looking for cameras. If they had been seen, Harris doubted he and Laila would be permitted to stay in the compound another moment. They'd more likely be with the American spy in the Cinder Block.

His attention switched to her mouth. He couldn't help it. She was staring up at him, looking worried and nervous, and he wanted to make her feel better. Kissing her had made him feel better. Alive. Relaxed. What effect had it had on her?

If he brought up the kiss, would she be uncomfortable? Or was it better to clear the air and mention it? Or not speak of it and test her reaction to another kiss? He took her hands in his, watching her face for a response.

She looked from their hands to his face. "What are you doing?"

"Reassuring you," he said, knowing the gesture had missed the mark if she had to ask.

"This isn't reassuring. It's unnerving."

He released her. "I didn't realize my touch made you uncomfortable."

She shifted on her feet. "It doesn't. It's not the touch. It's other things." She looked at the ground away from him.

"The kiss. You're worried that I've kissed you. Twice."

She met his gaze. "I'm worried that it happened, but you weren't alone. I was there, too, an active and willing participant. I'm concerned that you make me want to kiss you, even when I know it's a bad idea."

"Why do you feel that way?" he asked. Were her objections purely cultural? Or was it him that she objected to? He had plenty of strikes against him: American, FBI agent, unable to make a relationship work.

"We don't have a future."

He had thought about that. The plan had been to give Laila a new life in America to keep her safe from her brother or the Holy Light Brotherhood or her countrymen, if they intended to harm her. Harris had understood that he would cut ties so the investigation could never lead back to her. What if they could have more? What if starting over in America wasn't the end of their relationship? "Maybe we can still see each other. Now and then." As he spoke the words, he knew they were a long shot. He guessed his bosses at the CIA and FBI wouldn't react well if he mentioned it.

Laila pressed her lips together for a long moment. "Maybe now and then?"

"I told you I would be myself and honest when we were in this room. Now and then is all I can offer."

She played with the ends of the veil she wore over her hair. "We're working together. This could get messy."

"It will get messy whether I'd kissed you or not. We're playing these roles, and it's easy to get caught up in them."

Her eyes narrowed slightly. "Is that what fueled the kiss? You were caught up in the role you were playing? You told me when we were in my room, you would be Harris Truman, so don't lie to me."

He heard the edge in her voice. It wasn't how he'd meant it, as if the only reason he'd kissed her was because he was playing her boyfriend. He'd wanted to kiss her. She was a beautiful woman. "Not just the role. Your fire and passion call to me. I'm intrigued by you and your culture. I'm excited that I've met someone as genuine and caring as you. Even if you're only in my life for a short time, I've enjoyed, and will enjoy, every moment."

She looked away from him and retreated a few steps, folding her arms over her chest.

Closing herself off from him. "What did I say?" he asked, reviewing the words.

"You didn't say anything. You were honest. I'm disappointed in myself. You've probably kissed hundreds of women in your lifetime. For me, you're the first and only."

He'd played fast and loose with her trust, and hadn't considered the kiss would have real meaning for her. She was conflicted about relationships with men, and he should have been more restrained. "I'm sorry. I didn't mean to upset you. I haven't kissed hundreds of women." Every woman he had kissed had been special to him in some way. It sounded corny to think, much less say. Plus with age he'd become more discerning about each woman he chose to allow into his life. "I've learned to be careful."

"Careful? What do you mean by *careful?*"

Could he talk to her about this? His mistake with Cassie wasn't classified, but it was embarrassing. "The last woman I dated betrayed me. I was working an undercover case, and one of the men I was investigating paid her off to gather information about me and reveal who I was. It blew the case and nearly got me killed."

Laila's jaw slackened. "Why would she do that?"

Harris had asked himself the same question time and again. He had let Cassie into his life and into his heart. She had slept in his bed. He had trusted her. "The money won her over. She never said if she was angry with me or if she was looking to hurt me. Maybe she didn't foresee the consequences of her actions. She didn't love me as deeply as I believed or at all."

"What happened to her?" Laila asked.

"She's in prison. I don't speak to her, and she hasn't reached out to me." He'd learned a difficult lesson from his experiences with Cassie. He didn't trust his ability to judge a person who he had developed feelings for, and knowing how a friend could turn on him, he hadn't figured out how to incorporate a relationship into his life while he was undercover.

A knock came at the door. He didn't wait for a second one. Nothing would stop Mikhail or his security from entering the room without permission. He should not be in Laila's room alone with her.

He took her hand, kissed the back of it on the henna ink then fled to the balcony and waited only long enough to see her mother enter before bolting off the balcony and returning to his own room. He was inside for less than five minutes when someone pounded on his door.

Harris opened the door. Two of the emir's guards were waiting for him. "The emir requests a private meeting with you."

Harris smiled as if flattered. "I didn't realize he knew who I was."

"He knows," one of the guards said.

Harris pretended not to hear the ominous overtone in his voice. His wealthy-German-heir attitude wouldn't allow him to be intimidated. "Great."

Following the guards to Mikhail's library, Harris searched for Ahmad Al-Adel. Locating the terrorist was on his mind always, and now that he suspected at least one of Al-Adel's men was on the premises, he was determined to find him and others in the terrorist organization.

The silent guard opened the door to Mikhail's library. Harris entered and looked around as if it were the first time he was seeing the room. The emir was seated behind his desk. "It's a pleasure to meet you," Harris said.

Mikhail stared at him for a moment before coming

to his feet, circling the desk and extending his hand. Harris shook it. Mikhail gestured to the pair of chairs fronting his desk and sat in one. "Please have a seat."

Harris sat and waited for Mikhail to introduce the topic. One trick he'd learned during interrogations was that most people were uncomfortable with silence and would try to fill it with either nonsense or incriminating information. Harris could sit in silence for hours. Didn't bother him.

"Laila tells me you intend to marry her."

Harris smiled and folded his hands over his lap. He would talk about the marriage part first, business second. "I do intend to marry her. I'm learning my way around her culture, and I've been studying Islam. I want to be accepted by you and her family as her husband."

Mikhail nodded, and Harris thought he saw interest in his eyes. Harris waited again for the emir to lead the conversation.

"I'm interested in knowing more about you. What do you do for a living?"

"At the moment I'm a finance student at the University of Colorado, but after I finish my degree this next semester, I'm returning to Germany to work for my family's shipping business."

There is was again. The flare of interest in Mikhail's eyes. "Is the family business doing well?"

Harris would have thought Mikhail would have been more direct. Was he trying to lead Harris around to offering to help him? Was it appropriate for Harris to extend such an offer? "Despite the downturn in the economy, profits are up eight percent, and we're adding new areas to our standard shipping locations every month."

"Is your company able to handle special deliveries? Those that are sensitive in nature, and may require delicate handling and discretion?"

He'd gotten to the point. "Kuhn Freight can take any job, large or small. We're known for our discretion with our clients. We've moved historical artifacts, rare items and priceless works of art without incident." He lifted his head high and injected pride into his voice.

Mikhail looked pleased with himself. "I've been looking for someone to help me move some special items that are important to me. I haven't found a suitable transporter who I can trust to be discreet."

Harris didn't have to pretend to be enthused about Mikhail's interest. He'd passed another hurdle by capturing the emir's attention and opening communication about what Mikhail might want to move. Those "special items" could be destined for Al-Adel and the Holy Light Brotherhood headquarters or other bases of operation. Harris leaned forward to convey his attentiveness. "We'd be honored to earn your business. You won't be disappointed with our services."

Mikhail nodded. "We'll have more time to talk tonight. After dinner I've arranged for some entertainment for my closest friends. Please plan to join us. Transportation leaves the compound at ten."

Mikhail stood, and Harris followed suit. "Sounds like fun. Thank you for including me."

As Harris left the room, he was mentally fist pumping in victory. He'd found his way into the emir's private party. A private party that might include Ahmad Al-Adel and the members of the Holy Light Brotherhood.

Chapter 6

Harris wasn't responding to her text messages. Laila had even been so bold as to knock on his bedroom door. He hadn't answered.

She returned to her room, anxiety twisting in her stomach. Where was he? He hadn't mentioned having another meeting. Had something gone wrong?

Part of her worried she'd have to find some way to report to the CIA that Harris had joined the other American spy in the Cinder Block. Why hadn't she been given a direct contact in the event of emergency? Didn't the CIA and FBI trust her with this mission? If she'd been planning to betray Harris, she would have done so already.

When the balcony door slid open, Laila came to her feet, throwing aside the magazine she hadn't been reading.

"I got your messages. What's wrong?" Harris asked.

"I was worried about you. Where were you?"

"With your brother. He wanted to talk about our engagement and the family shipping business."

She let out her breath, knots loosening in her stomach. "I was so scared."

Harris came closer to her and pressed a finger over her lips. The contact was electric. "You worry too much. I'm fine. Your brother was making sure my intentions were honorable with you, and that I'd be open to helping him transport some sensitive items to difficult locations."

Emphasis on the words *sensitive* and *difficult*. Was Mikhail talking about weapons or supplies for Al-Adel and his terrorist organization?

Harris had made great progress. The situation was playing out as he'd wanted. "What did you tell him?" Laila asked.

"I told him I wanted to marry you, and my company would love to earn the business of the Emir of Qamsar however we needed to. He also invited me to a gathering tonight."

Disappointment speared through her. She'd hoped to spend some time with Harris this evening. His operation came first, and he couldn't pass up the opportunity to rub elbows with Mikhail and his inner circle. "Will you be out late?" she asked.

Harris inclined his head, his blue eyes searching her face. "I don't know what Mikhail has planned. Is something wrong?"

Laila wasn't supposed to grow attached to him. They were actors playing a part. Yet that kiss lingered on her lips, and she wanted to spend more time with him. She hungered for it. Which was ridiculous and would likely cause her more hurt in the long run. Their relationship wasn't leading anywhere except a dead end. Or a possible, improbable "now and then" visit. "My mom stopped by to see if we were attending Aisha's dessert party tonight. I was hoping you and I could spend some time together. Best desserts in the world by some of the top chefs. She has a pastry chef from France, a baker from England and a chocolatier from Belgium." Maybe she could appeal to his stomach, and he'd choose spending time with her over working Mikhail.

"I'll have to pass. If Mikhail's gathering ends early, I'll stop by."

It had been a long shot, but it didn't stop the disappointment from spreading over her.

Harris set his fingers under her chin and nudged her head up so she was looking at him. "Do we need to talk about this?" His voice was gentle, heavy with concern.

Her face gave away the disappointment she felt. She couldn't help it. She wasn't trained to hide her emotions the way he could.

"Nothing to talk about." She had understood the ground rules coming into this operation. The mission came first and finding Al-Adel could save lives. Her developing feelings for Harris weren't an important factor. At least they weren't important to him. She needed to get the reins on her emotions and keep them from galloping out of control.

He let out his breath. "We know that isn't true. What's going on here is a lot to talk about."

She was too afraid to ask about their future and press him about his feelings. She was afraid the honest answers would hurt. She didn't understand men and had no experience with them. What she was feeling for the first time was intense and honest. What if he didn't feel the same for her?

"We don't have a problem," she said. A lie. She still had the same problem, the same gnawing in her stomach like something was about to happen, but she didn't know what.

"If you need something that I'm not providing, you need to tell me," he said.

Confusion and insecurities muddled her thoughts. "I'm fine. We'll have time together tomorrow," she said, unable to keep her voice steady.

"You're even beautiful when you're lying to me."

She lifted her chin. "I'm not lying to you," she said. Her voice came out in a whisper, and she hated that she wasn't stronger about this. She should lock away her feelings and forget about them. Her father had raised her to be strong and in control. Losing control of her emotions was a weakness.

He traced his thumb over her lower lip. "You're a terrible liar."

"I told you that at the beginning. But I'm not lying."

"I know a way to get the truth from you."

She lifted her brow. "Oh?" Some secret agent trick? A lie detector test? Checking her pulse to see how fast her heart was beating?

He brought his mouth close to her neck and he kissed her, his lips brushing against the sensitive skin at her nape. She caught the game he was playing. She shivered. "You can't seduce the truth out of me."

He didn't say anything. His hands drifted down her sides, stopping and resting at her hips. The nerve endings in her skin tingled and danced. "Tell me what's going on in your head," he said.

The demand was soft and gentle, and Laila wanted to spill the truth. To confess that her life felt in flux, her ideas for the future had changed, her feelings for him had evolved, and that she wanted more than he could give her. She'd grown closer to him, gotten to know him, and she didn't want to end their relationship when this mission was over.

In other words, to tell him she wanted to alter their arrangement, and that he should trust her to be in his life in a real, concrete way. Trust her. Something he'd implied he couldn't do, not with the memory of the woman who'd betrayed him burning on his mind.

What could she say and not ruin their connection and send him emotionally fleeing? "I enjoy spending time with you. I was disappointed that I wouldn't see you tonight," she said.

The word "tonight" hung heavy between them. Laila had never spent the evening alone with a man. Had never gone to dinner and out dancing, and then returned to a man's place for kissing on the couch. Or other things. Those other things she hadn't explored, and for the first time, she wanted to explore. Or at least was curious about them.

"I'll see if I can find a way to see you," he said.

Excitement spread from her chest to her hands and feet. She leaned closer to him and gripped his shirt in her hands. Maybe he did understand he was important to her.

He was offering a compromise. He didn't have a mission-related reason to see her. It meant a great deal that he was willing to try. Maybe she was blowing the situation out of proportion, or assigning meaning that wasn't there, but he was taking a chance. Any time they were together like they were now, they risked being caught. The emir's guards had made it clear they didn't respect a closed door.

If someone walked in on them right now, with Harris's hands on her waist, her fingers fisting his shirt, his lips on her neck, licking, kissing, what would happen to them? She had no desire to be caught or to face the repercussions of behaving in a manner she knew was inappropriate in Qamsar.

Harris drew away from her. "If you're okay, I should go."

"You could stay for a few more minutes." A few more minutes in his arms wouldn't hurt.

He raised his eyebrows. "I could stay here for much longer than a few minutes. But we both know what would happen if someone finds us together. Alone."

She pressed a kiss to his mouth. "Be safe. I worry about you leaping across balconies. Someone might see you."

"I'll be careful. I'm always careful."

He dropped a kiss on the top of her head and he went to the balcony doors. He looked back once at her, winked and then disappeared outside.

Mikhail had arranged for his private party to take place outside the compound with transportation to and from the location for his guests.

Two large tents were erected in the desert sand, the sky was clear of clouds and filled with stars, and ornate rugs covered most of the area around the tents.

Most odd were the generators humming into the

night air and the portable satellites affixed to the top of the tents. If this was an outdoor adventure, it certainly lacked any of the features of "roughing it" or becoming one with nature.

Following the other guests inside a tent, Harris could only think of the word *harem* to describe the scene. He removed his shoes and stepped deeper inside. Mikhail's private "closest friends" party wasn't exclusive to his friends. A group of lovely, half-naked women danced to music piped over the speakers in the corners of the tent. Men played poker at two round green-topped tables.

Harris surveyed the room, and though the lighting was patchy, casting shadows into the corners where he guessed more carnal activities were taking place, he didn't spot Al-Adel. Also missing from the festivities was the emir's brother, Saafir.

More than one glass was filled with what Harris knew wasn't soda.

Apparently at this pre-wedding party, social, cultural and religious rules were forgotten. Half-naked women, alcohol and gambling were acceptable in this realm.

Though Harris was used to hiding his emotions, he let surprise show on his face. The setup was something he'd expect from a Western bachelor party, not in the middle of a desert in the Middle East. Some of the men in the room seemed intent on their card game, whether they were uncomfortable with the women's dance or loving the game, and others were openly enjoying the women's performance.

Harris quickly decided how to play his cards. His character wasn't a prude, although engaging with these women could put his relationship with Laila in jeopardy. If she, or any of the other girlfriends or wives knew what was transpiring in this place, he couldn't imagine how to explain it to her. That was how a boyfriend would think, right?

Harris didn't need to explain his actions or behavior to Laila, and anything he did on this mission was for the successful location and capture of Ahmad Al-Adel, and anyone else they could tie to his wrongdoings. Even as he composed the rational argument, guilt assailed him.

Earlier that day, he'd known Laila was upset when he'd mentioned this party. Though she wouldn't tell him all the reasons why, he caught the thread of the problem quickly. The kisses they'd shared had confused her. This situation had confused her. He couldn't blame her. It had scrambled his thoughts, too, and he'd made some questionable decisions when he was alone with her, like kissing her.

He was undercover, spying on the Emir of Qamsar and searching for a dangerous, internationally wanted terrorist. Those actions alone should occupy his waking thoughts. If it wasn't enough, he had the sharp experiences of Cassie's betrayal to remind him that his safety and the protection of his team and success of the mission required every precaution in bringing someone into his confidence. But those thoughts didn't shut out his feelings for Laila. She interrupted his thoughts during the day, and she invaded his dreams at night.

The mission had to come first. He was in Qamsar and at this party for his job. Getting into this tent was a milestone. The situation and the alcohol would loosen tongues. He scanned the room, looking for Mikhail, and found him sitting on a leather wingback chair, surrounded by a small group of friends with two scantily clad women perched on the edge of his chair like decorations.

Harris hid his disgust. He strode to Mikhail, avoiding colliding with the gyrating women. Holding his hand up several times to decline a personal dance, he navigated the room. He didn't find that type of entertainment sexy. It was seedy and awkward, both for him and the woman. A woman pretending to be interested in him for cash was as appealing as snuggling with a flatulent camel.

When he reached Mikhail's side, the emir turned to acknowledge him. "Harris, glad you could make it."

His demeanor was friendlier and more casual than it had been earlier in the day. Mikhail might have been pleased with the business connections Harris brought to the family. Or, while he didn't have a drink in his hand, perhaps he had indulged.

"I appreciate the invitation. Nice setup you got here." Harris gestured around the room.

It had to have taken Mikhail's staff hours to rig the tent and equipment, to move the furniture and supplies to the middle of the desert. It was a strange cross between the history of the country and the modernization of the culture.

Mikhail introduced him to the men sitting in the circle with him. One of the men caught and held his interest, a man named Tariq Salem. Harris had seen his face before and recognized the name. He was one of the men on the CIA's persons of interest list because he had ties to Al-Adel.

Harris eased into the conversation. He spoke the

language fluently, having no problem with the regional dialect or local slang.

"You've got to give this up, my friend," one of the men said, gesturing around. "Aisha's not the type of woman to turn a blind eye."

Mikhail laughed. "Aisha is a good woman. She knows her place."

One of the older men smiled. "All women know their place. But take it from someone who has been married for thirty-five years. It's a happier life when your woman is content. I never understand young grooms who want to prove a point by controlling their wives and making them miserable. Let the women have their fun and keep them happy. If you do, when they get into bed with you, they are more than happy to let you have your fun then."

The men broke into laughter.

"I know Aisha," Mikhail said. "She can have her women's events and her dessert parties and buy expensive things to wear. But I draw the line at involving her in my personal life."

"She is your personal life," the older man said lightly.

Mikhail nodded. "Maybe I can manage to have a life with her and a life to myself."

The men shared stories about their wives and lovers, some admitting having both wasn't worth the expense and effort, others talking about their second and third wives, and how it had made their life more complicated, but worth it.

"And what about you?" Mikhail asked, drawing Harris into the conversation. "Living in Germany, you must have a different perspective."

He'd been content to listen, both to the conversation

in front of him and those around him. Mikhail had invited him for a reason, to check him out and make sure he was for real, but perhaps also to get a sense if he could be trusted. If Harris didn't offer anything toward the conversation, he was losing his chance to build a relationship with the emir. "I've had to be careful. In the past I've gotten the attention of gold diggers and status seekers. It's one of the great parts of my relationship with Laila. She comes from wealth. Besides most of the relationships I've seen, at least the ones that are worth working for, one woman is more than enough. I don't see how I'd keep up with more than one."

"Are you calling my sister a handful?" Mikhail asked, amusement in his tone.

"A handful implies I need to handle her. That's not the case. She has a life and a world of her own, and I'm glad to be part of it." Speaking the words was easy because he spoke the truth.

"You're happy with her being independent? Fine that she's living in America?" one of the men asked.

Harris wouldn't have wanted it any other way. A woman who was dependent on him, needy to the point of not functioning alone, didn't appeal to him. "It works for us," Harris said, careful not to insult any of the men around him.

"If she gets out of line, beat your wife once, and then she'd know not to cross you," Tariq said. "Maybe twice if she's especially willful."

Harris controlled his temper and the angry retort that snapped to mind. Salem had to be baiting a reaction. Many of the men appeared uncomfortable. Why weren't they saying anything? Were they afraid to speak out against Al-Adel and his network of terrorists? Did anyone else know of the connection between Salem and Al-Adel?

Mikhail took a sip of his drink. "What goes on in a man's household is his business. But I think good Arabic women know their place without the need for fists."

Harris tasted bitterness on the back of his tongue. Growing up in a household where his mother ruled and strong, capable women were admired, he didn't agree with a woman needing to "know her place" or with ever, ever using his hands against a woman. A wife deserved to be touched one way by her husband: with loving, worshipful hands.

The image of running his hands over Laila came so quick, he didn't have time to censor it. He'd never touched the bare skin of her stomach, but he'd guess it was soft, like the threads of her hair running through his fingers. He physically ached to touch her.

When he forced his mind back to the distasteful conversation, Mikhail was laughing at something one of the men had said. "My mother is a good woman. When she becomes your wife, you won't have to do any training."

His mother? Harris had missed an important part of the exchange.

"Tariq has been patient, and his patience is running out," Mikhail said.

Tariq Salem? Mikhail was planning to match his mother and Salem? It would destroy Laila to see her mother in that man's hands. He'd admitted he treated a woman violently or at least was willing to. Why would Mikhail want his mother in Salem's hands?

Political reasons, Harris guessed. To establish strong ties between Qamsar and the Holy Light Brotherhood.

Was Mikhail that desperate for power that he'd offer his mother? If he was willing to hand over his mother to Salem, what was he willing to do to Laila?

Laila stayed awake until eleven, reading a romance novel on her e-reader. Half following the story, half waiting for Harris, she left her balcony door unlocked hoping he would show up. She hadn't heard anyone else in the hallway for the past few hours. Had he returned to the compound, or was he still out with Mikhail celebrating?

At midnight she gave up and changed into her pajamas. She slipped into bed and pulled the covers over her. Was Harris okay, or had something gone wrong at the party? It was a good sign that Harris had been invited to the emir's gathering, but Mikhail's temper could be volatile, and he had no tolerance for disloyalty, even suspected disloyalty. Did Mikhail believe something was amiss and want to keep Harris close while he checked into his suspicions? The desert was an easy place to lose someone, intentionally or not. What if Mikhail hurt Harris? He didn't have other allies to help him.

Laila took a deep breath and reassured herself. Harris could handle himself. He was smart and resourceful.

She awoke to the sound of her name and a hand brushing her hair away from her forehead. She recognized Harris's touch, knew his smell.

"Sorry to wake you. I didn't want you to think I forgot about you," he whispered.

The need for sleep fled once Harris was in her room, beside her on her bed. She rolled onto her back. He'd come to see her despite the late hour. "What time is it?"

"Three o'clock"

She stretched her legs under the sheets, trying to shake off her tiredness. "Did the party go well?"

"It was interesting. I have some information to follow up on."

"That's good," she said. "You could have called or texted me." She'd left her phone on the bedside table for that reason.

"I wanted to see you."

Her heartbeat broke into a sprint at his words.

"How was your night?" he asked.

She struggled to remember the dessert party. Now that Harris was in her room, her mind was absorbed with him and how close he was to her. "The food was amazing. Aisha is so happy to be getting married soon."

"I'm glad you had fun. Do you want me to leave so you can go back to sleep?" he asked.

She didn't. She wanted him to stay. It was wrong to ask something of him that could get them into trouble. Not only that, she wasn't sure what being alone with him would imply to him. She didn't want to take things fast, but she didn't want to call them to a stop, either. If he left her alone now, she would regret it. "Why don't you stay?" she asked. "We can talk. Make yourself comfortable." Was that clear? Or did women use those words to coyly invite a man to sleep with them? She was out of her element. Again.

"I'm not propositioning you," she added.

"I know that."

"I want to spend time with you."

"Hey, Laila, please stop worrying. I understand. I

won't do anything you don't want to do. I won't take advantage of a beautiful half-asleep woman in her bed."

She should have known Harris wouldn't have interpreted her invitation as an offer for sex. She didn't have to worry about things like that with him. He got her. He understood.

Harris pulled off his shoes and tossed them on the floor. He loosened his tie and unfastened the top button. He pulled the wicker chair in the corner of the room closer and took a seat.

"You can lay here with me if you want," she said, surprised at her boldness.

Harris hesitated a few moments before standing and circling the bed. He sat beside her, staying on top of the blankets. He adjusted the pillows behind his head so he was reclined.

"Do you want to hear about the night your brother had planned for himself and his friends?" he asked.

"I'm guessing it was wilder than a large sampling of desserts, teas and coffees. I heard a rumor from one of the women at the party that Mikhail wants big send-offs for his final nights as a bachelor."

"That's a good way to put it. Another way to put it is that your brother should not pass judgment on anyone else for drinking, smoking, dancing or gambling."

Laila hadn't expected the party to be demure, but she hadn't guessed the extent of the activity. "Tell me you're joking."

"I'm serious. It caught me off guard. It reminded me of a scene from an American fraternity house on a Friday night, except far fewer women."

Laila had never been to a fraternity house, but she'd

seen movies. "There were women at the party?" If Aisha found out, she would be angry.

"Yes, and they weren't family or friends. I'm guessing they were hired companions."

"Was Saafir there?" Laila asked. Based on the book they had found in the library, her brothers could have some relationship she didn't understand. Maybe Saafir and Mikhail were on the same page regarding their intentions for Qamsar.

"No, he was absent, and no one mentioned him."

Laila had grown up sheltered, but she knew men sometimes overindulged behind closed doors, and despite what Mikhail might preach and the rules he applied to his own house, he did his share of breaking those rules. "What did you do?" she asked, feeling a twinge of unreasonable jealousy.

"I talked to as many people as I could and found out everything they were willing to tell me. Which in some cases were their drunken escapades as youths." He grinned at her. "I had to share some of my own stories, of course, of growing up with two brothers in Germany."

"How much did you have to stretch the truth?" she asked.

"Except for some details, it wasn't hard to come up with interesting stories. I kept them PG-rated. I didn't want your brother to overhear and deem me unsuitable for you."

"Did Mikhail ask again about our engagement?" she asked. She hadn't gotten a sense of why her brother had invited Harris.

"He did. In a way. Mostly he and his buddies shared with me their views of a woman's role in marriage."

Laila almost scoffed. She could imagine that conversation. "Did they use the word *subservient* or was it just implied?" she asked wryly.

"The actual word might have been used a few times."

"What did you say about that? You couldn't have disagreed too loudly." Mikhail recognized Harris's culture and expectations would be different, but he wouldn't take kindly to open opposition.

"I tried to be as quiet as possible, and when I had to speak, I kept my comments neutral." His face turned serious. "I also overheard details about Mikhail's plans for your mother. I debated not saying anything, but if you have this information, it might help you convince her to leave Qamsar with you."

The hair on the back of her neck stood on end. This couldn't be good news. If it was, Harris would have blurted it out.

"Mikhail intends to have your mother marry a member of the Holy Light Brotherhood. Or at least, someone who had ties to it."

Laila stared at him. Her stomach turned. Her brother wanted her mother to remarry this soon? It would follow tradition to pair her mother with a suitable husband, but her mother was happy. She was taken care of, and she deserved more than a couple of years to grieve for her husband. "He wants her to marry a man from a terrorist group? No. No. You can't let that happen."

Harris met her gaze, fire snapping in his blue eyes. "The plan is to get her out of here before that, or anything else bad, happens."

He set his hand over her arm. It was a comforting touch she needed. She could have shrugged him off, or she could have pulled away. Relying on Harris to be there for her, to keep her and her family safe, had become part of her day-to-day reality.

Anger at her brother incensed her. "What is wrong with him? Why would Mikhail do that?" Laila asked.

"He's misguided. Maybe he wants to have ties to Al-Adel. Maybe he and Tariq Salem have some other relationship."

The man's name was Tariq Salem. Laila had never heard of him, but she already hated him. "Saafir will be furious if he finds out," Laila said. Unless he was on board with the decision. She couldn't picture it, but nothing about the past couple of weeks seemed real to her. Saafir's name was in the book with the Holy Light Brotherhood symbol on the cover.

Harris was watching her closely. "It won't happen. We won't let your mother marry a terrorist."

"When can I talk to my mom about leaving Qamsar?" Laila wanted her mother out of harm's way. If she could confide the truth to her mother, her mother could be more careful.

"At the soonest we have to wait until the emir's wedding to tell your mother our plans. If we need to get her out sooner, I'll pull every string I can to make that happen. For now we stick to the original time line. When we get the information we need, we'll tell her we have to leave."

Laila pictured her mother's reaction. She'd have to leave most of her things, but it would be for the best. Would her mother see that? If she was destined to marry a terrorist, she'd have no choice. Convincing her mother should be a matter of logic. "You'll let me know when I can talk to her?"

"Of course," Harris said, squeezing her arm lightly.

Along his jawline, the blond hair of his stubble gave him a roguish appearance. She wanted to trace her fingers along his face. She curled her hands into fists and kept them beneath her pillow. She couldn't help sliding closer to Harris. "I heard who Mikhail had planned to marry me off to."

"Are you disappointed that won't be happening?" Harris asked carefully.

The opposite. She was relieved. "Not at all. The man is an absolute troll, and I would have hated being his wife. He would have been a difficult man to love."

Harris appeared pleased. "I'm glad you have options now."

A world of options she'd never had before had opened up. Laila had assumed an arranged marriage would work, but perhaps the reality was harsher than she'd imagined. At the same time, she felt the urge to defend it. "My parents had an arranged marriage, and they were deeply in love."

"It's great that it worked out for your parents. They were lucky."

"My father had enough status and resources to take a second wife, but he never did. Do you know why?"

"Your mother wouldn't have liked it?" Harris asked.

Laila smiled. "That's true. She would have hated it. But in our culture, a man can only take multiple wives if all wives are treated equally. My father said he could never have loved another woman the way he loved my mother, and in that way, his wives could not be equals."

"Sounds like they had a good thing going," he said.

They had. Laila had hoped to find the same thing in her husband. "They had something precious."

"Arranged marriage or not, for two people to find each other in this world and make it work and be happy is amazing and rare," Harris said.

Was he skeptical of finding love? It saddened her to think his last relationship might have burned him too deeply for him to consider trusting and marrying a woman. "What about your parents? Are they happy together?" she asked, wondering if she was treading on a sensitive topic.

"They're together and love each other a great deal. So are my two brothers with their wives. I've seen it happen. I can't seem to figure out how to make it happen for me."

Their eyes locked and held for a long, lingering moment. She had so much to say, she wasn't sure where to start. She wanted to tell him maybe she could make it happen for him. That they should leave open the door to the possibility they could have something together.

She wasn't bold enough to make the suggestion outright that she and Harris could and should have a future. "I don't know what you've been looking for in a woman or why it hasn't worked out, but if you keep your eyes open, the right woman will find you."

Harris slid down farther on the bed, letting his head rest on the pillow. "For a person without much dating experience, you have a lot of confidence in my ability to find someone."

Whenever she pictured the future, she envisioned a marriage that worked. Was she wrong to be so optimistic? "I'm confident because I've never been in love and had it turn sour. I don't have those heartbreaks clouding my thinking. I can only imagine what love is like and assume that, if we want it and it's real, we'll find it and hold onto it."

"Never been in love," he repeated slowly.

He knew that about her. Nothing about her statement should have shocked him. Why did he sound confused?

"What about you? Have you been in love?" she asked.

He appeared pensive before he answered. "I've spoken the words, and I believed them when I said them. But looking back, I don't know if I was in love or if I was in lust or if I liked the idea of being in love."

In that way they were on equal footing.

"I imagine that love changes a person, and that's why it works. You don't have to change, but you want to. You meld together," she said.

He smiled. "Now that's a romantic idea."

She blushed, grateful the low lights hid her face. "Well, how would you describe it? Since you've almost been in love, tell me what it's like."

"Almost in love is not *in love*. The best I can do is tell you what I've seen in my brothers," Harris said. He shifted, and his body skimmed hers. Even with the blankets between them, heat and power surged beyond the barriers. "They each met a woman, and from the moment I saw them together, I knew they had something special. They only had eyes for each other, and even when they resisted, and they resisted hard at times, they couldn't stay away from each other."

"Did they have reasons not to trust, like you?" Laila asked. If he could answer that question, maybe it would give her insight into how she could gain his trust. She wouldn't betray him. She had promised she would help stop the Holy Light Brotherhood, and had put her life and her future on the line. That had to mean something to him.

"They had their reasons for being careful."

Just like he had his. "How did they overcome them?" Laila asked.

"Circumstances. Persistence and patience from the women who fell in love with them."

Was that what Harris needed? For her to prove time and again she was trustworthy?

The conversation lulled and sleep found her. When Laila awoke, she couldn't remember what they had last talked about or when they had drifted off. Harris was asleep beside her, fully clothed on top of the blankets.

It was early, the sun not quite risen in the sky. Laila took the comforter and tossed it over Harris, leaving the sheet and blankets over her.

The movement woke him. "What's the matter?" he asked, sounding groggy.

"I thought you might be cold," she whispered.

"But now you'll be cold."

"I'm okay."

The words weren't out of her mouth before he'd thrown the comforter back over her and lifted the blankets, sliding beneath them.

"Is this okay?" he asked.

They weren't touching, and yet it was the most intimate she had been with a man. Plumes of fire infused her body. His eyes were closed, and she let herself stare. He was a beautiful man, and sleeping beside him, she felt safe and protected, cherished and wanted.

What was he feeling? Tired? Had slipping beneath the blankets been to get comfortable or to get closer to her? The peaceful look on his face told her he wasn't scrutinizing lying in bed with her the way she was.

She closed her eyes and let herself snooze longer next to Harris. When she awoke a second time, she had moved her feet over to his side of the bed, pressing them to his calf. He didn't appear to mind. Was this what it was like to sleep beside a man? Her body intertwined with his, the brush of skin and the physical contact natural and warming, desire and craving humming inside her body.

She shifted to get out of bed, trying to not wake him. His eyes popped open. He must be a light sleeper.

"Good morning," he said.

"Morning," she replied.

"How did you sleep?"

"I slept great. How are you feeling?" she asked.

"Pretty amazing and pretty scared. I slept beside a beautiful woman, and if her family finds out, I'll be sent to the Cinder Block. The moment I let down my guard, that's when we're most in danger."

"Nah, you'd be stuck marrying me on the spot."

He twisted his lips in thought. "How do you know that wasn't the reason I stayed all night?"

Though his tone told her that he was teasing, a shimmer of happiness piped over her. "How will you get out of here?"

"Same way I got in. The balcony."

He sat up and rubbed his face. The light hair on his jaw had created a scruffy-looking beard. "If I'm caught en route to my room, I'll pretend I passed out in the garden."

"It would have been pretty cold outside overnight," she said.

"Good point. I'll pretend to be cold. The truth is much better. I was curled up warm and content next to you. We'll have to keep that between us."

Warm and content. Her nerves sparkled with awareness. Something had shifted between them. Was this what it felt like to fall in love, for the beginnings of love and intimacy to bloom? "This was a first for me."

The bright blue of his eyes seared into her. "I'm a lucky man. I've kissed you and slept beside you."

Two important firsts, at least to her. What did it mean to him? "Have you spoken to your boss about seeing each other when I return to America?"

Harris shook his head. "I haven't had the chance."

The mission was priority one now. But when they returned to the United States, if she had to, Laila wasn't sure how she would let Harris go.

Chapter 7

Harris shook off the remnants of sleep. He'd been dreaming with Laila at his side, the fresh scent of her skin wrapping around every thought. She'd captivated him, enough that he'd shared with her stories about his family, the people closest to him. Protective of his family and the people he loved, he was very careful about what he said about them. If a victim, witness or informant knew he had family, he made it clear they weren't a subject he discussed. Even with coworkers, he was sometimes reluctant to discuss them.

He didn't want his deepening relationship with Laila to cause him to make a mistake or overlook a critical piece of information. Devon had warned him that working closely with Laila could cause these problems, as if Harris's relationship with Cassie hadn't already taught him of those dangers. Harris wouldn't let emotions get ahead of logic or blind him.

Harris had made good progress in the few days he'd been in Qamsar. The more he observed Mikhail and the people around him, the more familiar faces appeared. Like Tariq Salem. He didn't want anyone or anything to impact his headway.

Leaving Laila's room via the balcony was becoming easier. He'd done so a few times, and at this point, he needed to get the timing right, and he could remain unseen.

He entered his room and was immediately aware it had been searched. The pillow on the left had been rotated upside down, and the dust patterns on the dresser gave away items had been shifted.

When had the search taken place? Last night while he was at the emir's party? He'd need to search again for listening or recording devices, and to be safe, he'd make a call to his "brother" explaining the previous night and where he had been. If someone had come into his room the night before and found him missing from it, he didn't want questions raised.

He swept for bugs and found only the one in place that had been in his room since his arrival. He sent a secure message to the CIA that he'd seen Tariq Salem speaking with Mikhail and relayed his suspicions about the American spy being held in the Cinder Block. He dialed Tyler under the pretense of talking about his evening at the emir's party. He didn't drop any names, and he didn't reveal anything the emir would object to him saying. The emir had invited Harris into his inner circle, and Harris didn't want to openly flaunt that trust.

He told Tyler that, the last thing he had remembered, he'd been en route to his room and had passed out in the garden.

After trading some friendly banter, he wrapped up the call. "I need to get a hot shower and something to eat," Harris said.

"Stay in touch. We hope to see you soon," Tyler said.

In other words, send a secure transmission with anything you discovered, and let's wrap this mission successfully and soon.

Harris went into the bathroom and turned on the fan. He opened his phone and logged into the CIA mobile application with the profiles of persons of interest to the CIA. He found Tariq Salem's picture right away. He was number seven on the CIA's list.

Harris read Tariq Salem's detailed profile. Most of the information he'd known. He was surprised to learn Tariq was a distant relative of Aisha's on her father's side. Was Tariq Salem at the wedding as Aisha's kin or as the emir's business associate? Why had Mikhail chosen him as a husband for his mother?

Harris logged out of the application, questions running through his mind. He took a shower, shaved and brushed his teeth. Though he had left her less than an hour ago, he was looking forward to meeting Laila for breakfast. He'd spent the night with a woman he was interested in sexually, but nothing physical had happened between them. Yet he'd felt as if everything was right with the world. Instead of frustration, his anticipation intensified. Though nothing could happen with her, he couldn't keep his mind off the idea of holding her, touching her and tasting her.

It would have been natural for him to pull her into his arms and make love with her. Were she any other woman with whom he had amazing chemistry, he wouldn't have stopped himself from kissing her. But this was Laila. She was working with him on this mission, and she was innocent. He couldn't take advantage of her, not again. Laila was risking everything for him.

She'd proven to be smart and trustworthy, but Mikhail was a powerful man. If he suspected Laila of deception, he wouldn't hesitate to punish her, sister or not.

Harris wanted to call one of his brothers, one of his real brothers, and talk to them. To ask if his need to be close to her and his excitement to see her was part of their experiences with their girlfriends-turned-wives. His brothers teased, they made fun of each other, but when he needed them, they were always there. Always.

Not to say he and Laila were like his brothers and their wives. But Harris had never felt this way. The intensity of the attraction was new. Harris had had good times and fun trips with other girlfriends, but what he was experiencing with Laila rose to a higher level.

Other relationships could go either way, and he wouldn't have cared much. With Laila, he'd care if they had to part ways. He would miss her. He would want to know how she was doing. He would want to see her.

That almost scared him more than the risks he was taking on this mission. He couldn't cut and run. Not with Laila. Knowing at some point she would be relocated and given a fresh start made the gnawing in his stomach worse.

Harris received a message from Tyler that the team needed to speak to him. Disappointed he'd miss breakfast, he texted Laila to eat without him.

Harris left the compound on foot to be sure he wasn't under audio or video surveillance. He didn't mention to Laila where he was headed, and he doubled back several times to ensure he wasn't followed. He called Tyler when he was a good distance from the compound.

"We got your message," Tyler said.

"Do you need me to do something else with him?" Harris asked. *Him* being Tariq Salem.

"No," Tyler said. "We're trying to confirm why he's attending the wedding. Is he a guest of the bride or is he there for Al-Adel?"

Harris looked around to ensure he was alone. "I can't be sure. I had the same question."

"Several other assets confirmed the rumor that the American spy is being held in the Cinder Block. The CIA also has a way for you to get inside, talk to him and find out what he knows. We're worried he might be relocated to the west side of the country to another prison or vanish completely."

"Why would he be moved?" Harris asked. Harris was more concerned that he'd be executed before anyone had time to intervene on his behalf.

"If too many people have heard rumors that an American spy is being held inside the Cinder Block, the embassy will get involved and contact local authorities. The emir still has the right to decide if the American will be permitted to speak to anyone, but he won't create an international incident over it," Tyler said. "The Cinder Block doesn't have the facilities to perform a quiet execution, and the guards can't give the prisoners another reason to stage a revolt. They'll move him somewhere and make a big deal about his transfer, and then kill him without anyone knowing or causing a problem. But we won't let that happen. Instead, you'll get the intel, and once you confirm he's inside, we'll work on a liberation plan."

The way inside wouldn't be simple. "If I'm caught, my cover is blown, and I won't be able to work the emir from my current position." Didn't the CIA have other agents in position to help the captured American spy?

"The way inside the Cinder Block involves Laila, and I doubt she'd work with anyone but you."

Harris mulled that over. Laila would help him if he asked. She'd been concerned to learn about the prisoner in the Cinder Block. Even so, he'd need to hear the plan first before he was willing to involve her. If it put her at an unacceptable risk level, the answer would be no. "Tell me how I'll get into the most locked-down prison in the country and with a woman no less."

Tyler sighed. "You don't have to sound defeatist. We need the intel the American has. He knows something, and we need to find out what."

Harris looked around again. A few cars passed along the street, but no foot traffic. The heat of the day kept most people indoors. "Assuming I get inside and manage to find him, how will I get this man to talk to me?"

"We have faith in you, and we can give you a few tools to use."

"I'm not torturing anyone," Harris said, not liking where this conversation was heading. Another reason he preferred working for the FBI. As a special agent, he'd never been asked to use extreme measures when questioning a suspect.

"Not torture. High likelihood he's been trained to withstand that anyway. We want you to use your profiler training and get inside his psyche. Prepare what you'll say to him and then get the information from him. We'll send you what we know for you to start with."

Harris was comfortable analyzing someone. But he didn't have background information on this man specifically, and he wouldn't have much time to talk to him. Any technique he used would be based on a generic profile and whatever impression he got of the man when they met. "Tell me the plan to get inside." He wasn't a Navy SEAL. He wasn't storming the gates and taking out enemies in an attempt to talk to the American spy. That scenario ended with both of them getting killed.

"We stumbled on to some lucky information. The emir's brother, Saafir, has been working with humanitarian groups throughout the world to bring compassion to the infirm and imprisoned in Qamsar," Tyler said. "He's working quietly, keeping his mission off center stage. The emir knows about it, but Saafir is trying not to flaunt it in his face. He's been having women hand out food, water and blankets."

The notebook he and Laila had found in the Emir's private library came to mind. If Saafir was a goodwill humanitarian, how was he tied into the Holy Light Brotherhood? Could be his humanitarian work was a cover. "I'm not asking Laila to go into that prison, and I don't know if we can trust Saafir." Laila had helped enough. She'd put herself at risk by coming to Qamsar, by assisting him in placing the bugs and by agreeing to their late-night rendezvous. Taking her into a filthy, dangerous prison didn't sit well with him.

"You won't tell Saafir anything about your objectives. You'll be with Laila, and you'll look out for her," Tyler said.

If she came, yes, he would. But why put her at risk? "Why would Saafir allow us to get involved?" Harris asked. Women in Qamsar could go more places and weren't seen as a threat. But he was a man and a foreigner.

"Tell him your family would like to make a contribution to support the good work he's doing. He cares more about his cause than he does about preserving some facade that their prisons are humane."

Unless Saafir's concern was feigned. "I can try it." He'd heard stories about the Cinder Block. It was an awful place, dirty and dark. Rats, roaches and who-knew-what-else inhabited that jail along with the inmates. It was no place for a woman like Laila.

"We'll wire some money into your account, and you can write a check to Saafir. Once he agrees, you can join their humanitarian trip, and when you get close to the American, you need to speak to him in Russian." Tyler described what Harris was to do, how he could reveal himself as an agent without tipping off the guards or anyone in their party.

"What if he shuts me out?" Harris asked. A few days in a hellhole could wreck a man. How would Harris gain his trust in a few seconds and convince him to talk?

"Then we're working in the dark about what he knows," Tyler said. "I know you can do this."

Harris would try it. He wanted a way inside the Cinder Block without involving Laila. "Why does Laila need to be involved? I can speak to Saafir directly."

"Saafir won't take a foreigner into the prison. But at the request of his sister, he will take her and her suitor."

"You sound confident."

"We are confident."

Now if only Harris had that much assurance in the plan and in keeping Laila safe in one of the most treacherous prisons in the country.

It was his turn to ask for a favor. "I need you to kick something up the chain for me," Harris said.

"Go ahead," Tyler said.

"When I get Laila, her mother and possibly her brother Saafir safely to America, I want to know where they're relocated to. I want to keep tabs on them." He'd start with making sure Laila wasn't swallowed up by the system. Then he'd figure out a way to see her.

A long silence followed. "I'll pass your request along. But, Harris, we both know the chances of anyone agreeing to that are nil."

Late that afternoon Saafir was alone in the gardens when Harris and Laila approached him.

He and Laila greeted each other warmly, and Harris noted how different her interaction with Saafir was compared to the formal and distant manner she and Mikhail had been with one another. She introduced Harris to Saafir. It was the first time Harris had spoken to the emir's brother.

"Please, join me," Saafir said, gesturing to the open seats across from him. In the middle of the table was a pot of tea and several drinking cups stacked upside down.

Harris and Laila each took a seat, and Laila poured them both a cup of tea, topping off Saafir's cup, as well.

Saafir smiled his thanks. "The weather is beautiful today. With the wedding activities, this is one of the only quiet places I could find to sit and think."

"I hope we aren't disturbing you," Harris said.

Saafir took a sip of his tea and then set it down on the table. "No, not at all." His mannerisms were slow and precise, calm and unhurried. Harris had trouble picturing this man as an ally of the Holy Light Brotherhood, but the most dangerous men were the ones who hid it best.

After talking for a few minutes, Laila brought the conversation around to their purpose. "Harris and I are interested in helping with your humanitarian mission in the prison system."

Saafir regarded his sister carefully. "You've never mentioned wanting to get involved. Why now?"

"Whenever you've emailed me, you tell me about your work. It's obviously something you care about a great deal. I want to help. We want to help."

Saafir wrapped his hands around his teacup. "What did you have in mind?"

Not an outright no like Harris had expected. Thus far the emir's younger brother was proving to be easy to get along with. Years living in his brother's shadow hadn't made him outwardly angry or bitter. He had carved out his own identity and found worthwhile work.

Harris leaned closer. "My family is eager to make friends in this country. They know how important Laila is to me, and they've written a check to your cause." Harris withdrew the check and slid it on the table to Saafir.

If Saafir was surprised, he didn't show it. He didn't

immediately reach for the check, either. "I am glad you and my sister are happy together. I don't expect a gesture to sway me. I'm not the person you need to win over, and from what I've heard, the family is pleased with this match."

Laila shook her head. "The money is not meant to buy you or your favor. Harris and his family want to help." The genuineness in her voice was believable.

Saafir smiled. "Then I accept your gift, and thank you from the bottom of my heart." He took the check and put it under his teacup. "The work we're doing brings better living conditions to the prisons. It's our tradition that the families of the imprisoned should care for them, send food and clothing, and necessary items, but too often the families can't afford to send anything or aren't given access to the prison to deliver the items. Packages get lost in transit, and prisoners go hungry for days or weeks on end. I wish to stop this. Even prisoners deserve essentials and respect."

Harris didn't see the connection to the Holy Light Brotherhood. But Saafir's dedication was almost too good to be true. "How did you convince the emir it was a good idea to go into the prisons and offer help?" Harris asked. He hoped Saafir would give away something in the manner by which he spoke of his brother.

Saafir leaned closer. "Mikhail is a good man with good intentions, but he feels that kindness is a sign of weakness. By taking on the project myself and keeping my distance from the emir and his administration, needed work can be done without my brother appearing weak. As much as my brother resists change, he knows our prisons are old and crumbling."

Harris understood the emir's thinking, though he

didn't agree with it. Kindness wasn't weakness. Sometimes it took a stronger man to be kind than to be indifferent or cruel. "I hope that this helps your mission. It's good work you're doing."

"It's needed work. I have more plans for the future. I'm a dreamer, and I believe in this country. I want to see social reform in schools and in the workplace. Change won't happen overnight, but it won't happen at all if no one does anything. Laila and I were born to privilege. It is my burden and my honor to use my influence to help my country."

"I'd like to see what you do in the prisons firsthand," Harris said.

Saafir looked between Harris and Laila. "You'd like to visit our prisons? For most visitors to our country, it's the last place they'd want to see. The conditions are bad. You don't have anything like this in Germany. It will be shocking to you."

Was he trying to talk Harris out of it, or was he telling Harris no? Harris decided to push further. "I've seen the most beautiful parts of Qamsar." He glanced at Laila. She was the most beautiful part of the country, inside and out. When her eyes met his for a moment, he read the longing in them and wished they were alone. Wished he could take her in his arms and carry her away from this. She deserved more in her life. More than he could give her. He was restricted by this mission, bound by the rules of being an FBI agent, by his position and by his personal life.

He refocused on the conversation. He could have spent an entire lifetime thinking about Laila and planning ways to touch her. "Now I want to see the worst. I cannot fully understand Qamsar without seeing both the good and the bad. Experiencing it for myself will give me a better appreciation of the work you're doing."

Saafir's eyes were wary, and he folded his arms over his chest. He wanted to outright tell them no, but he was considering the political and financial consequences of a denial.

"Please, Saafir. We can help. Let us try," Laila said.

At his sister's plea, his gaze softened, and Saafir appeared to consider it. "I suppose there isn't harm in coming along. Mostly women attend to the prisoners, but I join them to keep an eye on things and make sure no one gets the wrong idea about why we're visiting. Getting into the prisons, even for a visit, is a tricky maneuver."

They were taking a chance the Cinder Block was one of the prisons Saafir was planning to visit. What choice did Harris have? This was the CIA's plan, and he'd do his best to carry it out.

Laila squeezed his fingertips. "Thank you, Saafir. I am pleased to be included."

"I'm pleased someone takes an interest in the work we're doing," Saafir said.

Harris let the conversation drift to Saafir's ideas about the country. Harris found most of them logical and clearheaded. Saafir recognized the problems his country faced, and he had common sense solutions to fix them. Harris watched him speak, trying to get a read on Saafir's genuineness. Everything about his posture, facial expressions and tone spoke to honesty. But well-skilled liars knew their craft.

Laila remained silent on the issues Saafir mentioned, nodding when appropriate. In Qamsar, it wasn't her place to comment on social and political matters, but Harris wondered what she was thinking. Though some circumstances in this country required that she hold her tongue, she was smart, and he liked hearing her ideas.

Laila was the whole package: brains, beauty and a heart of gold. Knowing it didn't take the edge off his desire for her. It only made her more difficult to resist.

What if Saafir was working for the Holy Light Brotherhood, and reported the vulnerable position he and Laila would be in by visiting the prisons? An attempt had been made on her life once. If their objective was to pin her death on America, they might be safe while inside the borders of Qamsar. But if Harris and his team had misinterpreted the reason for the car bomb, visiting the jail gave the terrorist group an easy way to kill her.

Laila waited in her room for Harris. He'd texted her a time, another late-night meeting, to discuss the jail visit. He hadn't given her much of an explanation earlier in the day. He hadn't said why he had canceled breakfast, and her mind had flipped to the worst-case scenarios. Had something come up with the mission? Or worse, had he blown her off to put some distance between them after the intimacy they'd shared the night before?

Laila couldn't tell her mother about Harris's late-night visit, and she hadn't mentioned his abrupt departure that morning. She wished she could confide in someone about her growing feelings for him. The only person who knew the details of her relationship with Harris was Harris, and she couldn't talk to him about her riotous emotions.

When Harris slipped through her balcony door, relief rushed over her.

"Saafir agreed to allow us to help more easily that I expected," Harris said, dropping his German accent, and kicking off his shoes and setting them on the balcony. They'd be waiting if he had to flee. So far, the ugly shoes hadn't made another appearance. She was grateful.

"He's an easygoing guy, and he takes his work seriously. If you're becoming part of our family and your family is interested in helping by making donations, it's in his best interest to allow you to tag along."

"Unless he has an ulterior motive for allowing us to visit the jail," Harris said.

Did Harris think everyone operated with personal agendas and hidden intent? The book they had found in the library didn't make Saafir look good, but Laila wasn't ready to accept that Saafir had joined the Holy Light Brotherhood. "We asked him if we could come along."

"He could have grabbed the opportunity to get us to a place where making us disappear would be simple."

In Harris's world, the players were double agents and spies. In his personal life, women betrayed him and couldn't be trusted. In her world, not everyone was out to hurt everyone else, and friends and family could be trusted. "It will take more than scrawl in a book to convince me Saafir has turned."

Harris's eyes clouded with worry. "Have you ever been inside a Qamsarian prison?"

She'd seen pictures and heard stories. That was the extent of her experience. "I haven't. I know not to expect cleanliness."

Harris's chest rose and fell as he took a deep breath. "The conditions will be deplorable, the prisoners abused and malnourished, and the guards likely indifferent. It's the only way for someone to work in a place like that and not go crazy."

He was worried about her. He was taking his vow to keep her safe seriously. A tickle traced up her spine. Being under his protection made her feel special and safe. "I can handle it. I know it won't be pleasant."

Harris laid on the bed. "I've been thinking about you all day."

The words drew her closer. She peeled away the covers and climbed onto the mattress. "I've been thinking about you, too. About last night."

"Regrets?" he asked.

Qualms hadn't entered her thoughts. "None."

His body relaxed. "I'm glad. May I stay with you until you fall asleep?"

Her heart shouted an instant yes. She wanted to spend as much time with Harris as she could. Her brain screamed a warning. The more time they spent together, the closer they became, the harder it would be when he left. "After Mikhail's wedding I won't see you." Few precious nights remained for them to be together, nights to avoid being discovered. Tossing away caution, she made the decision on pure impulse and desire. "Yes. I want you to stay with me." She reached for his hand and took it in hers.

Laila drew him closer, wrapped her arms around his waist and rested her head on his chest. "I like being with you."

"Me, too." He kissed the top of her head. "I'd stay all night, but my room was searched last night. We need to be careful." Harris brushed his hand along her arm. "Your skin is so soft."

"I can hear your heartbeat," she said.

"Do you hear how fast it's pounding?" he asked.

She lifted her head and met his gaze. "Why is it fast? Are you worried?"

"Not about this mission. Everything about this mission is going fine. But, yes, I'm worried. I'm worried about what's happening with us. I'm worried if this continues, you'll get hurt."

She flattened her palm against his chest. "You've got nothing to worry about. I'm fine. I've known from the moment we left the States what we had."

"Come here," Harris said, his voice soft and quiet.

Laila shifted and crawled up his body. With her arms resting on his chest, she skimmed her lips across his. Harris closed his eyes.

"Do that again."

She repeated the action, and this time, Harris's hand crept to her lower back.

"You have me in a compromising position," Laila said.

"That goes both ways," Harris said.

Laila kissed him again. Feeling bold, she ran her fingers through his hair. It was soft between her fingers. She reveled in the feel of his mouth on hers. Harris shifted beneath her, bringing her body over his. Her dress moved up her legs, baring her feet, her calves and her knees. In some of her American clothes, she'd shown more skin, but she'd never had a man between her legs. Hot pleasure sizzled and burned across her body.

Harris's mouth moved to her chin, to her neck and

to the spot where her clothes met bare skin. He moved aside the fabric, and his tongue flickered against her overheated skin. The urge to tear off her dress consumed her. She wanted nothing between them, and she wanted to feel Harris's hands sliding over her body.

Laila took a deep breath and sat up. Her thoughts caught up to her in a rush. Too fast. This was moving too fast.

Harris stroked the side of her face. "What are you thinking? Is this too much?"

She wouldn't tell him that she'd been thinking about stripping naked. Coarse words she wasn't prepared to speak. "I think we need to slow down." She needed to take her time and make careful decisions. Spending time in bed with Harris was a slippery slope, and she wanted to be in control of where it might lead. At the moment, she wasn't ready for more.

"I understand. Slow is fine. You set the pace."

His understanding touched her. She was safe with Harris. He wouldn't push her. He wouldn't lie to her. Her trust was well placed with him.

"Tell me more about your family," Laila said. "You met mine."

"My parents are amazing. Growing up, I would have called them too nosy. They kept me out of trouble. And my brothers? There are no better men. As much as they hassle me, when I need them, they are always there."

"Sounds pretty ideal."

"Don't get me wrong. We're not ideal. We fight. We argue. We don't see eye to eye on everything. But what really matters is that we'd do anything for each other. When I told them I wanted to take this assignment and work jointly with the CIA, I could tell they were worried, but they supported my decision. My mom used to be a CIA operative, and she was nervous, but she knew I could handle it."

How different from her family! While her parents had never actively prevented her from doing anything, the culture in which she'd been raised was restrictive. Growing up, Laila had had a sense of where the boundaries were, and she hadn't pushed or questioned them.

She laid next to him on the bed, letting the conversation roll, sharing the occasional kiss until she drifted off to sleep.

When Laila woke, Harris was gone. She had another hour before she needed to prepare for her outreach trip with Saafir and his group. Her sheets smelled of Harris, and memories of both his gentleness and those scorching kisses kept more sleep out of reach.

At 6:00 a.m., Laila met the outreach group by the main gate of the compound where two black vans were waiting. For getting so little sleep, Laila felt refreshed and clearheaded.

In total the volunteers numbered fourteen. The females were dressed in dark dresses, simple footwear and head scarves, no jewelry dangling from their arms.

Laila sat behind Saafir and next to Harris in the passenger van. Her placement in that location was either Saafir's or Harris's design.

They visited two prisons, and Harris and Laila quickly learned the routine.

They returned to the vans to travel to the last jail of the day.

Saafir turned in his seat to face her. "This is one of the more difficult places we visit. Some call it the Cinder Block."

Laila forced herself not to look at Harris. She'd almost forgotten the Cinder Block was the primary reason they'd come on this trip. Her stomach roiled with nerves, and her palms dampened.

How much worse could the Cinder Block be than the other prisons? Laila had heard rumors about it. She dreaded seeing the inside and hated that people lived within the run-down building.

As they climbed out of the vans, Saafir pulled Laila and Harris aside. He paused and waited for two women to pass. "This is the worst of the prisons we visit. The conditions will not be as good as the previous ones. As a whole, the prisoner population is angrier and more restless. They have not been tried or convicted of any crimes, and they are often foreigners without family in the area to take care of them. They rely on us, and the generosity of strangers for food and clothes. Language barriers and difficulties between religious groups and cultures cause riots, which leads to swift, violent responses by the guards. If anyone recognizes Laila, she will be in trouble."

Harris's shoulders tensed. "How do the prisoners treat you?"

"It took me months to earn a sliver of their respect. They know I'm the emir's brother. They don't talk much to me."

Laila hoped for the same treatment. Ignoring her was better than attacking her.

"Please stay close and don't let any of the prisoners' comments upset you," Saafir said.

If she and Harris had to stay close to Saafir, how would they talk to the American prisoner alone? For that matter, how would they find him? The building was huge, with few windows to the outside. The American spy could be anywhere inside.

Laila glanced at Harris to gauge his reaction, and he appeared unconcerned. She knew he felt otherwise. His mind was working overtime to find a way to meet their objective.

They walked toward the entrance to the prison. Harris stayed close to her side, never touching her, but near enough he could have slipped his arm over her shoulder if he'd wanted to. If they were in America, would he casually take her hand? Would he pull her close into the secure circle of his arms? Her imagination was running away with her.

They entered the prison, and the differences struck her immediately. The security at the Cinder Block was tighter. No cursory glance into their boxes. Their supplies were searched, containers opened and rifled through. No one in the group appeared fazed by the search.

A large, brutish-looking man entered the security area. He crossed his brawny arms over his barreled chest. "Contained here are the country's most manipulative and unscrupulous criminals. Don't attempt to fraternize with them. Don't believe anything they tell you. They are born liars. The emir has granted access to this prison on a week-to-week basis. If we sense you are in danger or if your presence is a national security threat, that access will be denied permanently."

Laila's heart beat faster. If her and Harris's intentions were discovered, Mikhail would revoke visiting privileges, and the entire prison population would suffer more than they were, because of their interference.

With shaking hands Laila helped load the remaining supplies onto dollies and carted them past the sliding metal gates to where the prisoners were housed. As it had been at the other sites, the group worked in pairs. Harris and Laila were teamed together. Saafir lingered nearby.

Without windows, the only light came from dangling bulbs in the center of the hallways. The thick, humid air smelled of earth and human waste. Laila tried to breathe through her mouth and not gag.

They stopped at each cell and spoke briefly to the inmates, keeping their conversation to determining what provisions were needed. They handed out blankets and toothpaste, books, magazines, packages of food and bottles of water.

Most of the men seemed broken and worn with an edge of rage that surrounded their being. Some offered only a glare in their direction. The security guards walked up and down the hallways, assault weapons strapped across their chests. At the leers and taunts from the prisoners, the guards swung their weapons toward the cells in warning.

"Do you see him?" Laila asked quietly as she opened another box of water bottles.

"Not yet."

Other aid workers distributed goods to the prisoners, no one paying attention to Harris and Laila. The guards glanced in their direction, but their main focus seemed to be intimidating the prisoners.

"He could be housed away from the general population," Harris said.

They couldn't ask to see him. They didn't know his name, and they wouldn't have a reason to see him or to know he was in the Cinder Block.

Harris stiffened slightly, and Laila followed his gaze to the cell three away from where they were standing. Unlike the rest of the prisoners who sat against the walls in their filthy cells, laid on the floor on bed mats, or ignored her and Harris, this man was standing at the bars, gripping the metal in his hands, his face almost pressed between the slats.

His eyes held a wild and intense look.

Harris and Laila approached. Harris set his hand in front of Laila in a silent signal to stay back.

"You're not Qamsarian," he said to Harris.

Though his Arabic was flawless, the prisoner looked American. His nose was too small, his face flat and his hair cropped short. He wasn't as scrawny as the other prisoners, and his clothes were matted with grime but not worn threadbare.

Laila took her time gathering supplies from the boxes, buying Harris precious moments to speak to the man. Was this the American spy? Would Harris speak to him and get the information he needed?

Harris's gut tightened, his instincts telling him this man was the one he needed to speak with. This was the man they had been searching for. "Visitors to a new land," Harris said in Russian.

The man didn't respond.

"But you understand being a visitor. You don't belong, and few know you are here," Harris said.

Though the man didn't look at him, he was listening. He understood.

"The best way to find success is to share the load," Harris said.

To a black ops agent with no personal life, no identity, success and completing his mission would mean everything. Harris was staking his bets that to share the load, to tell what he knew about Al-Adel, the Holy Light Brotherhood and Mikhail's involvement, he would find some satisfaction. If he believed he wasn't getting out of the Cinder Block, talking to Harris would do some good. Harris could use the information the American had found to locate and stop Al-Adel.

Harris couldn't linger by his cell much longer. He would draw the attention of the patrolling guards.

"You won't have other trusted visitors like me," Harris said, keeping his words low and in Russian. "Trusted" being the key word.

The man reached through the bars and took the items Laila had brought him. "Thank you," he said to her in Arabic.

Harris waited a few beats to see if he would say anything else. Harris could feel the eyes of the guards on him, watching, staring. Was his voice carrying to them? He turned away from the cell and to the cart, ready to push it farther along. The man in the cell knew he had slim hopes of rescue. If he didn't care for sharing information, Harris had no pull over him.

"He will be at the wedding. He has powerful allies. No one in the emir's circle can be trusted," the black ops agent said in Russian so quietly if Harris hadn't been intently listening, he wouldn't have heard him.

Had the American spy stumbled on to who could not be trusted? Or had he gotten close enough to make that person nervous, nervous enough that he was now serving a life sentence in the worst prison in Qamsar? Saafir? Was the American referencing the emir's brother, a man who presented himself as working for the poor and powerless?

Harris took another book from the supplies box and brought it to the black ops agent. "Who can I trust?" Harris asked.

The man shifted his eyes to Laila and then back to Harris. "No one in the emir's circle. They are all dirty." Still in Russian.

Saafir? Mikhail's aids? Laila's mother? Aisha? Laila's uncles? How many people in the royal family were involved with the Holy Light Brotherhood?

Was he insinuating Laila was involved? Harris could trust Laila, couldn't he? The emir didn't hold Laila in his confidence. She was a commodity to trade for favors from his friends. Then again Harris had believed Cassie could be trusted, and she had sold him out to his enemy, knowing her betrayal could kill him and his team.

One of the guards looked in their direction and changed course, coming closer.

The American didn't share anymore of what he knew.

"I wish you the best. You have an ally in me," Harris said.

The man looked over Harris's shoulder and stepped away from the bars, taking his items to the back of his cell. The guards? Harris turned. Saafir was approaching.

"Everything okay here?" Saafir asked.

Harris nodded. "Fine."

"Don't linger. It makes the guards nervous," Saafir said.

"Understood," Harris said.

Laila pushed the dolly past, and Harris followed her to the next cell.

For the next three hours, Harris replayed the American spy's words. Who else in the emir's close circle was working with Al-Adel? Harris and the CIA had been following the emir, tracking his movements, but perhaps they had missed something—or someone—important. Did Al-Adel have someone on the inside, working with the emir, feeding the emir information?

Chapter 8

"What did the American tell you?" Laila asked, the moment Harris stepped into her room that night from the balcony. She rushed to him and took his arms. Touching him had become second nature to her, an instinct that warred with the values she'd been raised with.

They'd returned to the compound after their visits to the prisons and had parted ways. Harris had texted her that he'd stop in for a visit when the coast was clear. "He told me others in the emir's close circle are involved with Al-Adel."

Not surprising. Mikhail surrounded himself with a group of trusted advisors and often included them in his decisions. To make an alliance with Al-Adel, even in secrecy, would have been difficult without some around him knowing about it.

"Did he say who?" Laila asked. How many people? If many were involved in working with Al-Adel, the more allies the terrorist had in the country, the easier it would be for him to hide within the country and at her brother's wedding.

"No, he didn't tell me who."

Harris took a few more steps into the room and closed the balcony door behind him. This room was their sanctuary, the one place to be alone. Much nicer than lurking and hiding outdoors or trying to converse in public without anyone overhearing them.

Harris stared at her for a loaded moment.

"What's the matter?" she asked. "Did something else happen?"

A wary expression entered his eyes. "Have you told your brother we know about the connection to the Holy Light Brotherhood?" Harris asked.

Laila took a step back. She felt as if he'd slapped her. His question sounded like an accusation. She hadn't told her brother anything. Nothing to Mikhail, not a word to Saafir and heartbreaking silence to her mother. "I've been helping you."

"I know."

Doubt laced his words. As if she was doing this with another intention or lying to him. "I took a huge risk bringing you here. Why would I do that if I were planning to betray you? I could have refused your request."

"We put you in an awful position. We've forced you to betray your family for your country."

Insult squared her shoulders. She didn't see this mission as betraying her family or her country. She was protecting them from Mikhail's bad decision. "Do you hear yourself? I am doing this because, if the Holy

Light Brotherhood is in Qamsar, I want them out. For the people who live here. For my family. I did not turn on my brother. I recognize he has problems, and I am not willing to allow his extremism to harm an entire country of people." Anger heated her neck, flaming up her back. She'd done everything Harris had asked of her. How could he stand in front of her and speak this way?

Harris let his head fall into his hands. "I'm sorry, Laila. I had to ask."

She folded her arms across her chest and lifted her chin, tipping back her shoulders. He had hurt her. "No. You didn't. If you think you can find someone else to do what I've done, then maybe you need to do that."

Harris shook his head. "No other woman could do what you do. I don't know what's gotten into me."

The woman from his past. Her betrayal haunted him. A prick of compassion let some of the air out of her anger. "I am not the woman who sold you out. I am Laila. I am a different woman. I'm loyal and true, and I don't hurt people I care about."

He lifted his head and met her gaze. "You don't have a reason to care about me."

She threw up her hands in frustration. "I don't have a reason to care? What about our relationship makes you believe I don't care?" The kisses they'd shared? The time they'd spent alone? The worry and concern she carried with her every moment they were apart?

He said nothing for several long seconds. "You've given me plenty of reason to trust and none to suspect you."

"Will this be the last time I hear you draw comparisons between me and the faithless liar who broke your heart?" If he didn't want to talk about their relationship, the least he could do is not accuse her of being an untrustworthy wretch.

"I won't let those thoughts get the better of me again."

But had he moved past the situation? Or had this woman broken him forever?

Harris kicked off his shoes and sat on the edge of the bed. "I'm sorry. Please forgive me."

"Forgiven." When she spoke the word, she meant it, although she still wondered about his ability to trust. "Have you figured out how to get him out of the Cinder Block?" Laila asked.

"Not yet. I messaged what details I could recall about the prison to the team. Even when we were delivering items, no prisoners were allowed outside their cells."

Laila sat on the bed next to Harris. "It was a strange day. I will never get those places and those people out of my mind."

Harris's hand stroked her back, and her skin tingled under his touch. "I shouldn't have involved you. I could have gone without you."

Laila reclined against the headboard and took his hand in hers, interlacing their fingers. "Saafir might have found it odd that you wanted to go without me. He might have questioned why you were so interested. But he knows I have a bleeding heart. He probably figured I put you up to making the donation and then asking if we could come along."

Harris's thumb moved across her finger. "I don't want you to have nightmares about what you saw today."

"If I'm haunted by what I saw today, that makes me human. Knowing it's happening in my country is how I can help create positive changes." Though she'd have to leave Qamsar as soon as Harris located Al-Adel, she would find a way to give back. Perhaps she could donate anonymously to Saafir's organization, assuming it wasn't a front for dealings with the Holy Light Brotherhood. "It's awful for the people living the nightmare. I don't think prison should be a luxury resort, but at least the accused should have a fair trial and be given a chance to defend themselves. If they are incarcerated, they should be treated like humans, not rabid animals locked in cages. For that matter I've seen animals treated better."

Harris eyes glinted with amusement. "You sound like an American."

She took it as a compliment. "I've lived in the States long enough that those American ideals have started to rub off."

Harris's gaze softened. "That's good. I worried, after seeing your life here, about the difficulties of living in another place permanently."

Since arriving in Qamsar, Laila hadn't thought much about her early life here, about leaving her home country to further her education in the United States. In some ways, moving to America was returning to the life she'd built, one she was comfortable with—school and work. But it was also starting over. She would need to make new friends, establish new contacts, and because she'd need to hide from Mikhail's vengeance and her countrymen's anger, old friends would be out of reach. Starting over at a new school would be hard.

She liked her classes, her professors and her classmates. She liked having her aunt and uncle close.

How would it feel to know she couldn't return to Qamsar? She would no longer be safe or welcome in the country where she'd been raised. She'd be cut off from family, from weddings, from funerals and from visits. Her mother and Saafir would be with her, but thinking about how different their lives would be felt strangling.

It would be even more difficult for her mother, who was set in her ways, saturated and happy in the Qamsarian culture. American life would be better than the life she'd have in Qamsar, especially if her eldest son's and daughter's betrayals were discovered, or if she were married to a Holy Light Brotherhood terrorist. Those loyal to the emir could target Laila and her mother and deliver what they considered proper punishment. Or Mikhail could jail them in the Cinder Block. Or the country could revolt against the emir and his family, putting them all in jeopardy.

In America, Laila had seen how nervous Middle Easterners made some Americans. Though Laila had blended into the social scene, her mother, who'd wear traditional clothing as she always had, might be subjected to the fear and prejudice that surrounded the Middle Eastern community in some areas. Would that be taken into account when she was relocated? Bigger cities would make it easier to find acceptance.

"I'll adjust. I want to be an American. I want to have a life with happiness, and I don't think that happiness is waiting for me in an arranged marriage in Qamsar. Life won't be perfect in America, and it may be some time before I'm comfortable and settled, but I'm re-silent," Laila said, touched he'd considered how she would feel about relocating.

"I know you are. It's one of the reasons I knew you could handle this situation."

The softness of his words and the closeness of his body sent a shimmer of excitement along her spine. He was paying her a compliment, and she basked in it. It was rare to receive compliments from a man. "One of the reasons? How else did you know?"

A bemused expression crossed his face. "We have a profile on you. We did our research before we approached you."

Of course they did. But how did they find information about her, and how accurate was it? "What did the profile say about me?"

Harris grinned. "Maybe you don't want to know."

His evasive answer piqued her interest. "I do. Tell me."

Harris hemmed and then decided to answer. "It said you were compassionate and idealistic. Both traits that worked to our advantage. You'd see the problem we were trying to address and want to help. It also said you were intelligent and strong, which was important to keep your cover. The part I liked best was the section that addressed your beauty, humor and sophistication." His eyes glittered and he lifted a brow.

She laughed. "You're joking about the last part."

"It wasn't in the profile. But it was the part I had sketched in my mind about you. I like to know everything I can about my partners."

Beauty. Humor. Sophistication. Is that how he saw her? To think of herself in such a flattering light made her head swell. "You're such a flirt."

"No, I'm answering your question. But now answer one of mine. Tell me what about me made you agree to come here. Not the situation. Not the ethics. I know it was more than that."

Her instincts had told her Harris could be trusted. "I didn't have access to the information you had, so I didn't have a profile or a folder about your life. But I had gotten to know you from the café. When you came in, you spoke to me. You didn't talk on your phone while you ordered, and you didn't ignore my answers to your questions." That show of respect had meant something to her. "And not to put too fine a point on it, but you saved my life. If I had been closer to the car or if you hadn't been at the café that night, I'd be dead."

Harris nodded. "What about my charming good looks? Didn't that sway you?" He waggled his eyebrows at her.

She laughed out loud, and then remembered they were meeting in secret and put a filter on her volume. "I thought you were cute the first time I saw you."

He groaned and rolled onto his back, covering his eyes with his forearm. "Cute? Cute is for puppies."

She pried away his forearm and met his bright blue eyes. "No, cute is for American guys who are attractive. Cute is the first step to being interested in someone."

"I'm listening," he said, his tone urging her to continue.

"In addition to cute, I could trust you. You were smart and strong, and I felt safe with you. That meant the world to me in agreeing to help." She hadn't expected to develop feelings for him as anything more than an FBI agent pretending to be a man in love with her.

When they were no longer pretending to be in love, would they have feelings for each other? "If I'm going to live in America, I want to date more."

"Dating? What we're doing is not dating. If we were dating, I would take you out somewhere nice to eat dinner and listen to music. I would come up with interesting places you'd like to visit and then ask you to come along. I would bring you flowers and candy, and cook you dinner and dine with you by candlelight."

Her mind tripped over the idea of Harris romancing her. It couldn't happen in Qamsar, where their relationship was strictly controlled and monitored by watchful eyes in the compound. It could happen in America. If he stayed in touch. If she lived near him. If he stayed in a part of her life. Could those circumstances unfold?

If they weren't dating, what were they doing? The second question was far safer than the first. "If we're not dating, what do you call what's happening between us?"

"I don't have a word for it."

Helpful. He'd flirted, he'd touched her, he'd visited her in secret and he'd kissed her. But those actions didn't have a name. Without a name, she felt adrift in confusion. "This is new to me. I'm counting on you to give guidance." She didn't know how to navigate a relationship with a man. What she had seen from her mother and cousins wouldn't apply to Harris. Her family hadn't arranged their relationship, and Harris wouldn't like her to pretend to be subservient.

His eyes were filled with emotions she couldn't read. "I think it's better if we don't try to define it. That will put pressure on the both of us, and we don't need any additional pressure in this situation. Looking for Al-Adel and trying to figure out who we can trust is a full-time job."

Disappointment surged through her. Was he telling her that he wasn't interested in committing to her? Had she expected him to? He was closing off the conversation, and she didn't feel any clearer about their relationship. It existed in some undefined gray area, and insecurities rose in her chest. How much of their relationship and his emotions had she manufactured in her mind based on what she was feeling?

Harris looked around the room. "I wish I could take you somewhere. Somewhere not inside the compound, somewhere we wouldn't be watched, and we could relax and have fun."

"Aren't we supposed to stay in the compound and look for you-know-who?" Laila asked, her head spinning at the idea of leaving the compound with Harris without a chaperone, sneaking off somewhere dark and sensual. A belly-dancing club. A private dinner in an upscale restaurant, where women dined in gowns and men wore suits.

Harris sighed. "I don't think he'll arrive this soon. It's a few days until the wedding."

"Then let's chance it," Laila said.

"Chance what?" Harris asked.

"Let's have Mikhail's chauffeur drop us downtown. We'll say we're meeting friends. We'll ditch the security escort and take a cab to wherever we want to go." Her boldness surprised her, both because it wasn't like her to break the rules, and because she hadn't realized the depth of her desire to date Harris. To be alone with him and explore their relationship. To get to know him better and to prove to him she was worthy of his trust.

His eyes filled with intense heat. "What did you have in mind for us to do?"

"We can walk on the beach and have a late-night meal. Or dessert at one of the five-star restaurants along the water." She couldn't bring herself to suggest they walk to the shadier side of town and see what they could find. Laila wanted to spend time with him away from the prying eyes of her family. For a night, she could pretend as though they were in America, and the drama and tension of this mission was far behind them.

"Let's do it," he said.

Surprised he'd agreed, she hugged him, an uncharacteristic display of affection that had an unintended effect: searing heat pooled low in her belly and desire burned hotter in her heart.

Harris's arms slipped around her waist, holding her against the long length of his body. He pulled her head scarf away from her hair. "Why do you cover up your hair? It's so beautiful."

She should break away. She should stop him. Nothing in her could do so. His arms felt too good around her, the lean strength of his body against hers.

"I have to cover it. At least while I'm in public in Qamsar."

His eyes followed his hands as they moved along the fabric of her dress. "The clothes you wear are supposed to keep a man disinterested. You need to tell whoever made these clothes, it didn't work. If anything, I'm more interested in seeing what's underneath. I spend more time thinking about it than is right."

He released her, but his gaze never left her.

"You've seen what's under my clothes," she said.

She realized she'd chosen the wrong words. She'd meant he'd seen her in Western clothes.

"I wish that statement was true."

She read the kiss in his eyes and leaned into it. His mouth met hers, and she'd expected a hard, intense kiss. Instead, his lips were soft yet demanding, nudging her own apart. He shifted, moving his body on top of hers, tucking her beneath him. The kiss took on a carnal life of its own growing harder, deeper.

They'd slept beside each other, slept with his arms around her, but this felt different. Laila sensed this was leading somewhere, and she didn't want to stop it. She anchored herself to him, his amazing mouth moving over hers.

Her mind screamed for more. As if he'd heard her, he set his thigh between her legs, and she let her knees open as wide as her dress would allow. With his leg in such an intimate position, pieces of her control shattered. He braced his elbows on the bed on each side of her head, holding his body over hers.

This is what she had been missing for most of her life. Passion. Heat. She couldn't get enough. Laila sensed a change in Harris. He wasn't controlled and confined. Shifting his weight to one side, his hand explored her body. Need pulsed from his fingers into her, his hands stroking her in ways she'd never experienced, driving her body higher and bringing hot arousal into her core.

His hand skimmed under her breasts, and she arched, wanting his hands on her. He seemed tentative at first, his hand brushing lightly across her oversensitized nipples and, at her moan of encouragement, clamping across her breast.

The satisfied sound that escaped his lips almost made her vault off the bed.

"We need to slow down," he said.

"No, no, we don't," Laila said. Let them see where the attraction led.

"The longer we do this and the further this goes, the more difficult it will be to stop."

She wanted Harris, and her body had every intention of letting him make her feel good. Except this was a big decision for her. Her honor, her readiness and her heart would change if this happened between them. Was she ready to make love to a man? To Harris?

Her mind spinning and her heart pounding, she scooted back on the bed and sat up on her elbows. "Maybe we should see about going out." Being in public and adhering to Qamsar's social conduct laws would prevent them from openly pawing each other. She'd have time to think and not be swept away by her desires.

Some boundaries would help. Some boundaries would keep their desire in check.

Harris leaned back on his haunches and stabbed a hand through his hair, leaving the ends standing up in a mussed and sexy way. "Yes, let's go out."

"Are you mad?" she asked, trying to read his emotions.

"Of course not. I will never do anything you're not ready to do, and I want you to be comfortable and happy."

Laila knew he meant it and another part of her heart was lost to him.

Harris returned to his room to change for his night out with Laila and to throw some cold water on his libido. He had been close to making love to her, and he was glad they had stopped when they did. She wasn't looking for a one-night stand. She deserved better and more, especially for her first time.

Time away from the compound, the mission and the constant attention of Laila's family would be good for them. The stress of the day and their experiences in the jails had left Harris feeling cramped and on edge. If he were discovered as an American spy, he expected to join the other American in the Cinder Block. The conditions inside were worse than any jail he'd seen in America. He'd like to think he'd survive and escape, but how?

More maddening was thinking about Laila being discovered and joining him in jail. The Cinder Block wasn't a place for women, and Harris could only imagine what a woman might face under those conditions.

No matter how this ended, Harris wouldn't let it end with Laila being imprisoned. He'd protect Laila however he needed to, using whatever means and resources at his disposal.

Harris wasn't sure how they would break away from Laila's security escort once outside the compound. The emir had spoken to Harris about marrying Laila, giving Harris some privileges as her intended fiancé, but where was the line? Would he cross it with her and infuriate the emir?

The restrictions in the emir's compound were more severe than they might be other places. Could he have a private dinner with Laila? Hold her hand? Stare into her eyes and talk about whatever came to mind without censoring his thoughts, without the ridiculous fake accent?

His cell phone rang, and he glanced at it, expecting to see Laila's number. It wasn't Laila. He had a message from the CIA.

He logged into his secure message application and the words stopped him cold. "Al-Adel spotted in Qamsar. Location unconfirmed. D to deliver recon equipment ASAP."

Harris didn't have any exterior surveillance devices to place to watch the entrance, and exposing the devices he had to the elements and dark made them less reliable. He'd have to watch until Devon could deliver better equipment.

His plans with Laila disintegrated, but he had a new mission for the night. He needed to stake out the entrance to the compound and watch if anyone entered under a veil of secrecy. Al-Adel could be on his way to the compound. Harris texted Laila that he needed to cancel their plans for the night. She texted him a few seconds later.

Why do you have to cancel? she asked.

I need to stay in and rest.

It was a few minutes before she texted back. Understood. It was a long day.

Did she understand it wasn't exhaustion, it was mission-related?

A soft knock at his door. When he opened it, she had a smile on her face. She'd read between the lines on his message.

"I wanted to say good-night." She reached out and tucked a small slip of paper into his pocket. "Night, Harris."

She walked down the hall, and he opened the folded paper to read it. *I want to help.*

Could he involve her again? He needed a post where he could wait and watch. It would be long, boring work. If she was keeping him company, it would help pass the time. He could wait all night and see nothing. Finding a place to hide and watch would be difficult, and putting Laila in that situation for his selfish needs seemed wrong. What if they were caught?

Would she want to help if she knew what was involved? He sent her a text. Dress in layers. Courtyard. The *now* was implied. He'd explain to her, and if she changed her mind about assisting him, he'd understand.

He changed into dark clothes with layers. Qamsar was boiling during the day, but after the sun set, the temperatures dropped.

Harris waited by the gazebo where he and Laila had met before. She arrived in less than five minutes. She'd changed into a dark dress and pants peeked beneath it.

"What's going on?" she asked, sounding out of breath. She looked over her shoulder as if expecting someone to interrupt them.

"Al-Adel was spotted inside the border. I need to watch the entrance to the compound."

Laila's eyes were wide with concern. "I'll watch with you."

Having her with him was appealing, but the danger he was placing her in had him pausing. "If we're caught, we'll be in trouble. It will be difficult to explain what we're doing alone on the roof inside the emir's compound. It will look bad for us."

"We've been risking trouble since the moment I agreed to work with you," Laila said. She reached for his hand and squeezed it.

Twenty minutes later they were perched on the roof

of the emir's pool house, which gave them a direct view of the entrance to the compound. They'd had to climb onto an awning and pull themselves up onto the top level. It was too cold for outdoor swimming, and the area was vacant.

Spotting cars was made easy by the approaching headlights of the vehicles cutting into the dark.

"What will we do if he shows up?" Laila asked.

"Let my team know. We won't approach him. We'll take some pictures and send them on for verification."

"If he is here, what's the master plan?" Laila asked.

Harris hadn't been given specifics. "The team will involve the local authorities and arrange for him to be apprehended. Once he's in custody, we'll figure out what he's doing in Qamsar, and find evidence to tie him to your brother and any other groups he might be working with."

Laila shivered. None of the options he'd presented would end well for her family.

Harris wrapped his arm around her, tucking her against his body. "You don't have to stay out here with me."

"Sure I do." She rested her head on his shoulder. "It's better than being alone in my room."

"I'm sorry our plans changed. I owe you a date," he said.

Laila lifted her head, and he turned to meet her searing gaze. "You don't owe me anything."

"I told you I would take you out tonight, and then this came up. I'm a man of my word. I'll make it up to you."

"You don't have long. Mikhail's wedding is in a few

days, and Mikhail and Aisha have the days booked with events."

His time in Qamsar with Laila was growing shorter, and his feelings for her were growing deeper. She was open and honest. Even when he'd hidden behind his cover and worked the CIA's agenda, she hadn't closed herself off. She'd given him her trust and had risked her life for this mission.

He hadn't figure out how he would make it work and cut through the miles of red tape, but when they returned to the United States, he wanted to stay in her life. "Maybe I can take you out after the wedding. I put in a request to know where you'd be relocated."

Laila inhaled sharply. "Was it approved?"

"No answer yet," Harris said.

Sadness dropped the corners of her mouth. "We'll wait and see what happens rather than make plans we both know won't work."

Harris considered her words. Laila deserved happiness. The more time he spent with her, the more he wanted to be the man to give her that happiness. Would she want a man who would convert to Islam? He would be willing to do almost anything for Laila. At the start of this mission, he'd known he'd have to let her go once it was over. Facing that prospect now seemed impossible.

Harris settled in for a long cold night of watching and waiting for Ahmad Al-Adel.

Ahmad Al-Adel had never shown at the compound. Or if he had, he'd found another way inside besides the front entrance. Laila forced exhaustion from her mind. She'd been out all night with Harris, cuddled together on the roof of the pool house, waiting for Al-Adel to arrive. She and Harris hadn't seen anyone looking like Al-Adel. Harris had retrieved an outdoor video device around 4:00 a.m. from one of his contacts. They'd installed it to watch the entrance to the compound. The placement was a risk Harris was willing to take with Al-Adel being so near, their intel indicating he was in the country.

Tempted to cancel her plans for the day after getting to sleep at 6:00 a.m., Laila forced herself to forgo more rest. She'd made plans with her extended family earlier in the week and changes would invite questions. Mikhail and Aisha wanted family and friends, especially those who lived outside the country, to experience the culture and attractions Qamsar had to offer. Though none of the activities were new to Laila, as the emir's sister she was expected to participate.

Plus, Harris would be with her.

Aisha and Mikhail had arranged a private tour of the Qamsarian National Aquarium in Doha. The aquarium housed more than sixteen thousand animals and seven hundred species of fish, birds, reptiles and mammals. Visitors walked through tunnels of glass with fish swimming on four sides, creating an immersion experience.

Laila was meeting over two dozen of her family members, cousins near and distant including young children and older relatives at the aquarium. It had been closed to the public for the emir's exclusive use, and Mikhail and Aisha had planned to make a brief appearance later in the afternoon to have lunch. Laila had visited the aquarium several times in her life, but it had been years since the last time.

Laila had made polite conversation with her relatives on the ride there and had tried to keep the conversation away from Harris. She was grateful when they entered the lobby. At least her family would have other things to think about besides her relationship with Harris.

"How are you feeling today?" Laila asked Harris, keeping her voice low as their tour began.

Harris rolled his shoulders as if working out a cramp. "Like I slept for two hours." Which was about the amount of time she had.

She held back the urge to touch his arm. She had to preserve appearances. "We'll power through."

Laila took another deep breath and wondered if the aquarium served coffee.

Their conversation stopped as their tour guide explained the fish in the tanks around them. Laila had little interest in the description. She liked seeing the animals and watching them swim. She could let her mind wander to the nights Harris had held her and shown her things she had never experienced.

Would she feel this intensely if it were another man? Laila couldn't imagine every relationship would hold this level of heat and intimacy. She couldn't envision being with another man and feeling the same way.

On the tail end of that thought came a wave of sadness. What future could she have with Harris? He'd said his request to see her when returning to America had gone unanswered. He had asked the question, which meant something to her, but what good did it do if the answer was no?

Harris walked behind the group as they toured the aquarium. It was the best place for him to observe. A glass-enclosed bridge connected the main aquarium to the newer exhibits and the dining area where they were planning to meet Mikhail and Aisha. Their group was traveling across, looking out from the third-floor view. The streets below were heavy with traffic and the sidewalks crowded with people on their way to or from work, shopping and having lunch. Directly across the street was the symphony hall where a special concert was being held later that night in honor of the emir's wedding. At the corner of the street was the Qamsar National Art Museum, displaying priceless treasures from around the world. Several local artists had been commissioned to create works to celebrate the royal nuptials. That artwork would be unveiled the following day in a special exhibit.

A bright flash had every nerve in Harris's body tensing. He reached for Laila and pulled her against him, sheltering her with his body. The glass around them shattered, and the boom of an explosion pulsed through the air. Harris recognized the sounds and sights from his time in the marines. A bombing nearby, possibly close to or inside of the aquarium.

He clutched Laila to him, wanting to shield her from another blast, gunfire or whatever else might come next. Adrenaline surged hard in his blood. The people with them needed his protection, too. The children. The mothers. Laila's family. He needed to get everyone to safety.

First priority was to get off the bridge and out of the building. If it collapsed, they were dead. The main building was closer. How many seconds had passed? Laila's family looked stunned and confused.

Harris pointed behind them. "Pick up the children and run. Get off the bridge."

Forget protocol. He didn't let go of Laila's hand, needing her with him in a place where he could keep her safe. He surveyed the group. A mother with two small children was looking between them as if trying to decide. They didn't have time to waste. With his free arm, Harris grabbed the child closest to him, holding the little girl against him. The mother grabbed the other child, gratitude shining in her eyes. Laila stayed close.

Mothers and fathers picked up their children and raced toward the red door leading to the main aquarium from where they had come. Once inside the building, Harris scanned for a way outside.

He turned his attention to their tour guide. "Where is the nearest exit?"

The man appeared badly shaken. "The elevators."

"No, not elevators. The nearest stairwell." The elevators would be unstable and the possibility of losing electricity was high. White light from the exit signs hanging from the ceiling glowed in the darkened aquarium. Harris counted them lucky that they weren't wading through water or sharks or complete darkness. The fish tanks had withstood the blast, or at least hadn't shattered the way the glass on the bridge had.

Were the other aquarium employees finding a safe way out?

The tour guide pointed to one of the lit exits. Everyone followed Harris as he strode toward it. The little girl he was holding clung to his neck, her sobs loud in his ear. It was enough to tear his heart out of his chest. She was terrified, and he didn't know what to say to her to make her feel better.

He went for simple. "It's okay," he said. "We'll be fine."

Laila was singing softly to the girl and rubbing her back consolingly.

Harris pushed open the metal exit door. "Women and children down the stairs first," Harris said. He squeezed Laila's hand. He wanted her to get to safety. "When you get downstairs to ground level, move away from the crowds. I'll be right behind you."

"I'm staying with you," she said.

Mothers and their children filed passed him.

"Go with them," he said, nodding toward the women and children moving down the stairs. He handed Laila the little girl in his arms. "Be strong. They need a leader," he said in English.

A fire alarm shrieked through the building. Adrenaline shooting through his veins, Harris peered into the stairwell. He smelled smoke.

"Stop! Stop!" He flew down the stairs, getting ahead of the first person on the steps. Sending them back to the third floor was dangerous. They needed to vacate the building. Where was the fire?

Bright orange-and-red flames fanned into the stairwell from the first floor. He tried to recall the layout of the aquarium. If this stairwell wasn't an option, where was the next closest exit?

The second floor was their best option. If they had to break a window and jump, they'd survive it. He ached to think about the scared children and determination renewed inside him. He wouldn't allow anyone to be hurt. They would make it out safely, or he would die trying.

Harris yanked open the door to the second floor and

looked around. Though the alarms were shrieking, he didn't see flames ahead. "Come on!" He held the door as everyone raced through. This time, Harris counted heads. Thirty-three, including him. Thirty-three people would make it out of this building alive.

The lights flickered, and they were plunged into darkness. How could he be sure he hadn't lost anyone? He yelled over the sound of the children crying. "I want everyone to hold hands and stay together. We're getting out of here."

As each person passed him, he counted them again, touching their bodies as they passed him. With all accounted for, he ran to the front of the human chain. Laila was leading them, speaking reassuring words over the shrill of the alarm.

"I can't see anything," she said to him in English, panic shaking under her words.

"Doesn't matter. I know how to get out." A lie. But he needed everyone to stay calm and levelheaded. Running his hand along the tanks, he prayed another door would appear. He remembered one on the far side of the third floor and hoped the layout was the same for the second. They crept along the hallway, the children's crying drowned out by the alarms. Where was that door? The smell of smoke was filling the air, an indication their oxygen was being consumed by the fire. He had to find the exit.

His hand hit metal. He slid his hand down to a long bar along the door. He shoved it and the door swung open. "We're at the stairwell. I'll hold the door. Laila is leading you down the stairs. We're almost there. One flight and we'll be outside. Do not let go of each other's hands."

God help him if a child was lost. He would never stop looking for him or her.

Harris located the edge of the step. "Laila, I'll stay here and help everyone get started down the stairs. Go down and open the door to the outside. The sunlight will help."

Laila lifted his hand to her mouth and kissed the back of it, and then she was gone. Less than twenty seconds later, light flooded the stairwell.

Everyone moved faster when they could see the stairs. They broke into the sunshine and Harris counted. Thirty-three people. Scared, shaken but alive. Relief flooded over him. Now he had to decide what to do next.

They needed to get away from this area. Another bomb could explode, buildings could collapse or snipers could be waiting to shoot. He didn't know what or who they were dealing with, and until he did, he was proceeding with extreme caution.

Al-Adel was inside the country, and that gave him a strong suspicion of who was responsible. But accusations and anger would wait until everyone was safe.

Then Al-Adel would pay. He'd endangered someone Harris cared about. He wouldn't be allowed to hurt Laila again.

Chapter 9

After the explosion, the scene in the cultural district of Doha was chaos. The streets were knotted with wrecked cars. People were running, screaming and crying. Harris scanned for a safe place, somewhere away from the explosion.

Where had the bomb gone off? The face of the aquarium building was blown away, and the surrounding buildings and those across the street were damaged. Glass and concrete littered the ground.

The sounds of sirens filled the air, though Harris didn't see police or ambulances on the street.

"Do we have any injuries?" he asked, turning to the group.

Laila appeared okay, squatting on the ground next to the children and hugging them, whispering words of comfort.

Some of the children were wailing, and the sounds of screaming filled his ears. He tried to block it out and take stock of the medical status of the people around him. Then he could go back and help on the scene. Search-and-rescue missions would deploy after the police organized, and many people would need to be taken to nearby hospitals. Harris prayed the death toll had been small, or better, but more unlikely, zero.

"I think everyone's injuries are survivable. Cuts and scratches and terror," Laila said.

No one was bleeding profusely, and it was a good sign that everyone was walking.

Harris took out his cell phone and tried to dial the emir's compound to ask them to send help. He could relay the situation to the emir's switchboard operator and request assistance. The main operator would know the right people to contact. If he used his satellite phone, and no one else could get a signal on their cell phones, it would raise questions why he was carrying a satellite phone.

"Does anyone have a phone?" Harris asked. Cell service circuits were likely flooded, and others would have problems getting a connection.

Several people nodded.

"I want you to walk down this street as quickly as possible." He pointed along the sidewalk. "There could be another bomb. Or these buildings could collapse. Keep walking and trying to call the compound to give them your exact location. Traffic will be snarled for hours," Harris said. "You might have to walk for a few miles for a pickup."

Seeing the worn and scared faces of Laila's family, Harris looked around. The children couldn't walk for miles and carrying them would be difficult. Next door to the aquarium was a gift shop selling tourist items. "Give me a minute."

He spoke quickly to the three employees in the store who appeared unsure what to do. Their phones weren't working. The store had a few small shopping carts. He left the store with the employees and the carts.

"Put the children in these so they don't have to walk or be carried. You'll get farther this way," Harris said. Seeing the terror on the children's faces, Harris strove for something to distract them. "This is a great adventure. You get to ride through the streets in these carts. And when you get home, ice cream and cake for everyone!"

The children were calming down, and the group began moving down the street.

Harris waited a few moments and then turned in the direction of the bombing. He had studied Al-Adel's work. The man's terror attacks were usually confined to a small area, although often more than one explosion detonated. Was this orchestrated by the Holy Light Brotherhood?

"What are you doing?" Laila asked, taking his arm.

Harris stared at her. "Why didn't you go with your family?"

"And leave you here alone?" Laila asked.

He didn't want Laila in the thick of this. An attempt had been made on her life in America, and he didn't know if she had been one of the targets of the bombing here. "You need to be somewhere safe."

She gripped his arm harder. "I am safest with you."

Another explosion boomed through the air. Harris grabbed Laila and shielded her with his body, pulling them to the ground. Was that sound a building collapsing from the damage or another bomb? Harris guessed another bomb. Laila was shaking in his arms. Harris waited for the noise around him to die down and concentrated on listening for the rat-tat-tat of gunshots or for another flash of light or blast of a bomb.

His protective instincts roared louder. He wouldn't let anything happen to Laila. "I'm going to help where I can."

Her eyes widened with fear. "What if there is another bomb—"

He had some basic first-aid training, and he'd been a marine. Dealing with difficult situations had been part of his training. "There might be another one. There's no time to wait for help."

"I can help, too," Laila said, lifting her chin.

"You aren't trained for this," he said.

"No, but I'm capable and smart. I will be useful. Don't treat me like a crystal vase."

Laila wouldn't back down. She wouldn't leave the scene, not when her countrymen needed help. Arguing wouldn't get him anywhere. He'd seen her strength many times before. She might sometimes act like a shrinking violet in front of her brother or other males, but she had an iron core. "You're stubborn when you want something."

"So are you," Laila said, giving him a small smile.

Ambulances were arriving on the scene, and injured people converged on the first responders. They wouldn't have enough equipment and staff to triage every case, and the most dire would be treated first.

"Oh, no," Laila said, her voice a whisper. She pressed her hand against her head. "Harris, we were supposed to meet Aisha and Mikhail in the dining area. Do you think the bomb was meant for them? Do you think they got out of the building?"

It would be a huge coincidence if a bomb had gone off near the place where the emir and Aisha were scheduled to be, and Laila and her extended family weren't the targets. Harris didn't believe in coincidences, large or small. "We'll look for his car first and see what we can find out." No point in being reckless and running into an unstable building if no one was inside.

If Al-Adel was working with Mikhail, why try to kill him? Had their relationship soured? Or was Al-Adel attempting to force the emir's hand in a show of strength and dominance? Based on what Harris knew of Mikhail, he wouldn't respond well to being coerced or forced. What was the purpose of the bombing?

Laila bit her lip. "Maybe he and Aisha hadn't arrived yet."

Possible. "Let's hope they are safe and sound elsewhere."

They maneuvered through the crowds, some fleeing the area, others staring, looking unsure what to do next or where to go.

"I don't see his driver on the main road. Could be parked around the back," Harris said.

The stability of nearby buildings was in question, and he and Laila could spend the afternoon searching for the emir. Harris decided to change his tactic. "Let's find a policeman on the scene. They'll have radios and can get a message to everyone who can help. We can tell them the emir and his fiancée were scheduled to be at the aquarium this afternoon, and their whereabouts are unknown." If the police were not already aware of the matter from the emir's private security, the information would light a fire under them.

Harris again took Laila's arm. They couldn't risk being separated in the mounting confusion. More people were arriving on the scene to assist. Harris spotted a police officer rushing toward one of the buildings. Harris stopped him, and though he looked irritated at the interruption, he listened.

"The emir was scheduled to visit this area today. We're trying to confirm he is safe," Harris said.

His eyes wide, the officer pulled his radio from his belt. He would take their information seriously and act upon it. It took a few moments for the line to clear, and then he sent the message he needed to confirm the safety and whereabouts of the emir. "We'll find him," the officer said to Harris and then brushed past them in the direction he'd been headed.

Laila threw up her hands, worry plain on her face. "We still don't know anything. What if he's hurt somewhere?"

"It's likely Mikhail's private security knows where he is." Harris hoped, for Laila and her family's sake, it was true.

"Unless the security team with him was hurt or killed by the explosion."

If Mikhail was working with the Holy Light Brotherhood and they had planned this attack, this was a taste of more to come. Even so Harris tried to reassure Laila. At the moment, Mikhail wasn't a traitor and a liar. He was her brother. "If Mikhail was in that building, we'll see every search-and-rescue person in this city converge on the aquarium. They will make contact with the emir's staff and track him down. The best we can do is offer our assistance to this effort. Do you know how far it is to the nearest hospital?" Harris asked.

Laila thought for a moment. "There's one a few miles from here."

No one had taken charge of the scene yet. Groups were working independently, doing what they'd been trained to do. Harris tasked himself. "We need to check these cars for bodies or trapped civilians."

He looked around for a piece of cement he could carry in his hand. If he had to smash glass to get someone out of a car, that's what he would do.

They walked through the cracked and crowded streets. People were trickling out of nearby buildings, some looking wounded and others dazed. They were staring at their phones in confusion as if they would somehow contain the answers of what had happened and what to do.

"The national emergency response team will arrive soon," Laila said, biting her bottom lip.

"It'll be okay. We were lucky," Harris said, trying to assuage some of her fears. He would do whatever it took to keep her safe. He'd sworn to protect her, and he took that vow to heart.

"Or unlucky that the explosion happened in the first place," Laila said.

Most of the cars along the streets were empty. Some were mangled into nearby cars and poles, but the occupants had escaped.

In a blue sedan, the hood smoking, the driver was hunched over the wheel. Harris pulled the door handle. Locked. He tapped on the glass. The man didn't move.

Harris's heart fell. He looked for the rising and falling of his chest. Due to the position of the body, Harris couldn't see if he'd survived the wreck.

"Is he alive?" Laila asked, trepidation shaking her voice.

She shouldn't be here. Harris had seen gruesome and terrible situations. He was callused to them when he needed to be. This was new to Laila. "I'll check." He wouldn't suggest again she leave the scene. First, she wouldn't, and second, he didn't want her wandering the streets without protection. Fear could bring out the worst in people—violence, looting and anger. If she was recognized as the emir's sister, it could be even worse. "Why don't you go to the gift shop and grab some bags, fill them with bottles of water and whatever supplies you can find, and give them to people who need them? We'll explain to the store owners later and make reparations." He could watch her go to the gift shop and make sure she wasn't hassled.

She lifted her chin. "I will not leave you. I can help. Don't tell me to leave again, and I won't tell you the same."

Strength. She showed it again and again. Why had he underestimated her? "We've got to get into the car. Give me your head scarf."

Without hesitation, Laila removed it and handed it to him. He wrapped it around his arm. Using the piece of cement in his hand, he slammed it into the passenger side door. After two strikes, the glass broke, and Harris cleared away the shards. He reached inside and unlocked the doors.

Racing to the driver's side, he opened the door and felt for a pulse. It was erratic and light. "He's alive,"

Harris said. "He needs medical attention." If the man had a spine injury, he shouldn't be moved.

Harris waved over an EMT, who jogged to the car. "I have a man who's unconscious, but alive."

Laila was telling the man he would be okay. She stepped away so the EMT could get closer.

The EMT assessed him. "We need to get him to the ambulance. I think he's bleeding somewhere, but in this position I can't tell. Can you help me get him out of the car and carry him?"

Harris, Laila and the EMT worked the man out of the car, taking care not to jostle him any more than was necessary. No stretchers were available and the three of them carried him to the ambulance for further treatment.

For the next five hours, Harris and Laila, along with other volunteer civilians and medical professionals, assisted the search, rescue and treatment effort.

It seemed the number of people who needed help was endless. The police took control of the scene and searched for more bombs and other threats. Volunteers who had vehicles transported people to the nearby hospital. Roads were closed to everyone except emergency vehicles and the volunteer transporters of the injured. A tent had been set up on the site with emergency medical equipment, and was staffed to treat the walking wounded and those with less serious injuries.

The search and rescue teams were asking civilians without the proper equipment to vacate the scene. They were methodically looking for survivors and couldn't risk more injuries.

Reporters had arrived, and Harris stayed out of their

view. His face couldn't be on the news where he could be recognized and identified by someone who knew him.

Exhausted, grimy and thirsty, Harris and Laila sat on the curb three blocks from ground zero. Though the sounds of horns and emergency sirens followed them, they were alone. Laila handed him the bottle of water she was drinking. "I can't believe this happened."

Blood, sweat and dirt were smeared on their clothing. As many as they had tried to help, more waited. As time passed, the more likely those who were found would be dead. It was a reality that haunted him. At this moment he would give anything to hear his family's voices. They had been involved in desperate situations during their careers. He could communicate what he was feeling without saying much at all.

"My brother might have some information from the news," Harris said. His *brother,* meaning his CIA contact, Tyler.

Tyler answered after one ring. "Intel is going nuts here trying to get information on the bombing. Are you okay?" Tyler said.

"I'm fine. We were in the aquarium in Doha when the bomb exploded."

"When you're clear to talk, we'll need a report from you. The news media is speculating that the Holy Light Brotherhood is responsible for this tragedy. We have reports that the emir is secure, though he might have gone underground until his security can confirm it's safe for him to appear in public. We've also heard whispers that some groups in Qamsar are blaming America for the bombing."

"Say that last part again," Harris said. How was

this bombing being twisted into a crime committed by America?

"We've heard some chatter that some media outlets believe it was either an accidental, misdirected missile or overt scare tactic by America to force the emir to agree to the terms of the trade agreement."

Frustration coursed through Harris. Count on the media and separatists groups to speculate and start rumors blaming America. Trouble would come if those lies were believed and accepted by the public.

Would they have to reschedule the emir's wedding? If it was canceled, it reduced their chances of catching Al-Adel. If Al-Adel had been involved in the bombing, why? Where was he now? He'd been known to be hands-on with other bombings. He could be in the vicinity.

"I can't talk much now, but I wanted to let you know I'm okay. I'll call later," Harris said.

"No problem. Check your email when you can," Tyler said. "I'll send you anything I can find about the incident."

Tyler and the team would compile the information Harris needed to assess the level of threat to his personal safety and to Laila's. If they had to abandon the mission, the CIA would pull Harris and Laila out of the country as soon as possible.

"Hey, anything about my earlier request?" Harris asked. He glanced at the strong, beautiful woman next to him. He wouldn't forget her. He couldn't lose her.

Tyler cleared his throat. "You'll get the official response from someone other than me, but it's a no. I know you got involved, and you care about Laila, but you have to let her go. I'm sorry."

Harris closed his eyes. He'd heard the words but couldn't process them. Couldn't accept them or begin to think about what they'd mean for him and Laila. He was emotionally wrung by the scene around him, by seeing the devastation and now this. He said goodbye and disconnected the call.

Harris took a deep breath and hid his sadness from Laila. He couldn't accept never seeing her again. She meant too much to him. "My *brother* says the media is reporting the emir is okay, and they don't know who is responsible for the bombing, but they suspect it was Al-Adel."

Laila shoved her hair away from her face. Her long hair was braided, but strands had come loose during her work. It was the first time he had seen her hair while she was in public in Qamsar. In the wake of the disaster, cultural modesty was unimportant. "Why would someone do this? What's the point? So much destruction and death."

Harris put his arm around her shoulder. It felt like a rebellion against the CIA even if they couldn't see him. "I know it seems senseless. I can't explain it." Even as a profiler, he couldn't fully explain the psyche of a mass bomber. He could give textbook reasons, but he didn't understand them.

If someone was trying to kill the emir, they had gone to a lot of trouble and made a mistake at the last moment. Or had the bombing been about something else?

"Let's call the compound and ask for a ride. We could attempt to walk, but all of a sudden, I'm exhausted," Laila said. She rubbed her thighs and the back of her legs.

His eyes followed the movement, and he ached to replace her hands with his own. The present situation had given way to more liberties, but now that the immediate danger had passed, the rules were in force. He couldn't touch her publicly, and he shouldn't touch her privately. In the past several days, they had crossed the line too many times, and he didn't know if he could rein in his desires again and again without going crazy.

If the CIA had their way, Laila would disappear from his life. How could he stop that?

He placed his concern for her at the forefront of his mind, behind the lust that consumed his thoughts. "When we get back to the compound, take a long, hot bath. Drink as much water as you can stand. We worked hard today, and your body will feel it."

He called the compound and requested a car pick them up. "Do you think you can walk farther? The police have the area secured, and we need to get outside the lockdown."

Laila groaned, but stood. "I can manage. But tell me, how will you unwind? I don't see you as the hot bath type."

No, he didn't like hot baths. "Hot shower and stretches for my muscles. Food. Water. Sleep."

"I could give you a back rub," she said.

Harris's overtired body wasn't too exhausted to ignore her invitation. Excitement quivered along his spine. "That would be forbidden."

"You and I have done some forbidden things. I don't know of any reputable masseurs in this area. I'm your best option."

Even if other masseurs in the area were available, she'd still be his best option, his top pick. "We'll see what we can manage. But you'll have to let me return the favor."

He felt her gaze on him. He glanced to meet it. "Tell me what you're thinking."

She brushed her braid over her shoulder and straightened. "This relationship is American. I never thought I would have this."

Interesting observation. "What about this seems American to you?"

"I lived in America for two years. I had friends. I heard stories. I saw movies. Americans are much more liberal with touching." Behind the dirt on her cheek, he caught her blushing. He loved that about her, spirited and innocent at the same time.

"That's one way to put it," he said. "Most relationships I've seen in America are less conservative. That might not always be a good thing."

Her eyebrows lifted. "Meaning?"

"Meaning, you're less jaded, and your heart is more open." Laila was different from the women he'd dated, and he liked those differences.

"This is new to me," she said. "What we have now, and the life I'll have soon."

Her new life in America would be filled with changes. "You'll love it. You'll do great."

She rolled her shoulders as if trying to unknot tension. "I wish I had your confidence. It's a big adjustment."

"You won't be alone," he said. "You'll have your mom and Saafir."

She stilled for a moment. "And you? Did your team agree you could see me?"

He couldn't tell her the CIA had denied his request.

He was too devastated to comfort her. Too angry to admit defeat. He wouldn't lie, either. "It's not a done deal. Give me time to work something out."

Harris and Laila were greeted at the compound like heroes. Word of what had happened on the scene had spread, thanks to the other thirty-one healthy people who had made it safely to the compound.

Though the emir was not present, Aisha and Saafir welcomed them. Saafir tugged his sister into his arms and hugged her close.

"Mikhail cannot be here to thank you for what you did," Saafir said to Harris. "But please accept our warmest gratitude for looking after the members of our family as if they were your own." The look of gratitude in Saafir's eyes ran true, but Harris wasn't ready to discount the possibility of his involvement with the brotherhood.

Harris accepted his outstretched hands and squeezed firmly. "I did what anyone would have done."

The look in Aisha's eyes could have turned sand to glass. Harris didn't know Aisha well, but she seemed more annoyed than anything. Perhaps she didn't like having attention stolen from her wedding. He didn't get a strong reading from her one way or another. She was probably worried about Mikhail and scared that Qamsar was under siege.

"I am sure you'll want to get clean and rested. I will send meals to your rooms, so you might relax tonight. Please call on me directly if you need anything," Saafir said.

Harris thanked him for his kindness, assuring him it was unnecessary. He wanted time alone to process what had happened. He couldn't shake his anger and frustration regarding the bombing, and also knowing the CIA planned to cut him off from Laila when this was over. Both events were demoralizing.

He glanced at Laila. Her head was down and her hands clasped in front of her. She had been amazing at the scene, and she'd returned to being demure when the situation called for it. The change was remarkable. He wasn't sure he liked it.

He returned to his room, tired and beat. Harris sat on the wooden chair in the corner facing the window. He didn't want to mar the lovely white sateen sheets with his dirty clothes and shoes, but he didn't have the energy to get in the shower.

A tap sounded on his door, and he called out, "Come in."

He expected dinner and was surprised to see Saafir. After an initial moment of awkwardness, Saafir entered and closed the door behind him.

"I know you want to marry my sister," Saafir said. "Yet her ring finger is bare."

Saafir wanted to get into an argument about his intentions for Laila now? Harris stood. "I haven't had the chance—"

Saafir held up his hand. "Please sit. I know you are tired. I haven't had the opportunity to speak with you much. My brother prefers to handle these matters, but with him away, I wanted to give you something." He withdrew a box from his pocket. "My sister is a princess. Both in the literal sense of the word and in our hearts. This is a ring that belonged to our great-great-grandmother. It has been worn by four generations of women before they were married. Though it is simple in its design, all who wear it have happy marriages. I understand you may have your own family heirloom to present to Laila or perhaps something else in mind entirely, but this is a promise you may give to her now. It comes with our family blessing."

Saafir held out the ring, and it took Harris a moment to catch Saafir's meaning. "You want me to give this to your sister along with a promise?"

"Only if it is your desire to marry her."

Harris took the ring box and opened it. Inside was a gold band with an intricate scrawl on it. Lovely. Simply. Elegant. Like Laila. Saafir was offering a family treasure for Harris to give to Laila. It had meaning to their family. Harris hated the lie he was living, but he couldn't blow his cover. He accepted the ring, his heart heavy.

Harris had been right. After scrubbing the grime off her body and washing her hair twice, Laila filled the oversize tub with water and bubbles, and climbed in. It felt amazing to relax. Her back ached, her feet hurt, and her arms and legs were worn to the bone. If only she had a distraction. Something to busy her mind from the shocking images she'd seen that day.

It was the second time in her life she had been a victim of a bombing. She and Harris had helped some. Others were beyond help. The injuries and the hurt clawed at her heart, followed quickly by anger. Why had Al-Adel done this? Though the Qamsarian government hadn't released information pinning the bombing on Al-Adel, she believed he and the Holy Light Brotherhood were to blame.

How could her brother, either brother, work with

Al-Adel and his network of terrorists? Didn't they see the horror Al-Adel's actions caused?

Laila closed her eyes and tried to think positive thoughts. She would go crazy stewing on the awfulness of the day. *Think about the thirty-one people who had gotten out of the aquarium, my family. The people who had evacuated buildings in the area and had helped others get to safety. The dedicated first responders who were working the scene and would work the scene until they had done everything they could.*

And Harris. Think about Harris. He was a hero.

His body. His strength. His ability to give commands and to take commands when the situation was appropriate. He'd looked out for the people around him. He'd put himself last and the safety of others first. Those were the actions of an admirable man.

Their relationship was fragile and new, even more precarious because she didn't know what she was doing. She couldn't interpret what Harris planned, and she didn't have anyone with more experience with men she could ask.

When the water was too cool to be comfortable, she let it drain and climbed out of the tub. She put on her softest, most comfortable sleepwear, fixed her hair and called the concierge for dinner to be brought to her room.

As she heard a knock at her door, she pulled a scarf over her head and wrapped a long robe over her pajamas.

Her dinner was wheeled in on a two-tier silver cart. "Is all this food for me?"

The woman who'd brought the food laughed. "Yes. The chef said the family heroine is probably hungry.

He's prepared for you his specialties and made sure I'd tell you not to hesitate to ask for seconds."

Laila blushed. She wasn't accustomed to such hospitality. Even when she'd lived in the private quarters of the compound, she wasn't given this much service. "Thank you for this. This is so kind."

The woman left the room, and Laila pushed the cart bedside.

She jumped when she saw a shadow move in the corner of the room. Harris.

He stepped into the light. "Almost got caught," he said in English.

He'd also showered and changed, his light hair wet and his clothes formal. Where was he planning to go in a western-style black suit, stiff-collared white shirt, no tie, open collar, all handsome? "What are you doing here?"

"Everyone thinks I'm dining on my five-course meal in my room and then grabbing some sleep. Perfect excuse to slip away and check on you."

Something in his tone caught her attention. Exhaustion? Worry? "Everything okay with you?" she asked.

Harris rolled his shoulders and glanced away for a moment. "Rough day. Can we pretend for a few hours that we're alone and all that—" he pointed to the doors to her room "—doesn't exist?"

She took a bottle of water from the cart and tossed it to him. "We are alone, and yes, we can pretend." She understood what he was going through. She was experiencing some of the same troubling emotions. He needed understanding and gentleness to combat the day's horrors. She would do what she could to soothe his restless thoughts. Be a compassionate ear. Be a sounding board. Whatever he needed.

He took the cap off the water bottle. "Have you eaten? You've worked hard today."

"Not yet. Do you want to join me? There's enough for both of us."

"I ate in my room, but I won't turn away more food," Harris said.

Laila pulled back the bedspread and laid the plates of food in the middle. "Help yourself. We can eat buffet style."

The kitchen staff had outdone themselves with the selection of foods. Fresh fruit, perfectly cooked meats, flavorful vegetables and warm fresh bread were artfully arranged on the platters.

"This is amazing room service," Harris said. "I've stayed in five-star hotels with far less impressive dishes."

"That's the benefit of having a private chef prepare the meal," Laila said, taking a bite of melon. "Everything is prepared to please."

They ate until they were full, and then Laila pulled the platters that contained dessert from the tray.

Harris set his hand over his stomach. "I can't eat anything else."

Laila gathered up the platters and set them on the serving cart. "We'll save them for later, then."

"How about that massage now?" he asked, waggling his eyebrows at her.

She flexed her fingers. "I'll give it a try."

Harris grinned, pulled off his suit jacket and flipped onto his stomach, stretching out and making a sound of contentment. "I would ask you to start where it hurts, but everything hurts."

Laila had never given a man a massage before, but she understood the concept. She knelt next to Harris and started at his neck. She rubbed her fingers over the knotted muscles.

"Is this okay?" she asked, a pang of insecurity striking her.

"Feels great," he said, his voice low and calm.

Two simple words that tripped her into an emotional free fall. Instead of worrying about doing it wrong, she focused on Harris, on massaging his shoulders and along his spine. She skipped over his buttocks, not feeling right about touching him in such a private place.

He shifted and let out a long breath. "Everything you're doing is amazing. I haven't felt this relaxed since we arrived."

She let her fingers work over the taut muscles at the back of his thighs. "It's been a tense few days." A gentle prompt if he wanted to talk. Their visit to the jail. The bombing. The mission.

"You got that right." He skimmed his hand along her leg. "Let me give you a massage. You don't have to do all the work."

She wasn't sure if she was prepared to have his hands on her. Whenever she was in his arms, he unhinged her. Her body reacted so easily to his touch. "I had a hot bath. I'm fine."

He rolled slightly to the side and let his head rest on his propped hand. "You seem tense. Give it a try. If you don't like it, we'll stop."

Sounded reasonable except when factoring in the slightest touch could evoke an immediate physical response. But what could a few minutes hurt? Her muscles were aching, her body feeling the physical effects of the day. "I'll try it sitting up."

"Sure, no problem."

She turned and gave him her back, letting her legs dangle over the edge of the bed.

He took her head scarf and carefully removed it from her head. "I saw your beautiful hair today. You should wear it loose all the time." He touched the end of her hair where she had wound a braid into a bun. "May I?" he asked.

She nodded and he carefully removed the bobby pins she'd used to hold her hair in place. He untied the end of the braid and unwound her hair. Running his fingers through the dark strands, it fell around her shoulders.

Then his hands were against the bare skin of her neck. She shivered at the contact.

"Is this okay? Is the pressure okay?" he asked.

"Yes," she said, closing her eyes against the onslaught of emotions. The tenderness with which he touched her, the softness of his voice and the caress of his fingers had a tranquilizing effect on her racing thoughts.

His hands slid over her shoulders and the tension of the day melted away. Her body singed with white-hot awareness, every inch of her skin crying out for his attention. She wanted to lay beside him and curl her body into his, to feel his arms around her and the strength of his body against hers. The day had been difficult, and she needed something to anchor her, to reaffirm to her that life was good, and that decent people and happiness was part of it.

"I can't believe I've never done this before. It feels great," she said.

"It was a rough day. You must be exhausted."

Gradually excitement was overtaking tired. Though she'd expended every ounce of energy she had had helping at the scene, a second wind fluttered through her veins. "The shower and food helped." And his hands. His magical hands melted away some of the day's horror and fear.

Laila leaned against him, letting him support her weight, the small circles from his hands sending plumes of pleasure over her.

"Do you want to lie down?" he asked.

The question should have alarmed her, and on some level she was aware she was shifting to rest her head on the bed. His hands moved over her, slow and methodical, her body going boneless into the mattress.

When she awoke, the room was dark. She rolled over and found Harris sleeping beside her, facing her. He'd left off his jacket, but wore the rest of his clothes. He was beneath the sheets with her.

Trust.

The word flew into her mind. Harris trusted her. Though he hadn't wanted to talk much, he'd wanted to be with her. Had she gotten through to him? Had she made him see that she was a woman worthy of his trust? His history with women made it difficult for him to let anyone into his circle.

If he did, it wasn't one-sided. She trusted Harris. She had fallen asleep, and he had put a pillow under her head and covered her with the sheet. He'd stayed with her, not touching.

He'd taken care of her. Her eyes adjusted to the dim

light, and she noticed some of his hair had fallen over his forehead. She brushed it away.

"Hey, you," he said, not opening his eyes. "Do you want me to leave?"

No. She didn't. "Stay with me."

She slid closer to Harris, and he draped an arm over her.

Chapter 10

Harris awoke at 4:00 a.m. He was in Laila's room. She was tucked against him. He reached for his phone which had slid out of his pocket and onto the mattress. He checked his messages from his team again. The last he had heard, the emir was hiding underground, and the police were placing responsibility for the bombing on the shoulders of the Holy Light Brotherhood.

His questions about the incident returned. If Mikhail was working with Al-Adel, why would Al-Adel set off a bomb in the middle of Doha's art and social district when Mikhail was scheduled to be there with his family? Had something gone wrong in their relationship? Or was Mikhail on board with the bombing?

If the emir was involved, what purpose did the bombing serve? From what Harris's team knew of Mikhail, he loved Qamsar. He loved the culture and people. If he wanted to stall change, he could affect it through his position.

Unless Harris and his team had been wrong about Mikhail working with Al-Adel and the Holy Light Brotherhood. The jailed American spy had warned him that someone in the emir's inner circle—at least one other person—couldn't be trusted. Could Saafir be behind the bombing?

A violent attack was contrary to Saafir's nature, or at least to the persona he portrayed. If Saafir was working with the Holy Light Brotherhood, he could be setting the stage to take over as emir if something happened to Mikhail. Perhaps the bombing in the cultural district had been targeting Mikhail, and he and Aisha had been unreasonably lucky.

Every time Harris had interacted with Saafir, he had seemed kind and considerate. He'd given Harris a family heirloom to present to Laila. How could the same person work with a cold-blooded mass bomber?

Harris gently shook Laila's shoulder. He hated to wake her, but he wanted to run his theory past her.

"Do you think Saafir had anything to do with the bombing?" Harris asked.

"What?" Laila asked, exhaustion underscoring her words.

"If Al-Adel and Mikhail were working together, then Al-Adel tried to kill him. Their relationship either went south, or we were wrong about Mikhail being involved." He shouldn't be talking to her about this. She wasn't on the team, and she didn't have clearance, but she knew her brothers.

Laila rubbed her eyes and yawned. "Do I think Saafir, one of the most easygoing, kindhearted men in the country, is working with an international terrorist to kill people in Qamsar? Arranging violence against the people he's working to protect and serve? No, Harris. I don't think Saafir is involved." She sighed. "But we did see his name in that book in Mikhail's library. I don't know what anyone is capable of doing to push their agenda."

Saafir's work with the prisons was the perfect cover if he was involved with the Holy Light Brotherhood. No one would suspect him. "What was Al-Adel's reasoning behind setting off that bomb?" If the CIA and FBI's intel was correct, he was getting what he wanted from Qamsar: their cooperation to stop an agreement with America, safe harbor in Qamsar and halting cultural changes.

"If you ask me, there is never a reason to set off a bomb."

Harris had had similar thoughts earlier. "I'm trying to figure how these puzzle pieces fit, and I'm missing critical pieces of information."

Laila stretched beneath the sheets. "How do you know Mikhail didn't want the bomb to go off? Maybe he wants change but doesn't want to use his position as emir to make it public. If he can pin the bombing on America, which some in the media already have, he has the perfect excuse to end trade agreements."

Harris considered it. Mikhail could be two-faced. Plenty of leaders were. Standing in front of his people as a portrait of nationalism and pride yet working with a lowlife to achieve another agenda. "Could be. I don't know what he expected to happen. It seems risky that he'd arrange for the bomb to go off in a location where he was scheduled to be along with his own family."

Laila rolled to her side. "If he knew it was going to explode, he could have found reasons to delay his arrival. I wonder how much the family means to Mikhail. He never liked me, he doesn't get along with Saafir and he wants my mother to marry a terrorist. Those are not the actions of someone who loves their family."

"He might postpone the wedding," Harris said. "Do you think that was his plan? Is Aisha too progressive for him?"

Laila's eyes widened. "I can't imagine. She's the perfect subservient wife, and she doesn't have power over Mikhail. If he doesn't like what she says to him behind closed doors, he can ignore her." Laila grabbed his arm. "If the wedding is canceled, what will you do? Will you return to America and come back when it's rescheduled?"

Harris didn't know what his team would want him to do. He had a good excuse to give Laila's family for why he was leaving the country now. He could claim he was anxious about the bombing and wanted to return to America to keep himself safe. It might make him sound cowardly, but other wedding guests had fled the country, including Laila's uncle Aasim. But Harris wouldn't leave, not without Laila. "We believe Al-Adel is in the country. We know from his past behavior he likes to be nearby when he causes a disaster. He enjoys the scramble and the chaos. We still have a chance of finding him, wedding or no wedding."

"Does that mean you'll stay?" she asked.

Harris wasn't eager to abandon the mission. He hadn't accomplished his goals, and he wanted more time with Laila. He still hadn't figured out how he'd make arrangements to see her in America. "I'm not leaving until I have no other choice, or we find Al-Adel."

Laila relaxed. "I'll talk to my mother soon. Find out how she'd feel about a trip to America to see where her daughter goes to school and work. Start to prepare her."

Harris didn't see a problem with that. A concerned daughter would want to remove her mother from a potentially dangerous situation. She could tell her mother about her concerns about the family connections to a terrorist organization. Tariq Salem didn't hide that he was friendly with Al-Adel. "That might be a good idea." If they had to leave quickly, and her mother was somewhat more prepared for the trip, it would make the trip more comfortable.

Their time in Qamsar was ticking to a close and, along with it, his relationship with Laila. He didn't trust the CIA to tell him where she'd been relocated or to permit her to contact him. He didn't want to create a security risk by subverting the CIA's procedures. He wanted to work within those policies to be part of her life.

Everything in him rejected the idea of Laila not being in his life, of never seeing her again and of handing her over to strangers and putting his faith in them to keep her safe. She was safest close to him and in his arms.

Laila met her mother in her suite at the family's country house. After fixing tea, they sat outside on the balcony on plush chairs. Laila was worried about surveillance bugs inside the house, and this conversation needed to remain confidential. She didn't want to tip off anyone to her plans.

"Tell me what's on your mind," her mother said. "Is it the bombing? I've been told by your brother's guards he is safe."

She hadn't given her mother the details of what she and Harris had experienced in Doha, but her mother knew she had been visiting the aquarium when the bomb went off. "No, it's not the bombing. I'm worried about our life in Qamsar and about returning to America."

"Are you happy in America?" her mother asked, resting her hand on Laila's arm.

Her mother had shown interest in her studies, but had never asked much about her life there. "Yes, I love it at the university. I feel blessed to be studying there. I like living with Uncle Aasim and Aunt Neha. I'm content with my life." At least she had been before meeting Harris. Now Laila couldn't return to the life she'd had with the same expectations. She wanted more for herself and her future.

"What about Harris? Do you love him, too?" her mother asked.

Lying to her mother was difficult. Laila had been carrying on the ruse and hadn't made many slipups, but alone with her mother, she was tempted to tell her the truth. The whole truth. This would be over in a couple of days, and then she and her mother could leave Qamsar and start a new life. "Harris is special to me." Not a lie.

Her mother gave her a knowing look. "I see how you look at him. I've caught him looking at you. When I see you two together, I see the love that I had with your father."

Surprise shot through her. Laila hadn't expected her

mother to draw a comparison like that. How *did* she look at Harris? She was fond of him. She liked being with him. She looked forward to seeing him every day. She imagined a future with him. When she thought of him, warmth spread over her body, and when she imagined him touching her, desire hammered in her blood. Was that love? "I've never been in love. I had always imagined you and Father would arrange a marriage for me and love would follow."

Iba took Laila's hands in hers. "Your father and I want you to be happy. That is the most important thing. We would have found you a good man, and we hoped you would find a lifetime of love with him. I am glad Mikhail approves of Harris. He is a good man, even if he isn't the man we would have chosen for you."

"Why wouldn't you have chosen him?" Was she overlooking a great character flaw in him?

"He isn't from Qamsar, and we don't have close ties with his family. That would have affected our decision."

Of course. They would have matched her with someone in their social circle. "I don't know if I love Harris the way you loved Father." Or even if she loved Harris. Her feelings for him were strong. She cared for him and trusted him. Her heart stirred and tightened. Was she lying to herself, pretending she wasn't in love with him? Was her mother seeing something she couldn't?

Iba wrapped her arm around her daughter. "Of course you don't love him the same. Your father and I built love over many, many years. The freshness of new love is exhilarating, but as time passes, our love deepened and grew, and it was more than excitement. I found comfort and stability, a friend to be at my side every day through life's challenges." Iba wiped at tears that welled in her eyes. "I want you to have those things with a kind man. When I heard Mikhail wanted you to marry Noor, I was devastated. Noor is not a good man. He is cruel, and you would have had unhappiness with him."

Laila agreed. If nothing else, Harris had saved her from a marriage to someone she would have grown to hate. "Then what should I do? Are you telling me it's okay to marry Harris and move away with him? I mean more than okay with Mikhail, is it okay with you?"

She met her mother's eyes and found sadness in them. Iba let out a heavy breath. "Find your happiness. Grab on to it with both hands. I want my daughter with me, but I will be fine here. I have friends and wonderful memories of your father and my children. Knowing you are somewhere in the world, happy with a man who is good to you, will give me the happiness I need. You will visit me, and I will visit you, and when you give me grandbabies, I'll stay with you for nice long visits."

Tears came to Laila's eyes when she thought of her mother staying in Qamsar without her. Knowing that her mother would be with her in America had kept her from losing her mind and had focused her on the mission. "Come with me," Laila said.

"Where?" Iba asked. "To America? To Germany?"

She hadn't planned exactly what she would say to her mother, but she acted on instinct. "Come with me to America, and if we move to Germany, you can move with us."

Iba shook her head. "I cannot impose on your relationship that way."

"I've talked to Harris about it. He's fine with it."

Iba lifted her brow. "You want me to live with you and your husband?"

If it kept her mother from being killed in the fallout of Mikhail's involvement with the Holy Light Brotherhood, Laila would take her mother anywhere. "Come with me to America. Stay with me and learn the culture. At least come for a visit until Mikhail has sorted out who is responsible for the bombings and if there will be others." Or until someone uncovered the emir's ties to the Holy Light Brotherhood, and they were distanced from the immediate backlash.

Iba wrung her hands. "What confidence would I show in my son to leave now? I couldn't do that. I've lived in Qamsar all my life. I can't abandon my home and my family."

If she told her mother the truth, would she feel differently? Staying in Qamsar would be dangerous if anyone learned of Laila's involvement with the American government. The secrets she and her brothers were keeping were dangerous to their family. "Please think about it. We'll be safe with Harris."

"I know you are nervous about marrying someone and starting a new life, but I can't impose on you. We'll have visits, I promise."

The truth rose higher on her tongue. "What if the bombing yesterday was the beginning of something terrible? What can you do then?"

Iba appeared troubled, but she forced a smile. "We have to pray that Mikhail will behave as the leader he was born to be."

Mikhail was out of control. Mikhail wanted her mother to marry a terrorist. "Harris overheard something during a gathering in the desert. Mikhail wants you to marry a man named Tariq. He's an associate of Ahmad Al-Adel. I've heard speculation that the Holy Light Brotherhood is responsible for the bombing. Those ties to Mikhail are not good." Huge understatement. Devastating. Destructive.

Iba mouthed Al-Adel's name. "How can that be? Why would Mikhail permit someone like that in his presence? Is he not careful about the company he keeps? Why would he want family connections to a terrorist?" Iba dropped her voice on the last word. "And what will I do as the wife of a man like that? How will I survive?"

Laila wanted to confess the entire story, starting with the American government approaching her to help them find and stop Al-Adel, believing he would be in Qamsar for Mikhail's wedding. Anything to convince her mother to leave Qamsar. The only part preventing her was Harris's trust. He had trusted her with that information. If she betrayed that confidence, she was no better than the woman who had nearly killed him. "You will survive because you will come with me. We will be safe in America or in Germany. You won't have to be married to a man you'll despise. Mikhail is confused and not making good decisions."

Iba's face turned stern. "If you know something about your brother that could hurt us, you must tell me."

How much could Laila reveal without betraying Harris? "Harris can keep us safe. He's a good man." Partial truths were making her stomach hurt.

"I cannot leave Qamsar. You must know that. It is my job to stand by my son. If I leave in the wake of Mikhail's decision for me to marry, I am telling the country the ruling family is weak. I cannot allow that to happen."

Laila looked around, expecting to see Mikhail's guards hovering close by or one of Mikhail's cronies spying on her. "Harris knows the situation is bad, and he wants to protect us. Please come with us when we leave Qamsar."

"You are not asking for a visit. You want me to flee the country I've loved all my life without telling me why," her mother said.

Laila could tell her mother only so much without betraying Harris. She tried another route. "If you stay here, you could be in grave danger."

"Anyone can be in danger at any time."

"But if Qamsar is no longer safe, how will I know that you're okay?" Laila asked, desperation burning a hole through her chest.

"I was raised to be a strong woman. I've survived the death of my husband, and I'll survive whatever life sends to me."

Laila could see in her mother's face she was determined to stand her ground. She wouldn't be convinced, at least not today. Something more would need to transpire for Iba to turn her back on Mikhail and Qamsar.

Laila blew out a frustrated breath.

If Iba refused to leave Qamsar, Laila would lose her mother. If Laila stayed in Qamsar, she would lose Harris. Every scenario ended with her losing someone.

Mikhail addressed the nation, the broadcast shown on every news channel and streaming live from local websites. He did not reveal his location, and nothing about the background gave away where he could be hiding.

Harris listened, knowing his team in America was also tuned in and analyzing every word he spoke. The Qamsarian government was accusing terrorists of the bombing, though they did not mention any one person or group by name. The bomb was a deliberate and deadly attack, killing over two dozen people and injuring many others. The search for the missing was still underway, and the country's emergency response team and volunteers were working nonstop.

Mikhail mentioned Qamsar's intelligence community and their efforts to gather more information to bring those responsible to justice and to prevent future attacks. The emir offered condolences to those who had lost someone in the tragedy and thanks to those who had come together to support the rescue efforts. He asked for vigilance and prayers.

"But it is most important that we not allow fear to prevent us from living our lives," Mikhail continued, "or from doing the things we love. We are a strong country, an able country, and we won't be crippled by the cowardly attacks of terrorists. The group or country responsible for this will pay. Because of my belief that we are safe, that the local and national police and protection agencies are doing everything possible to prevent another incident from occurring, my wedding will take place as scheduled. It is time for us to band together and celebrate the richness of our culture, the peaceful people that we are, and Qamsar's bright, hopeful future."

Mikhail's words were ones Harris expected from a leader of a nation. A rallying cry for support to prevent the bombing from turning into a politically decisive disaster or causing panic.

Harris wanted to talk to someone about the speech. He needed a sounding board to see if he had missed something important. He could call Tyler. The CIA was likely running their algorithms and reading for hidden meanings in Mikhail's words.

Harris didn't want to talk to Tyler. Reading the messages waiting for him from his team and listening to them tell him that his relationship with Laila was over in a matter of days had zero appeal.

He changed into running clothes and sneakers, and left the compound on foot. Doubling back several times, he made sure he wasn't followed. Part of him wanted to run until he was physically exhausted. He needed to excise the emotions that had been taking their toll on him. Working with the CIA, staying undercover, living with his lies, dealing with the secrets and playing by the CIA's rules grated on his sense of integrity and who he was. The events of the week were piling on top of him, crushing him, making it hard to breathe. Blotting out the images from the bombing was impossible. The victims of that terrible day and the prisoners from the jails haunted him. Thinking about losing Laila was destroying him.

He hadn't felt this low in a very long time. Not even when Cassie had betrayed him had he wrestled with these demons. Her betrayal had brought on white-hot anger. What he faced now was more complex.

Asking for help had never been his strong suit, but if he didn't reach out to the people he loved, he would go berserk. He needed someone to ground him.

He dialed his parent's secure line. His mother answered on the first ring. "Harris." She sounded relieved.

"Hey, Mom," he said. He didn't hide the exhaustion. The hurt. The weakness. He couldn't.

"Are you okay? What's happened?" she asked.

His mother had a sixth sense about her sons. She knew when they were in trouble. "I'm still undercover."

His family understood he couldn't talk about his work. He'd told them about joining the joint task force with the CIA and that he'd be OCONUS.

"I know you can't say much, but I've had calls into every contact I have in the agency about you. I heard you were fine, but a mother needs to hear it from her son's mouth."

Harris let out a soft laugh. "I'm fine, Mom." He was hurting, but he would get through this. Reaching out to his family was helping.

"I hear the stress in your voice. Is it a woman?" she asked.

Perceptive. "Partially."

"What's the other part?" she asked.

"This isn't the job I expected," Harris said.

Her mother sighed. "It rarely is. Operating within the rules isn't easy. Most can't or don't want to for long."

He had newfound respect for his mother for working as a CIA operative for so long. "I wanted this to…" He didn't know how to finish the statement.

"Advance your career. You told us. But, Harris, what was wrong with what you were doing? You're good at being a special agent. Why do you need the change?"

"Something wasn't right." He had been struggling with feeling as if something was missing for too long.

"I don't like to tell you boys what to do. I don't give advice when it's not wanted. But I have to say this. You work too much. Working more or somewhere else or for someone else won't fill the emptiness or the loneliness. You need a personal life which brings me back to my first question. Who is she?"

"I met her here." No need to explain *here* was the mission.

"Is she who you're investigating?"

No. That would have brought a different set of problems. "She's on my side. But she'll be gone when this is over."

"Then don't let her get away."

"I might not have a choice."

His mother laughed. "There's always a choice. Hold on a minute. Brady and Reilly are here. They want to talk to you. Let me switch to speaker-phone."

After reassuring his family he was physically okay, Reilly jumped in. "It's a woman. Who is she?"

"I can't say," Harris said.

"Intriguing," Brady said.

"Speaking of, where are your wives?" Harris asked.

"Dad's showing them how to grill steak properly. He says they have a chance of actually getting it right, unlike his sons. You know how he gets about steak. But don't change the subject."

Harris smiled. A genuine smile. His father loved his steak and treated cooking it like a fine art.

"Are you in love with her?" Reilly asked.

His brothers never spoke like that. Being married had made them more open to talking about love and relationships.

"Don't make this a gossip session," Harris said.

"I'm going to answer for him with a *yes,*" Brady said. "In which case, whatever the problem is, whatever you think stands in the way, get rid of it."

"It's not that simple," Harris said. Ignore the CIA and their rules? Quit his job?

"Never is," Brady said. "Anyone worth having is worth working for. Don't let someone you love get away because you're worried about your job. You'll find another job if it comes to that."

Harris was surprised to hear his brother's suggestion. Brady had defined himself by his career and had lost the woman he loved because of it. It hadn't been easy for him to get his life back on track.

"It's not just the job. She doesn't know," Harris said. Laila was unaware of his feelings for her.

"Tell her," Brady said.

"She might not feel the same," Harris said.

Reilly groaned. "Dude. Man up."

"I don't know how to tell her," Harris said.

"Try using words," Reilly said.

This from his brothers who, up until a few years ago, were as unlucky in love as Harris. "Easy for you to say. You lucked out."

"Not luck. Skills," Brady said.

The brothers laughed and Harris wished he was with his family at his parents' place, Laila by his side. He wished he could bring her home to meet them, put his arm around her and call her his wife.

Wife. Flaming perfect. A few minutes ago, he wasn't sure what he felt. Five minutes into a phone call with his family, he was facing the fact that he was in love and wanted to marry her.

"This woman has it all," Harris said.

"Then she's too good for you," Reilly teased. "But seriously, don't forget you're a Truman. You have a lot to offer, too."

Harris expected more ribbing. "What if I can't make it work?"

"Unacceptable thinking," Brady said. "Make it work. If it's your job, quit. If you or she are into something bad, go off the grid for a while. Do whatever you need to do. You've got an entire team here to back you up. Whatever you need, we'll be there. When it all works out, Mom can stop worrying about her oldest son and instead focus on being a grandmom."

"A grandmom? Susan's pregnant?" Harris asked.

"She sure is," Brady said, his voice bursting with pride.

A picture of the life he wanted formed crystal clear in his mind. He and Laila with a family of their own, hanging out with his brothers and their wives, his parents and his future niece or nephew. Holidays, weekends, vacations. A family man.

He'd been trying to squeeze more from his career to fill the emptiness he'd been feeling. He couldn't get what he needed from it, not from more working hours and not from taking more cases.

He needed Laila to complete what was missing in his life.

Laila stood in the hot shower, letting the water beat down on her. Her mother hadn't agreed to come with her to America. Despite knowing she would face a difficult life in Qamsar, she wanted to stay. Her mother had said she would think about Laila's offer, but Laila knew her mother. Iba wouldn't leave. Why had she believed it would be easy to convince her? What about Saafir? Would he stay in Qamsar?

Laila would start over in America alone. Staying in Qamsar was too dangerous. It would come out that Harris was not Harris Kuhn, heir to a German shipping fortune, and her deception would be discovered. If Harris connected Al-Adel to Mikhail and Mikhail was jailed, Mikhail's supporters would make it too dangerous for her to stay. If the country turned on her family in anger, they would all be killed.

She could claim ignorance. Pretend Harris had duped her. But she didn't want to lose him in her life. And yet when the truth came out, Laila knew her family wouldn't support her relationship with a man they believed to be a liar.

It came down to that choice. She would lose Harris or lose her family.

She wiped at the tears of sadness that pooled in her eyes. Before she'd agreed to help Harris, she hadn't considered her feelings for him would grow to this depth or that her mother would decline to leave Qamsar.

Laila couldn't put her finger on the precise moment she had fallen in love with Harris, but talking to her mother had clarified her feelings.

Love. Unending, unyielding, inconvenient love.

A light tap on her bathroom door had her jumping. "Who's there?"

"It's me."

Harris! "Just a minute."

"You sound funny. Are you okay?"

Her throat was tight with emotion. "I'm okay. I need a couple of minutes." Laila checked her hair for soap, gave it another rinse and grabbed her robe from the hook in the bathroom. She wrapped it around her body and used a towel to dry her hair.

When she left the bathroom, Harris was sitting on the edge of the bed, his elbows on his knees and his hands clasped together.

His eyes narrowed when he saw her. "What's the matter? I can see it in your face. Something's happened."

Laila sat on the bed next to him. Her emotions were raw. "I talked to my mom about leaving Qamsar and coming with us, that is, with me, to America for a visit. She doesn't want to come. She wants to stay here and support Mikhail. When I pressed her, she said she would think about it, but I don't think she'll leave. She believes she has an obligation."

Harris's eyes darkened with concern. "She might change her mind."

Laila rubbed her temples. "She has a life here. Friends. Family. Her home. Her position as the emir's mother puts her in the spotlight. She worries leaving would raise too many questions and throw doubt over Mikhail's rule. If Mikhail's ties to the Holy Light Brotherhood are made public, he'll have more doubts and questions than he can handle. She didn't even seem that bothered about the idea of marrying a terrorist. She accepts it as her fate."

Harris wrapped his arm around her and kissed the top of her head. "Do you want to stay here with her?"

If she stayed, if she denied that she'd known Harris was an American spy, she would live in fear that the truth would be uncovered and she would have to live the lie every day for the rest of her life. If she stayed, she would never see or speak to Harris again. "I can't. It will come out that I assisted you. Those who support my brother and Al-Adel will mark me as a target for revenge. Those who don't will want to see my family jailed or dead."

Harris's breath brushed against her hair. "I know this is hard. We'll find a way to work it out."

How? Laila wanted her mother happy and safe. She wanted to be happy and safe. Those weren't both possible. "My mother kept saying she wants me to be happy. She thinks I'm in love with you." Laila laughed, though it sounded forced even to her. It was a test. How would he respond to the idea?

Harris's arm tightened around her. "What did you tell her?"

"I told her what I could. I kept our cover. I didn't risk our mission." She turned her head to gauge his reaction.

"I meant, what did you tell her about being in love with me?" Harris asked, his voice tight, his intelligent eyes watching her.

A pointed, direct question. One she didn't want to answer. "I told her I had feelings for you." In so many words. She felt the tip of her ears burning. Could he sense the omission or read into her words? Was the truth plain on her face? She wished she knew how he felt about her.

Emotion clouded his eyes. "It's good that you do, because I have feelings for you. Actually, I have more than feelings. I've fallen in love with you, Laila. We have a lot to face in the future, but I want to face it together." He slid to the floor, kneeling in front of her. "I talked to my family today. I had to call them. I had so much in my head. I finally got it. I know what I need. I know what's been missing from my life." He met her gaze and held it. "I need you. You're what's missing."

Laila watched him, her heart beating fast. Love and desire swelled inside her. He had spoken to his family about her. He'd let her into his circle of trust. Nothing could have meant more to her.

"Saafir stopped by to see me. He gave me a ring that belonged to your great-great-grandmother. It's simple and elegant, like you. I want you to accept it along with my promise that when I can, I will buy you a ring fit for a princess. I will do and give you everything I can to make you happy. I want you to be my wife." He withdrew a gold ring from his pocket.

Her eyes filled with happy tears and emotion tightened her throat. She hadn't expected this from Harris. Her great-great-grandmother's ring. Her mother had worn it before marrying her father. The gesture was more important than the ring. "I don't need another ring. I just need you."

He slipped the ring on her finger over her henna art, and she launched herself into his arms. She clung to him, exchanging long, slow, deep kisses. The more she kissed him, the more she wanted him. She hoped the kiss communicated what she felt: love, hope, excitement, tenderness.

"What about the future? What if we can't be together in America?" she asked, running her index finger down the side of his face.

"We'll be together. We'll find a way," Harris said. "It won't be easy. I know I'm not who you thought you'd marry." His arms looped around her waist, holding her against him, while he buried his face in her hair.

"Maybe not. I think you're better for me. My parents wanted me to be happy, and with you, I am. I won't believe there's anything wrong with that."

He tilted his head back to look at her. "You should have everything you want and every happiness," Harris said. His voice poured over her, hot and thick.

A tremor shook her. "Every happiness? You know what makes me happy? You. I want you in my life. In my heart. This ring means I am yours. It also means that you are mine."

His eyes flickered with provocation. A moment later, his lips again found hers, and she sank into the kiss. His breath tickled her neck, and she held his head in her hands. The magnitude of what they were doing wasn't lost on her. She had waited for the right man, and though he didn't come courtesy of an arranged marriage, she had found him.

She turned her body over to him and let him take the lead. He stood, setting her lightly on her feet, and drew back the bed sheets. Taking her hand, he led her to the bed. She sat, and he lifted her legs, running his hand along each calf as he moved them on top of the mattress. Heat blossomed where his hands stroked her bare skin.

He joined her on the bed. With unpracticed fingers, she unbuttoned his shirt. He slid out of it and peeled off his white T-shirt. She had her first look at his bare torso. Running her hands over the hard planes of his broad shoulders, masculine chest and pumped biceps, sharp pleasure seared her with longing.

He delivered another passionate kiss that left her breathless and needy. He unzipped his pants, slid them down his legs and tossed them to the floor. Off with his socks, and he was naked.

He moved over her, and Laila drank in the sight of him as he held himself over her. His iron biceps, his hard, taut stomach, his lean waist and oh... The evidence of his arousal was undeniable.

Fixing her gaze on him, she reclined into the mountain of pillows at the head of the bed. She touched his light hair, forking her fingers through it.

He unknotted the belt at her waist and opened her robe, taking time to run his hands over every inch of exposed skin. His lips followed in their wake, and the slowness and the care made her feel unspeakably precious. Skin to skin, nothing between them, her senses felt on fire and arousal scented the air.

His mouth drifted lazily from her lips to her cheek. "Is this okay?" he asked, cupping her breast in his hand. The caress was mind-blowing and her body responded, wanting him to touch her everywhere.

A current of heat ran between them. "Yes," she said, both thrilled at how unhurried he was and anxious for him to go faster.

Harris kissed her mouth, her cheeks, her chin. Laila couldn't do anything except feel. She couldn't get enough of him. If she had tried to picture this in her mind, she never would have imagined the perfection of the moment. She had made the right decision. Falling for Harris had been an unexpected joy.

She was relaxed and weightless against the bed, the sheets soft at her back, his hard body on top of her. He touched her hair and moved the long length of it to the side of the pillow.

He positioned himself over her, pushing her legs

apart gently. The muscles of his body flexed, every movement edged with barely restrained control. He took her left hand in his and touched the gold ring on her finger. "I like the way it looks on you. I like knowing what it means. Your henna is beautiful beneath it. You are beautiful."

She closed her eyes and thought about marrying Harris, about being his wife and about the future they would have together. "I like that I am yours." Every image that flickered in her mind was laced with happiness and love.

He kissed the tip of each finger. "You have delicate hands."

"Yours feel a little rough."

He slid his nose along her jawline. "Too rough?"

"No," she said. "They're perfect."

His hand slipped between her legs. After an initial moment of astonishment, she was right with him, his talented hands evoking a response.

She held back the moan that sprang to her lips. Someone might hear them. She had to remain quiet.

"Look at me," he said, nudging her chin up to meet his gaze. He brought his mouth down, brushed his lips to hers and then tilted his hips against her, his hardness sliding between her thighs. It felt so good she wanted to scream. She bit her lip and waited. She understood the mechanics of making love, but this was so much different. So much better than she had expected.

"Relax," he said. His low voice was soothing.

Laila closed her eyes and took a deep breath.

"Tell me this is what you want," Harris said.

Brown eyes met blue ones. "This is what I want."

He slid inside her and a shockingly sensuous feeling

ripped through her. He stilled. Waited. Then pushed farther inside her. The pain dissipated quickly, the un-comfortable pinch and tightness fading away as plea-sure and warmth consumed her.

Harris arched and closed his eyes, a sheen of sweat breaking out on his forehead. He seemed to grapple for control.

"You feel amazing," he said, withdrawing slightly.

The muscles of his arms flexed underneath her hands. The scent of spices washed over her, a clean, male scent.

Laila shifted her hips, taking him deep. Nothing could have prepared her for this moment. The hot blaze of arousal and passion urged her forward, beckoning for more. She slid her hands to his back, wanting to hold him against her and never let go. She wrapped her legs around his waist.

Harris answered her body's silent plea, and he rocked against her, slow at first, the pace building, their bodies finding a synchronized rhythm. Her breath escaped on a whispered sigh. His body coaxed wicked pleasure from hers, every movement escalating her enjoyment, every stroke of his hand fueled an already blazing fire.

"Tell me what you need," he said.

She didn't have words, and he seemed to understand.

"We'll go slow tonight. I promise," he said.

He used great care with her, building her anticipa-tion until it felt like too much, as if the pressure would burst in her chest. She grabbed his hips and urged him faster. Forget slow. She needed more. Deeper. Harder.

She clamped down on him as her body exploded in frantic pleasure. Harris stilled as her climax eased.

Breathless and spent, he rolled to the side, tucking her against his body, their skin in contact, heat simmering between them.

"Are you okay? Was I too rough?" he asked.

"I've never felt more like a princess," she said. Her skin was pulsing with excitement, and her mind was hazy with delight.

"I am yours to command," Harris said.

She made a noise of contentment and fell asleep in his arms.

Chapter 11

Laila checked her appearance in the mirror for the tenth time. Did she look different? She felt different. Her body was sensitive from making love with Harris, her stomach fluttered with excitement and the moments they'd shared were branded on her heart. The golden band he'd given her glimmered on her finger, a sign of his promise and commitment to her. She glanced over at Harris still asleep in her bed. Waking him didn't seem fair. Should she say goodbye before she left to help with wedding preparations?

She needed to help Aisha get ready for the processional through town before the wedding ceremony. Glancing at the clock, Laila had only a minute to spare.

She circled the bed and leaned over Harris. She brushed his light hair away from his face and ran the back of her index finger down his cheek.

He opened one eye. "Where are you going? Come back to bed."

She was tempted. His tight abdominals disappeared under the sheet covering the lower half of his body. "I wish I could. But I'm meeting Aisha to help with the processional to the mosque. I'll meet you outside the Grand Mosque. We won't be sitting together once we're inside, but I want to see you." Waiting to see Harris would be distracting. She wished they could spend the whole day together.

"Give me a minute. I'll come with you," he said.

"No, no, it's not appropriate. Trust me on this," she said.

He reached out and snagged her wrist before she could go. "Be careful. Please keep your phone on you. Al-Adel hasn't been spotted near the compound, but if the bombing in Doha is his work, he's in the area. We're banking on him making an appearance today, and his appearance might not be pleasant."

Cold water on her romantic fantasy. She hadn't forgotten about Al-Adel, but she'd wanted to focus on Harris. Thinking about Al-Adel brought to mind that she could be fleeing the country soon and starting over in America. "I'll keep my phone on me. If you learn anything, call me."

"You do the same," Harris said. He pulled her closer and kissed her on the mouth. A long, lingering, need-to-have-you kiss.

Laila slipped out of the room, feeling as if she was walking on air.

The scene in Aisha's parent's house was chaos. People were coming and going, carrying gifts, decorations, flowers and trays of food. At least a dozen people were talking on their cell phones, likely arranging final wedding details and coordinating the processional. Security was heavy around the house, guards patrolling and checking packages and people who entered the home.

Aisha's bedroom was in the back of the house, her windows overlooking a large swimming pool covered by a white trellis wrapped in flowers and greenery. Laila tapped on her door, and Aisha beckoned her inside. In contrast to the scene outside her bedroom door, Aisha appeared calm and unfazed. She was surrounded by three friends.

"Aisha, you look beautiful," Laila said.

Aisha's hair was styled in an elaborate updo, and though no one would see it beneath her veil, it was for Mikhail's benefit that night. She was wearing her wedding gown, a gold dress with long sleeves and a high neck. The designs within the dress were sewn of the same golden beads threaded through the fabric in an elaborate display.

"How can I help? Do you need something to eat or drink?" Laila asked, hugging the woman that would soon be her sister.

Aisha shook her head. "Could you check with my mother that the processional car has the right flowers? This morning they were blue. Unsightly. I don't want to drive through town and have those pictures in the newspapers."

Laila nodded. Though the detail had likely been rearranged to the bride's preferences, this was a big day for her and for everyone in Qamsar. The wedding would be a happy day and lift morale at a time when the country desperately needed it. "I will check on it. Don't worry. I'm sure it looks great now," Laila said.

Aisha turned in her chair away from the vanity. "Thank you, everyone, for your help. The processional is leaving in about twenty minutes, and I want to be alone for a few minutes to meditate and pray."

The pressure on Aisha was tremendous. She was marrying the emir. Her life would be easy in some ways, challenging in others. A few of her friends protested, asking if she was upset or nervous. Aisha shook her head at their worries. "I'm fine. This is a big day, and I'd like a few minutes alone. It might be the last moments of quiet I have as a single woman."

Her request for privacy was reasonable. The women in the room left quickly.

One of her friends dropped a kiss on her forehead. "I'll fix you some tea for the trip."

Laila followed after them and was halfway down the hallway when she realized she hadn't asked what color or type the flowers were supposed to be on the processional car. "Not blue" wasn't detailed enough to be sure the task was done to Aisha's liking. Laila debated returning to the room and interrupting Aisha's prayer or conferring with Aisha's mother about the detail.

Laila guessed Aisha's prayers included a wedding day free of explosions and mishaps courtesy of the Holy Light Brotherhood and anyone else who decided the emir's wedding was the opportunity to make a scene.

After another moment of internal debate, she decided it was best to check with Aisha. No point in starting the processional with an unhappy bride. Laila turned and saw someone slipping into the bride's suite. A man. Her breath caught in her throat.

Was it a servant? Or Mikhail sneaking in to see his bride? How had anyone gotten to Aisha's bedroom door past her security without been seen? Then again, in the chaos, one more person milling around wouldn't draw attention.

Feeling uneasy about the man who'd gone into Aisha's bridal suite, Laila crept to the door. What if it was a stranger? Or an attacker? Could Al-Adel have sent someone to harm the emir's bride? If he wanted to send a message, hurting Aisha would do it.

Laila opened the door a fraction of an inch and stifled a gasp when she saw the man Aisha was speaking to.

It was Ahmad Al-Adel. Aisha was locked in an embrace with him. They weren't strangers. She wasn't screaming for help or fighting him.

Laila couldn't take her eyes off the sliver of the scene shown from the crack between the doors. She focused hard to hear the conversation, trying to drown out the noise around her.

"I am so pleased you could make it," Aisha said, clasping his hands.

Surprise reverberated through Laila. How did Aisha know Al-Adel? Did she realize who he was?

"It wasn't easy slipping inside the borders of Qamsar. Your betrothed seemed intent on keeping me out. I've been here a few days."

Aisha laughed. "His security measures aren't half what they should be if you got inside. I knew you were here when you managed to set off the bomb in Doha. I delayed Mikhail enough that we hadn't even left the compound." She gave Al-Adel a wicked look. "When I am the emir's wife, I can make everything easier. We'll work together, and I'll have access to the resources you need to meet my goals. Our goals. America will not control us."

Laila stumbled back, her mind reeling, her heart slamming hard. Nausea and a sudden sharp headache sliced in her brain. Aisha had been playing Mikhail for a fool, pretending to be a loyal bride while plotting against him to use her position to help Al-Adel.

How had no one seen her deception? How had the CIA not known or suspected her?

Saafir wasn't working with Al-Adel. Mikhail wasn't, either. But it was someone in Mikhail's close circle, just as the imprisoned American spy had warned Harris. They hadn't considered Aisha, not even for a moment. Why?

The answer came immediately. For a woman in Qamsar to wield any power, hold any status or have any connections with powerful men was unheard of. Aisha was overlooked and dismissed. She'd played the subservient role of dutiful female to perfection. She'd fooled Mikhail. She'd likely fooled her parents. She'd fooled an entire country of people.

Why would Aisha do something like this? The bombing in Doha had almost caused the cancellation of her wedding. It could have injured or killed the people Aisha had invited as her guests.

What should Laila do now? What could she do?

Harris. She needed to find and tell Harris. Should she stay and listen to anything else they discussed? What if they were planning another bombing? If she was discovered, she would be killed. She needed to talk to Harris and then pretend everything was normal until Harris could do something to help.

Laila fumbled for her phone and started typing a text message to Harris. She had typed a few phrases when the door to Aisha's room swung open. Laila pressed Send and came face-to-face with one of the most dangerous men in the world.

Harris switched his cell phone to his other ear. He was listening to the world's longest conference call, and it was going nowhere. Every CIA director involved in the mission wanted an update. A dozen field operatives stationed throughout Qamsar were on the call, giving what information they could. The FBI was interjecting when they could. It was a last-minute scramble to see if they had missed an important element in locating Al-Adel.

The CIA's operatives in Qamsar were working their assets and information networks looking for more on Al-Adel, the Holy Light Brotherhood and the bombing in Doha. At the CIA district office in Colorado, Tyler and the team were analyzing the chatter on the channels they monitored.

Harris's mind wandered to Laila for the hundredth time that day. His future. His wife. Though he had already been thinking it, last night had cemented it. He would find a way to be part of her life when she returned to the United States. Even if it meant going off the grid and starting over with her, he would do it. He couldn't lose her.

He didn't know how this day would play out, but his instincts told him something big was going down soon. None of Harris's bugs had picked up a visual or audio on Al-Adel. Rumors post-bombing spread fast and furious, and sorting reliable information from wild gossip was time-consuming. For his sake and Laila's, he had to focus.

"Maybe we should pull Harris out," Tyler said. "We've had unconfirmed reports that Al-Adel is planning a bombing at the Grand Mosque during the emir's wedding. We don't know why he'd want to destroy his ally, but if he's successful, we're looking at heads of states, ambassadors and politicians from around the world being hurt or killed. It would be a show of his power."

"The emir's guards are checking every person who gets within a hundred yards of the mosque. They have the perimeter fenced and secured," Harris said. Even as he spoke the words, he knew Al-Adel would get inside if it was his intention. He would buy off people and pay for favors.

"We caught word that some of the countries with high-profile politicians attending the wedding sent extra security," Tyler said. "We have more help on the ground in that area."

More discussion and more demands for Al-Adel's location from the top-level CIA directors. Harris didn't state the obvious. He couldn't give them what he didn't have. No one had pegged Al-Adel's location.

"I need to interrupt," Tyler said. "I just received a message from our analysts that they've picked up critical information from the video feed from one of the bugs Harris placed. A few nights ago, Tariq Salem was in the emir's library and read from the book with the Holy Light Brotherhood symbol on the front. Devon retrieved the book, and our analysts say it's a covert way the emir or someone with access to that library is communicating with the Holy Light Brotherhood. They believe the emir's brother Saafir is in mortal danger. Based on the schedule I've seen, Saafir should be at the Grand Mosque. We need to get him protection. You on it, Harris?"

"I'm leaving now. I'll get to him and make sure he's okay." Staying on the line, but not listening, Harris was moving in the direction of the emir's fleet of cars. If he couldn't get a ride to the Grand Mosque, he'd steal a car.

Harris searched for a free vehicle and driver. Not finding anyone, he popped the lock on a vacant car and climbed inside. Two minutes later he'd hot-wired the car and was pulling out of the emir's compound. Harris sped through the streets of Qamsar. He'd find Saafir before Al-Adel did.

His phone beeped, and he glanced at the display. Laila had sent him a text message: Send help. Al-Adel.

Al-Adel what? She hadn't finished the message. She'd been interrupted. Fear struck him hard and fast. If Laila was anywhere near Al-Adel, she was in danger, and he had to get to her. She was his to protect. He wouldn't let anything happen to her.

Harris interrupted the conversation in progress. "I need to call my asset. She's reporting an Al-Adel sighting. Her last known location was the emir's fiancée's house. Send backup." His words set off a storm of discussions. Harris disconnected. Laila was his priority. He looked up the address of Aisha's parent's house on his phone and changed directions. At his current speed, he'd be there in five minutes. Five minutes too long. Too many bad things could happen.

He called Laila's phone. Once. Twice. She didn't answer. He left a voice mail for her to call him as soon as possible.

He should have gone with her. She'd said it wouldn't have been appropriate, but Harris should have ignored protocol and gone anyway. He should have stayed close to her.

Harris's phone rang. It wasn't Laila. It was Tyler. "You need to be our eyes and ears on the ground until we can get more operatives in the area. I'm trying to get someone else to lock down Saafir. We've alerted Devon, although he's dealing with another issue at the moment. We've called this in to local law enforcement and let them know Al-Adel's been spotted. All available staff are assisting with wedding security," Tyler said.

"Someone else will recognize Al-Adel if he's at the bride's parents' house," Harris said. If Qamsar's police force was looking for problematic guests, Al-Adel had to be on that list. After the bombing in Doha, Harris would bet Al-Adel was number one on that list. Unless Mikhail had paid his police and security team not to report in if they saw him.

"As long as any person who recognizes him approaches with caution and in the right way, we'll be fine. But we've got to assume Al-Adel has security and a backup plan if he's approached," Tyler said. "We don't know who is on whose side, either. We don't know who we can trust."

Laila. Her name sprang to mind immediately. She was in his circle of trust. He trusted her. He loved her. He couldn't lose her.

* * *

Al-Adel dragged Laila into the room and clamped a hand over her mouth. His hand smelled of gunpowder.

Aisha held a gun pointed at Laila's midsection. She'd never had a gun pointed at her before. Could it go off? If it did, wouldn't everyone hear it and come running? Would Aisha be so bold as to shoot Laila in her bedroom?

"Don't scream," Al-Adel said, removing his hand from her mouth.

"Just relax. I know you're tense about the wedding, but everything will be okay," Laila said, pretending to be confused about the situation and unaware of who Al-Adel was.

"Everything will be okay, because I'm in control of every aspect of this ridiculous charade," Aisha said.

Laila inclined her head. She'd never head Aisha speak with such heat and anger before. The submissive, adoring bride-to-be persona was gone. "If you don't want to get married, why are you?" Laila asked.

Al-Adel's grip tightened on her upper arm.

Aisha waved the gun at Laila. "I want the power. I couldn't have it without the man."

Keeping the gun trained on Laila, Aisha pulled the heavy maroon curtains over her windows, blocking the view of the pool and the sun.

"Why are you snooping around my room?" Aisha asked.

Laila's palms were damp with sweat and heat flamed up her back. Had she managed to send part of her text message? She'd dropped her phone in the hall. Would Harris understand the message? Could she stall long enough that someone would interrupt them? "I'm not snooping around. I had a question about the flowers."

Al-Adel shook her. "Don't lie. Do you realize I can make you disappear? No one will ever find you. I have a special place in the ground for women who lie."

Fear thrummed in her chest. Why would Aisha work with this man? What did she have to gain that she couldn't get as the emir's wife? Power of her own? How would Al-Adel sell that to his antiprogress followers?

"Tell me who you were sending a message to," Aisha said.

"Harris." From what they knew, he was her boyfriend. It made sense that she would be in contact with him. They hadn't uncovered Harris's identity, had they?

"Give me your phone," Aisha said.

"It's in the hall."

Aisha retrieved it and looked at the phone. When she raised her eyes, rage was hot in them. "You told him you saw Al-Adel. Who else is looking for him?" she asked.

Most of the world was looking for him, and after the bombing in Doha, all of Qamsar was on alert. "I don't know who is looking for him."

Aisha narrowed her eyes at Laila. "You shouldn't have gotten involved. I knew you were trouble when you showed up for the wedding with your German boyfriend and your American ways. Disgusting. All of it. How can you live in a country that is trying to destroy ours?"

Laila didn't know how to answer her. Her words could be the difference between survival and death. She had to make up an excuse. "I've tried to recover from my father's death. I've been looking for meaning. I realized it's in Qamsar."

Al-Adel shoved her to the ground and let go of her arm. "I haven't gotten as far as I have and survived this long without being able to read a liar. She knows something, and she needs to be silenced. It wouldn't surprise me to learn she's sympathetic to America's plan to destroy Qamsar."

Laila's heart hammered against her chest. America's plan to destroy Qamsar? Wasn't America trying to work out a mutually beneficial arrangement with them? What would destroying the country accomplish? "I don't know anything. I'm here for the wedding and to help Aisha."

Was Harris on his way? Would he find her? Would anyone step into the room and interrupt them?

Aisha needed to leave to join the processional soon. Laila had to buy time. "I don't know what's going on, whether this is wedding jitters or some misunderstanding. Aisha, we need to leave in ten minutes for the Grand Mosque. Thousands of people have lined the streets waiting to catch a glimpse of you." Laila wanted to convince Al-Adel and Aisha her main concern was the wedding. Could she make Al-Adel believe her?

"Aisha, go, before someone comes looking for you. I will meet you at the mosque, and our plans will continue as designed," Al-Adel said.

What were they planning? Aisha wouldn't be so foolish as to agree to set off a bomb during her wedding. She'd be risking the lives of her guests, which included her family.

Aisha handed the gun to Al-Adel as she left the room, smirking at Laila with distaste and closing the door behind her. Laila was alone with Al-Adel. Al-Adel didn't move for a long moment. "Who knows you are here?" Al-Adel pulled her to her feet, holding her face close to his, the anger crisp in his voice.

"I don't know," Laila said, looking around for a weapon, some way to defend herself. She couldn't outrun a bullet.

"Lying again," Al-Adel said. "We have plans today, and I won't let you ruin them. You're fortunate so many people are here. I won't shoot you." Al-Adel tucked his gun in the holster at his side.

Surprise flickered and then fear took over. Laila tried to run, but Al-Adel grabbed her in a choke hold and reached for Aisha's flat iron, wrapping the cord around Laila's throat.

Laila clawed at the cord around her neck. Al-Adel pulled tighter. She couldn't breathe. She was getting dizzy. Kicking her legs and twisting did no good. Al-Adel was holding her too firmly and had the cord tight around her neck.

The door to Aisha's room banged open, and Harris stepped inside. He rushed at them, tackling Al-Adel to the ground. The cord around her neck loosened, and Laila drew in gulps of air.

"Run, Laila. Get help." Gone was the German accent. Harris was all-American, all strength and aggression and protection.

Harris and Al-Adel were locked in a struggle. Laila was torn between screaming for help and trying to assist Harris. She saw Al-Adel reaching for his gun. Her vision was blurry, and though her throat felt raw, she yelled and threw herself into the fray, trying to kick him in the head. She got to the gun first and pulled it free of its holster.

The weapon felt heavy in her hand. She aimed it at Al-Adel and Harris.

"I'll shoot," she screamed.

Harris landed another punch across Al-Adel's face, and the terrorist went limp on the ground.

"Don't shoot," Harris said, breathless. "Just give me the gun." He rose to his feet and took the gun from her hand.

Three of the emir's guards ran into the room.

Laila scrambled to Harris's side, identified herself and Harris, and explained the situation. Having the country's most wanted man in Aisha's bedroom was shocking and terrifying. The emir's guards put handcuffs on Al-Adel and dragged him from the room, unconscious.

"Stay where you are," one of the guards said. "Backup is coming."

Laila and Harris were alone. "Are you okay?" she asked him. He had red welts on his face.

Harris pulled her into his arms. "I'm fine. But I've never been so scared. If I had lost you, I don't know what I would have done."

"You won't lose me. Not ever." She kissed Harris, grateful to be alive and in his arms.

Devon entered the room. "I raced here as soon as I received the message about Al-Adel. Are you two okay?"

"I'm fine thanks to Harris," Laila said.

Devon jammed a hand through his hair. "We've got storms in every direction. There was a jail break at the Cinder Block. The American spy is gone. Disappeared without a trace. We found a bomb in the Grand Mosque. We're working on an evacuation now. All members of the royal family are accounted for and safe. What happened this morning?"

Laila explained what she had seen and heard in Aisha's bedroom. Harris stayed at her side, and Laila knew everything would be all right as long as he remained there.

Even with an ocean between her and Qamsar, Laila couldn't ignore the news stories about her family, and the changes taking place.

Aisha had turned on the Holy Light Brotherhood for a lighter prison sentence in Qamsar. She had admitted she had planned to kill Saafir and hoped to convince Mikhail to join the brotherhood. She had confessed she'd pressed Mikhail to arrange a marriage between Iba and Tariq Salem. Aisha's plans to use Laila's death in America, the bombing in Doha and the planned bombing of the mosque to sway public opinion, and to force her agenda by showing the strength, reach and power of the Holy Light Brotherhood had failed. The bombings were a threat against entering a trade agreement with the United States.

Unable to handle the shame of his betrothed's betrayal and the scandal of her involvement with a terrorist, Mikhail had abdicated the throne and now Saafir was at the helm. Negotiations on a trade agreement with America were progressing.

Al-Adel was claiming to his few remaining followers that Aisha had been a weak, but necessary tool he had used to get what he wanted, and they should stay fast to the cause. Because Aisha had told the Qamsarian authorities what she knew about the Holy Light Brotherhood, most members, including Tariq Salem, were jailed or in hiding. Al-Adel's message had difficulty finding ears. Without fear of reprisal from the Holy Light Brotherhood or her countrymen, Laila hadn't needed a new identity.

Laila took another sip of her tea and closed the news site on her web browser. Her thesis proposal was due the following week, and she wanted to wrap it up tonight.

She smiled when Harris entered the café. His eyes scanned the room and landed on her. The entire room heated. Harris took a seat next to her and slipped his arm around her shoulders.

"How's it going? Ready to take a break?" he asked.

She playfully pushed him away. "No, I have to finish this. I can take a break tomorrow. We'll have the whole drive to your parents' place to talk." They were driving to Montana to spend a week with his family. It was a long overdue vacation for Harris, the first he had taken in years. He was working exclusively for the FBI as a profiler now, and most nights he was home in time for dinner. His priorities had shifted, and Laila was happy she was at the top of them.

"I plan to use that time to talk about wedding plans," Harris said.

Laila rolled her eyes. "As if my mother hasn't talked you to boredom about our wedding enough." Harris had confessed his identity to Saafir and her mother, and they had still given Laila and Harris their blessing to proceed with their marriage.

"I'm just glad she's happy for us," Harris said.

"She won't be happy if you don't let me finish this paper," she said.

He groaned. "You're too good a student. It's quieter at my place. Why don't you work there?" He nuzzled her neck.

"I like working here," she said. "It's where we met. If I go to your place, you'll be too distracting. If I wanted quiet, I could work at my aunt and uncle's place. Although with my mom staying there, it's a lot less quiet." Her mother and her aunt had been having fun reconnecting. Saafir thought it was best for his mother and sister to stay out of the country for a few months, until the aftermath of Aisha's betrayal and the politics that followed settled.

"I'll wait. But when this paper is finished, you're mine," Harris said.

Laila shook her head. "You don't have to wait for the paper to be finished. I'm already yours."

* * * * *

If you loved Harris's story,
don't miss his brothers' stories:
HIDING HIS WITNESS
and
SHIELDING THE SUSPECT.
Available now from C.J. Miller
and Harlequin Romantic Suspense!

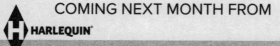

COMING NEXT MONTH FROM

H **HARLEQUIN®**

ROMANTIC suspense

Available December 3, 2013

#1779 COLD CASE, HOT ACCOMPLICE

Men of Wolf Creek • by Carla Cassidy

Detective Steve Kincaid had no idea his latest case would bring the alluring Roxy Marcoli into his life, along with a danger from his past that could destroy them both.

#1780 COLTON CHRISTMAS RESCUE

The Coltons of Wyoming • by Beth Cornelison

To solve the crimes at the Colton ranch and protect Amanda Colton's infant daughter, Slade Kent goes undercover. But to earn Amanda's trust and love, he must risk his heart.

#1781 SEDUCED BY HIS TARGET

Buried Secrets • by Gail Barrett

Nadine Seymour's worst nightmare comes true when she's kidnapped by the powerful family she's hidden from for years. Will the sexy, enigmatic rebel be her salvation or her undoing?

#1782 COVERT ATTRACTION

by Linda O. Johnston

A rugged FBI agent. A determined U.S. Marshal. Both undercover, unaware of the other...at first. Can they work together to uncover a deadly conspiracy while fighting their sexual attraction?

REQUEST YOUR
FREE BOOKS!

2 FREE NOVELS
FROM THE SUSPENSE COLLECTION
PLUS 2 FREE GIFTS!

YES! Please send me 2 FREE novels from the Suspense Collection and my 2 FREE gifts (gifts are worth about $10). After receiving them, if I don't wish to receive any more books, I can return the shipping statement marked "cancel." If I don't cancel, I will receive 4 brand-new novels every month and be billed just $6.24 per book in the U.S. or $6.74 per book in Canada. That's a savings of at least 22% off the cover price. It's quite a bargain! Shipping and handling is just 50¢ per book in the U.S. and 75¢ per book in Canada.* I understand that accepting the 2 free books and gifts places me under no obligation to buy anything. I can always return a shipment and cancel at any time. Even if I never buy another book, the two free books and gifts are mine to keep forever.

191/391 MDN F4XN

Name _____ (PLEASE PRINT) _____

Address _____ Apt. # _____

City _____ State/Prov. _____ Zip/Postal Code _____

Signature (if under 18, a parent or guardian must sign)

Mail to the **Harlequin® Reader Service:**
IN U.S.A.: P.O. Box 1867, Buffalo, NY 14240-1867
IN CANADA: P.O. Box 609, Fort Erie, Ontario L2A 5X3

Want to try two free books from another line?
Call 1-800-873-8635 or visit www.ReaderService.com.

* Terms and prices subject to change without notice. Prices do not include applicable taxes. Sales tax applicable in N.Y. Canadian residents will be charged applicable taxes. Offer not valid in Quebec. This offer is limited to one order per household. Not valid for current subscribers to the Suspense Collection or the Romance/Suspense Collection. All orders subject to credit approval. Credit or debit balances in a customer's account(s) may be offset by any other outstanding balance owed by or to the customer. Please allow 4 to 6 weeks for delivery. Offer available while quantities last.

SUS13R

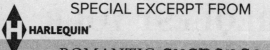
"I need to buy a gun," she said as Steve pulled out of the
Roadside Stop parking lot.

He nearly snapped her neck with his fast stop. He turned
in his seat and frowned at her. "You are not getting a gun.
You can be anything you want in the world, but you can't be
a gun owner. You'd wind up shooting a customer or yourself
by accident."

"Or you," she said, knowing he was right.

"There's always that, too," he agreed.

"It sucks being a target of somebody and not knowing who
they are or why they want to hurt me."

"It's odd that whoever it is hasn't succeeded yet. I mean,
instead of just locking you in the freezer, why not stab you to
death or beat you with something?"

"I know. I thought of that already."

He turned down the lane that was Amish land. "It makes me wonder again if maybe the attacker is a woman."

Roxy frowned. "I just can't imagine any woman who would want me hurt or dead." She turned and looked out the window, where young and old men in black trousers, long-sleeved white shirts and wide-brimmed straw hats worked in the fields.

Steve drove up to a modest white ranch house with a huge dairy barn behind it. "This is Tom Yoder's place. He's the bishop, and we need to check in with him before we speak to anyone else."

He pulled to a halt before the Yoder house and cut the engine. He unbuckled his seat belt and then turned to look at her. "And, Roxy, just for the record, you should never have to change a thing about yourself for any man. You're perfect just the way you are."

He didn't wait for a reply, but instead turned and got out of the car. It was at that moment Roxy realized she was more than a little bit in love with Detective Steve Kincaid.

Don't miss
COLD CASE, HOT ACCOMPLICE
by Carla Cassidy, available December 2013 from
Harlequin® Romantic Suspense.

ROMANTIC suspense

COLTON CHRISTMAS RESCUE
by Beth Cornelison

Single mother and ranch veterinarian
Amanda Colton teams up with undercover agent
Slade Kent to uncover family secrets and find
the mastermind behind the crimes at the
Colton ranch in order to protect her daughter
from the people intent on kidnapping her.
Together, Amanda and Slade follow the loose
ends and new tips about the family's illicit past
as they hunt down the mastermind behind the
plot to destroy the Colton family. But to earn
Amanda's trust and love, he must risk his heart.

Look for the exciting conclusion in the
Coltons of Wyoming miniseries
next month from Beth Cornelison.
Only from Harlequin® Romantic Suspense!

Wherever books and ebooks are sold.

Heart-racing romance, high-stakes suspense!

www.Harlequin.com

HRS27850

HARLEQUIN®

A *Romance* FOR EVERY MOOD™

Love the Harlequin book you just read?

Your opinion matters.

Review this book on your favorite book site, review site, blog or your own social media properties and share your opinion with other readers!

Be sure to connect with us at:
Harlequin.com/Newsletters
Facebook.com/HarlequinBooks
Twitter.com/HarlequinBooks